Windigo Thrall

What Reviewers Say About Lambda Literary Award Winner Cate Culpepper's Work

"Culpepper's writing style can only be described as fluid and soothing. This is a multi-faceted book that will fascinate even the staunchest non-believer. Culpepper is a born story teller, and the reader can imagine her spinning this yarn of ghosts and evil spirits to friends around a campfire."—*Lambda Literary Review*

"There's a lovely ebb and flow to their courtship, a dance that is refreshingly healthy and mature. Of itself, River Walker is a fine romance. ...But wait, there's more. Throw in the cyclic killings of abusive men and you have a tight little mystery. ...As if a sweet romance and intriguing murder mystery aren't enough, Culpepper throws in a good, old-fashioned ghost story. Romance, mystery, and ghost story—Culpepper does it all."
—*Kissed by Venus*

"*The Clinic* sets the tone for what promises to be a terrific series. Culpepper's writing style is spare and evocative, her plotting precise. You can't help but feel strongly for the Amazon warrior women and their plight, and this book is a must-read for all those who enjoy light fantasy coupled with a powerful story of survival and adventure. Highly recommended."—*Midwest Book Review*

"Culpepper's writing is crisp and refreshing, even in the midst of the difficult subject matter she has chosen for this story. Her turns of phrases are unique and resonate like harp strings plucked to create a beautiful tune."—*Just About Write*

"[*The Clinic*] is engaging and thought-provoking, and we are left pondering its lessons long after we read the last pages. …Culpepper is an exceptional storyteller who has taken on a very difficult subject, the subjugation of one people over another, and turned it into a spellbinding novel. As an author, she understands well that fiction can teach us our own history without the force and harshness of nonfiction. Yet *The Clinic* is just as powerful in its telling. "—*L-Word.com*

Visit us at www.boldstrokesbooks.com

By the Author

WINDIGO THRALL

by

Cate Culpepper

2014

WINDIGO THRALL

ISBN 13: 978-1-60282-950-3

This Trade Paperback Original Is Published By
Bold Strokes Books, Inc.
P.O. Box 249
Valley Falls, NY 12185

First Edition: January 2014

Credits
Editor: Cindy Cresap
Production Design: Susan Ramundo
Cover Art By Richard Gerhard
Cover Design By Sheri (graphicartist2020@hotmail.com)

Acknowledgments

I give thanks to all the gods that be that after eight books, I haven't managed to kill off my long-time editor, Cindy Cresap, with my penchant for comma splices and perpetually confused modifiers. Betas Connie Ward and Gill McKnight proved their usual indispensable selves in the writing of *Windigo Thrall*, though I declined Gill's suggestion that I change the title to *Eat Me*. A fond personal nod to Amy Kruetzman-Bernheisal and Pam Goodwin for their amazing support of all my books.

Dedication

For Sarah Dreher and Stoner McTavish

Prologue

1828
Snow Moon
Minnesota

She called on the last of her will and ran faster, her breath bursting from her laboring lungs in the frigid air. A raging wind gusted through the forest, slapping her face. The rough path wending through the trees was snarled with dead vines and fallen branches, and her feet and legs were scratched and bloody. She no longer felt pain or hunger or anything but cold, terrible cold.

But she was Chippewa, and her people knew winter and cold. Her people knew courage.

She ran on, cradling her newborn in her arms, his cries a thin, tired mewling against her breast.

The young brave who shared her furs, her life, ran after her, screaming. Ravenous.

The long, dark season had been cruel to her tribe. Great hunger. Death. And with great hunger came the unrelenting agony, the gnawing craving for the last taboo.

With great hunger came the Witiko, the Spirit of the Lonely Places. The Cannibal Beast.

A nursing mother, she was one of the lucky women the tribe tried to keep strong, but even her legs were spindly and weak.

She fell at last, as she knew she must, slipping on iced moss and crashing to the snow-crusted earth. He was on her in seconds, the handsome warrior she had loved all her life, the father of the child in her arms.

He crawled over her, gibbering, saliva dripping from his jaws, his sweet body and spirit like a spider's now. The Witiko had taken him, and there was nothing of the laughing Chippewa brave, the husband and father, left.

Except for one brief moment. She lay gasping on her back, squeezing the squalling baby in her arms as the man straddled her waist. His mad eyes found hers, and for one breath too cruel to endure, he was her love again. He knew them for his wife and son. His face filled with shock and horror and sure knowledge of what was to come, and he lifted his arms to the merciless moon and roared, in terror and loss and farewell.

She sobbed his name as his teeth found her throat.

CHAPTER ONE

Present day
Washington State

Grady looked at her young wife, whose eyes were clenched shut, lower lip clamped in her teeth. Elena held her hand in a death grip, and Grady gave it another comforting pat.

"Hey," Grady whispered. "You don't want to miss this."

Elena squinted one eye open. "We're crashing?"

"Nope, not crashing." Grady had offered this reassurance several times during the flight. "Just saying hello to an old friend."

She nodded out the plane's window. Elena frowned, but leaned forward and followed her gaze. Then her eyes widened and a smile tugged at her generous lips.

"*Madre de Diosa,*" Elena whispered. "Grady, she's beautiful."

The crystalline clarity of the day offered an amazing vista of snow-cloaked Mt. Rainier out the oblong window as they descended toward Seattle. It didn't surprise Grady that Elena deemed the old volcano a woman; Elena's kind eyes found the feminine in most of nature's creations. Rainier had always seemed more male to Grady, austere and remote. At least sixty climbers had lost their lives trying to scale its craggy peaks, but she decided to keep this particular tidbit to herself.

The plane dipped lower through a heavy blanket of clouds, darkening the cabin and sealing them in mist. Elena's smile faded as she sat back, her throat moving as she swallowed.

"Most crashes happen either during takeoff or landing," Elena pointed out.

Grady knew Elena had just summarized the whole of her knowledge of air travel, as this was her first flight. She still marveled that a woman could live for twenty-five years in this world and never board a plane, but Elena's world had always been a small desert town in southern New Mexico. "We're not going to crash. I absolutely guarantee it."

"An easy promise for you to make, Professor Gringa." Elena squeezed Grady's hand again. "If we crash and we both die, I will be too busy to hold a lie against you."

Grady raised Elena's hand to her lips and kissed it, then looked around to check their privacy, belatedly and out of sheer habit. They couldn't live openly as a couple in Mesilla, and that still grated on her. She wasn't a particularly physical person, but it would have been nice to comfort her frightened wife without worrying about hostile stares.

The plane, of course, was filled with weary travelers preparing for landing and paying them no mind, and they were floating down into a city where gay couples were no novelty. As foreign as a large urban center would seem to Elena, Grady was returning briefly to her home ground. She'd earned her doctorate in anthropology at the University of Washington and remembered Seattle fondly.

She was glad Elena kept her eyes shut as they emerged from the heavy overcast sky and thumped down onto the runway. While the sunlit air in the higher elevation had been sweet and clear, the cloud cover over Seattle was the dark, unbroken gray typical of long winter months in the Pacific Northwest. It already felt oppressive after the open skies of their desert valley, Grady's adopted home. Elena didn't stop whispering prayers until they rolled to a stop at the terminal, and Grady was finally able to gently extract her aching fingers from her damp grip.

She worried that Elena would be overwhelmed by the midday clamor at SeaTac, but as at most times, Elena proved open to new experience. Once she was sure they weren't about to plunge to their fiery deaths, she began to look around with interest. The easy sway returned to her full hips and the sparkle to her dark eyes as they weaved through families welcoming passengers home.

"We could live at this airport! Yes, let us live at this airport." Elena turned in a circle as Grady steered her toward baggage claim. "Look. Food from four different countries, in the last ten yards! Also stores for clothes. A whole store for cinnamon buns. And how many coffee shops does one city need?"

"Seattle will always have an insatiable need for salted caramel macchiatos. In this, they are my homies." Grady juggled their heavy coats over one arm and the case carrying her laptop with the other. "Listen, I'll grab our bags. Why don't you see if our ride is—"

"Sí, grab our bags, but let me carry these, *chica*." Elena took the coats and the case from Grady. "You don't have to butch me, remember? Sometimes I'm stronger than you. Plus, I need to get a souvenir for Mamá."

Elena trotted toward a shop and Grady watched her trot, grinning. Even with her arms full, Elena moved with the natural sensuality of a healthy woman at home in her body. Grady felt a pang and lay her hand over her heart. No one she knew in the Northwest would call Grady Wrenn fanciful, but she could testify in court that it was possible to love someone so much your heart actually hurt.

She still gave herself butch points for wrestling their luggage back to the souvenir shop. Dr. Chambliss hadn't told her how long this strange study might take, just to prepare for winter mountain weather, and they had packed for a siege of several days.

She found Elena chatting happily with an older woman wrapping her purchase on a glass-topped counter. Grady would have paid the cashier, thanked her, and left, but Elena chatted happily with just about everyone. She counted out several of her hard-earned bills on the counter, and Grady sighed. Elena was a respected curandera in Mesilla, but spiritual healers were not particularly well compensated these days.

"Grady! You'll love this." Elena rested her hand on the woman's wrist, then lifted the tissue paper away from a small, colorful mask constructed of thin pine and feathers.

Grady nodded, pleased. It was quite well made. "Hey, a good choice, given our assignment. That's a Makah mask, isn't it? The legend of the Cannibal Woman."

The cashier looked impressed. "That's right. You sure know our local tribes and their myths pretty well."

"Grady is a cultural anthropologist." Elena smiled proudly. "She knows so much about Native people. Grady, this is Trudy. She told me this little mask is of an evil woman who was a cannibal, and she wreaked havoc on the Makah until the children of the tribe defeated her."

Grady peered at the mask and tried hard not to say what she was thinking.

"And she looks *exactly* like my Mamá!" Elena finished.

"It's uncanny!" Grady agreed, and they cackled together. The sharp-toothed, half-crazed face did hold a remarkable resemblance to Inez Montalvo.

A hell of a long walk finally delivered them outside the sliding glass doors of the lobby to the arrivals pickup area. Cars were swerving in and out of the loading zone, but Grady saw none with anyone like Dr. Chambliss waiting for them. They hustled as well as they could toward the pedestrian shelter to await their ride.

"Your Seattle doesn't know how to rain, Grady." Elena shook out her long hair. She seemed to be enjoying the city so far, and their only view was the parking garage.

"Seattle's going to be disappointed to hear this. It thinks it's a fiend for rain."

"But no drops fall. I feel nothing; I just walk ten feet and I am suddenly wet!"

"Hate to break this to you, but it's not raining. That's normal Seattle air making you wet."

"I don't think so." Elena leaned briefly into Grady. "It's the company I keep."

Elena had been practicing sexual innuendo. She had been terrible at it when they first got together over a year ago, as she would be the first to admit, but they both had fun with it now.

"Elena, I am not going to have carnal knowledge of you on a stone bench outside of SeaTac."

"No? Then the women of Seattle must learn to be the fiends for carnal knowledge that the women of Mesilla are." Elena quirked one distinctive eyebrow at her, and Grady melted.

"I'll learn," Grady promised.

"And I will teach you." Elena bounced lightly on the bench. "We have a whole week for these lessons."

A week. It still seemed an impossible blessing, a week alone with Elena in the snowy grandeur and privacy of a mountain cabin. Grady taking this study meant the trip was comped by the university, and talking Elena into coming along was manna from heaven.

Speaking of hell, Elena's cell chimed. Her smile turned wry as she groped in her pocket. "Don't glare at me. This is your fault. You are the one who gave us all cell phones for Christmas. And you are the one who set mine to play 'Season of the Witch' when she calls." She flipped open her cell. "Hello, Mamá; we didn't crash."

The mental demons that haunted Inez Montalvo took the form of the most cantankerous nature Grady had ever known, and an absolute inability to leave her home. Her mother-in-law relied entirely on Elena for income, shopping, and daily assurance that she was safe and unlikely to be murdered. Inez was the reason her daughter had never set foot out of the Mesilla Valley, and it had taken some stamina for Elena to insist on her right to this rare vacation.

"Mamá, my *gringa wife* did fix the window, just like you asked. No one will get in."

Grady lifted the little Makah mask out of Elena's open bag and unwrapped it. She waggled it at Elena's face, as Inez's voice harangued her through the cell's speaker.

"And you know Cesar and Sylvia are going to stop by every day to see how you are." Elena closed her eyes and bit her lip as Grady shook the mask at her in an eerily accurate imitation of Inez. "Yes, they can be Grady's students and still be good Catholics. You'll be fine."

Laughter almost bubbled out of Elena, and she took the evasive action of kicking Grady's ankle, rather hard. Grady snickered and rewrapped the mask in its tissue paper.

"Go make some posole, Mamá." Elena's voice was infused, as always, with more fondness for her mother than frustration. Grady's affection for Inez was more grudging, but it was there. "And call me only if there's an *emergency. Te amo*, Mamá. I'm going to go have more carnal knowledge of my gringa wife now. Good-bye."

She snapped her cell closed and snorted laughter into Grady's shoulder.

❖

Pat Daka brushed the prayer stick in her pocket with the flat of her thumb. She had dreamed of the warrior and his woman again last night, their terrible deaths. Odd for her. She wasn't given to fancy, to creating people out of whole cloth. Having nightmares about them. It was this Windigo bullshit, invading her sleep.

She shifted her hips against the side of the Outback, glad for the idling SUV's warmth. It would be more comfortable inside her ride, but it was already too crowded in there for her liking. She didn't relish adding two more passengers. A crowd streamed through the glass-paneled doors of SeaTac. Arriving flights were heavy this afternoon. She didn't know how she was supposed to recognize this anthropologist when she saw her.

One of the back side windows purred down next to her elbow.

"Pat." The voice was terse. "Close your jacket, please."

Pat looked down into the piercing eyes of Joanne Call.

Jo gestured to the blond woman sitting on the cushioned seat beside her. "Becca is uneasy with guns."

Pat caught Becca's apologetic smile as the window slid up, and then she was staring at her own reflection in the glass. An impassive woman gazed back at her, rock-jawed, her blunt features framed by thick black hair, jagged above her pressed collar. She zipped her Park Service windbreaker shut, hiding the pistol holstered in her belt. Whenever Pat was off the mountain she preferred to be visibly armed, but she could accommodate Becca Healy's discomfort. She didn't know why Becca was uneasy with guns, but any woman who had to put up with Jo Call on a daily basis deserved a little indulgence.

The sprawling airport was far enough from Seattle to avoid heavy city traffic, but Pat was still restless without forest and rock and snow beneath her boots. Too many people down here. Mt. Rainier was blocked from her gaze by the tall parking garage nearby, but there was still light in the sky. The mountain would loom to the southeast as soon as they pulled out of SeaTac, beckoning on the horizon. Her spirit yearned toward it like a lost child for its mother.

A sharp rap sounded on the side window and she straightened. The glass lowered a mere inch and Jo's long finger emerged, pointing at a bench beneath an awning. Two women sat closely together, laughing. From Jo's curt signal, one of them must be their anthropologist. Pat slipped the toothpick from her lips and sauntered to them.

"Dr. Wrenn?" Pat eyed the slender white woman and the plump Latina with her.

"Grady. That's right." The woman got to her feet and peered at Pat through her glasses.

"Pat Daka. I'm a ranger with Mount Rainier National Park. I'm here to give you a lift."

"Yeah?" Grady looked puzzled. "Well, thanks. This is my friend, Elena Montalvo."

"Ma'am."

"Hello, Pat." The Latina was younger than Grady by about ten years. She stood, struggling with an armload of coats they should have donned before leaving the terminal, and extended one hand. "It's nice to meet you."

"Pleasure's mine." Pat shook her hand briefly. Elena's palm was cool and smooth except for the mild calluses that indicated she worked for a living. The other one, Grady, would have hands like silk. She had that academic vibe, like Jo. "Let me help you with those bags."

All this courtesy came naturally after three years in the Park Service, but she was glad to turn to the physical labor of hauling their luggage to the Outback. The vehicle Jo had purchased for her had been fully outfitted for Park mountain service, and it could accommodate five passengers easily. Pat just hoped none of them were big talkers.

One of the side doors of the truck swung open, and Becca Healy stepped out. "*Oh,* for heaven's sake. Your arms are six feet long, Jo. Please lend a hand with this stuff."

Jo unwound her limbs from the recessed seat, and all six feet of her stood beside Becca, biddable as a lamb. Grady came to an odd dead halt on the sidewalk. Curious, Pat tipped her mirrored sunglasses up and watched the two white women glare at each other.

"Hello, Dr. Call," Grady said. "I hadn't realized you were coming along on this jaunt."

"As you see." Jo lifted one large suitcase effortlessly and carried it to the rear of the Outback. "We're parked in a loading zone."

Pat pushed aside bags of groceries to make room, her curiosity unsated. These two had some history, that was obvious, but their apparently mutual hostility wasn't surprising. Pat had known Jo all her life, and she had that effect on everyone.

"*Gracias*, Dr. Call." Elena's tone was friendly, but Jo bypassed her offered hand and slipped into the front seat.

"*De nada*," Becca answered her. "You've now heard every word in Spanish I know."

Jo's new girlfriend carried the social graces as naturally and lightly as a second skin, and how that awkward geek had won her heart was a complete mystery to Pat. Becca went to Elena and clasped her hand in both her own. "You've met Pat and Jo. I'm Becca. You're Elena and Grady. Welcome to Seattle!"

Becca stepped back to include them all in her warm smile. "You guys ready to catch a cannibal monster?"

❖

Becca noted Jo's fast slide into the shotgun seat, leaving her to share the back with their new colleagues. She didn't mind; prolonged physical closeness to anyone other than Becca was difficult for Jo.

Riding with Pat was like traveling under the protective guard of a butch Lone Ranger. Becca took in the square, strong set of the young Makah woman's shoulders as she steered them skillfully out of SeaTac. Ah, women in uniform. She wished she knew more about Pat and her family, the odd relationship between Pat and Jo. Perhaps this weekend would provide time for some private coffee conversation.

Elena was gazing out the window with a dreamy smile, her cheeks flushed with color. She looked excited as a kid, and not much older than one. Grady Wrenn sat flipping slowly through screens on her iPhone, a scowl on her handsome face. Becca had wondered if they were a couple, and the identical rings they wore, beautiful swirls of silver and turquoise, cinched that notion.

Grady glanced through the window as they turned south on I-5. "They've moved the university?"

"We're not meeting Dr. Chambliss this afternoon. He's sending us straight to Rainier." Jo was texting rapidly, her voice impassive.

Grady didn't look pleased with this announcement. "Hey, we planned to spend the night in the city. I wanted to show Elena a few sights."

"Change of plans." Jo closed her cell. "Heavy snow is forecast for the lower elevations this weekend. Time is a factor here, and Chambliss wants us on the mountain before the roads are iced in."

"I see." Grady frowned at the back of Jo's head.

"Don't we have time for a quick dinner before we go up, Pat?" Becca asked. "Fresh salmon at Ivar's?"

"I'm afraid they close the gates to the foothills at Longmire at five p.m." Pat kept her eyes on the road. "We'll make it, but there's no time to stop."

"Ach," Becca sighed. "I'm sorry your plans were wrecked, Grady."

Grady's face cleared and she returned Becca's smile, gracious enough to allow an awkward moment to pass in response to friendliness. "I guess they're only postponed."

"Yes, the city will still be here when we come back." Elena plucked Grady's sleeve. "Look, chica! Already you are showing me marvels undreamed of in our little valley."

Becca ducked her head toward the forested hills flanking the highway. "You mean trees?"

"Trees," Elena repeated reverently. "Green, everywhere you look, even in winter. You live in such a beautiful place, Becca."

"That we do. I love it here." Becca saw Pat flick Elena a smile in the rearview mirror and she agreed with her; she liked Elena, her eagerness, the warmth in her eyes as she regarded her more reserved partner. "Wait till you see the land around Jo's cabin, Elena. Trees thick as bristles in a brush. It's gorgeous. Pat lives on the property and she keeps it in excellent shape."

"Jo's cabin?" Grady's tone was polite. "I didn't realize you owned the cabin Dr. Chambliss secured for this study, Dr. Call. Will you be staying there with us, then?"

Becca thought she detected rising horror in Grady's expressive features, but it was quickly hidden. She answered for Jo, a habit she'd fallen into because she usually managed not to piss people off by merely speaking, and Jo would rather not communicate, period. "Yes, we're all helping Pat with this investigation. Don't worry. The place is huge. There's more than enough room for us. I kind of begged my way into this little jaunt. I'm a social worker, and Jo felt I might be helpful in talking to the family."

"Begging wasn't necessary." Jo seemed so formal, so unlike her relaxed animation when they were alone. "You deserve some time off. You work too hard, Becca." She glanced back at her. "I wish you would fasten your seat belt."

Becca heard Jo's protectiveness, her concern for her, her real pleasure that Becca was along on this trip—all of that in those few terse statements. She doubted their new friends heard the love in Jo's curt words, but it was there. "Well, we don't get to work together very often. Our fields don't blend that much, so I jumped at this chance."

"I'd think your field would be an unusual match for this study, Dr. Call." Grady folded one leg over the other on the spacious back seat. "Dr. Call is an expert in afterlife communication, Elena."

Elena's expression was an interesting blend of fascination and acceptance. "Yes? Then we are in the same field."

Grady nodded. "Elena is a curandera in our home in New Mexico. An herbalist, a nurse, and a spiritual healer." She reached over and clasped Elena's hand. Elena's eyes flew to Becca and her smile faltered, but then she relaxed again and pressed Grady's fingers.

"Hey, I'd love to hear more about your work, Elena." Becca meant it. "Jo's taught me a lot about what might lie beyond—"

"I have only the most peripheral connection to the anthropology department," Jo interrupted. "I teach a course in transpersonal psychology to Chambliss's graduate students. That involves the self-transcendent or spiritual aspects of the human experience."

Becca noted, with both amusement and consternation, that Grady mouthed this definition silently as Jo spoke it.

"Chambliss commissioned me for this study because I specialize in capturing recordings of sounds generated by afterlife entities," Jo went on. "And apparently, those sounds are manifesting in this Chippewa family."

"This Chippewa family is hearing a voice from the dead." Grady's expression had closed again. "The voice of the Windigo."

Becca saw Pat's shoulders tense, a subtle stiffening.

"That's correct," Jo said.

"The Chippewa aren't native to the Pacific Northwest," Grady said slowly. "And neither is the Windigo."

"That's correct."

"So we're thinking this Chippewa family relocated cross-country, all the way from Minnesota, and brought the Cannibal Beast with them?"

"Correct." Impatience had entered Jo's tone as Pat turned off on the smaller highway toward Mt. Rainier, and Becca thought again, as she had so many times since she fell in love with this difficult woman, that she would spend her life helping Jo navigate the treacherous territory of human interaction. If she had fallen in love with a partner who was physically disabled, Becca reminded herself, she would spend her life steering her wheelchair over cracked sidewalks. Willingly. She and Jo were dealing with a disability that could be just as challenging, and it merited equal compassion and patience.

"This family feels they're suffering from some kind of curse." Becca was filled with uneasy wonder at the prospect of such a burden. "They fled their home tribe to escape this Windigo, and they're afraid that somehow it followed them here."

"And can I ask how the Park Service got involved in all this?" Grady asked the back of Pat's head.

"Some local called in a complaint about the Abequas squatting on Park property," Pat said. "When I talked to the family, they were all focused on this Windigo curse. I passed the recording of our interview on to Jo. I knew she was experienced in such things."

Pat volunteered nothing else, but then Pat generally volunteered little, Becca noted. Jo seemed to speak directly to her only to issue one instruction or another. She treated Pat like a paid servant. But then, with the exception of Becca, Jo treated most people that way.

"Pat has arranged for us to meet with the family tomorrow morning." Jo glanced back at Grady. "I hope you're accustomed to rising early, Dr. Wrenn."

"Seriously? We're going to be 'doctoring' each other for three days?" Becca's voice was teasing. "Can we make it Grady and Jo?"

"I'm fine with that," Grady said. "If she is."

Becca saw Elena stroke Grady's wrist, the same comforting touch Becca offered Jo on a daily basis. There was a definite prickliness between their two doctors, even more palpable than the discomfort Jo's brusqueness usually inspired, and Becca didn't understand it. Grady didn't seem the type to be prone to easy annoyance, to disliking people on sight. The laugh lines were deep around her mouth, and her gray eyes were friendly and kind, at least when she looked at Becca.

Silence filled the lush interior of the vehicle as the powerful motor purred beneath them, carrying them deeper into the hills. Pat clicked on the strong wash of the headlights, pushing back the gathering darkness that fell so early on the mountain this time of year. Becca sat back in her seat, content with the beauty of the twilight scenery and the quiet to enjoy it.

They drove past the poignant Morton's Loggers' Memorial, dedicated to the men who lost their lives in that once vital, often lethal profession. At a crossroad a few miles farther north, Becca saw the lonely roadside shrine to a park ranger who had been killed only the winter before.

"Damn, that's a gruesome image." Jo shuddered visibly as they passed the monument. "You'd think they could do better than that for her."

Becca lowered her eyes, annoyed. She found the laminated photo of the young officer resting on a simple pine altar poignant and fitting.

Elena looked back. "This is a tribute to a ranger who was lost? Did you know her, Pat?"

"Margaret Anderson was a mother of two," Pat said. "She was shot by a man trying to escape the police."

Becca winced in sympathy. Of course Pat had known that young woman. She had probably worked with her. She regretted Jo's insensitivity all over again.

"Did they catch the man?" Elena asked.

"Yes," Pat said. "The guy who shot her died himself, later that night. He froze to death in a stream."

"Good," Elena said, and Pat nodded.

Becca gave herself a mild shake. What in any god's titties was wrong with her today? Of all the beautiful sights she could be pointing out to their guests, they were chatting about memorials and murder. It was unlike Becca to dwell on sadness, cruelty, and loss, yet it was suddenly all she could see on this pretty drive. Pat's vehicle was Outback's best. It cost twice what Becca made in a year, and its heater was a blast furnace, but she was shivering nonetheless.

The wind wasn't helping. Gusts were picking up, punching lightly at the steel skin of their chariot, creating periodically ghostly whistles. Pat drove with a sure and practiced hand, and Becca trusted her to deliver them safely through a blizzard, if it came. She wasn't afraid for their physical safety; she just didn't like the wind.

Becca pulled her eyes from the window and met Elena's gaze. Elena was watching her with mild concern, one eyebrow lifted in a way that made her seem more mature, almost maternal. Becca grinned and winked at her, feeling a little foolish. She was fine, she told Elena silently. They were all fine, and a hot tub and s'mores and a crackling fireplace awaited them. She couldn't wait to show Elena the cabin.

❖

Not many people could wink at Elena without making her feel like either a prostitute or a child. But this Becca created a good thing—this nice, friendly wink with no trace of condescension—so it was fine, and Elena winked back at her.

She knew what was disturbing Becca. She only wondered why Grady and Pat and this strange Joanne didn't seem to hear it. The winds around the old mountain teemed with ghosts. They howled with a sense of loss that filled Elena with wonder and sadness. There were so many of them.

But then the winds in her desert valley had always been rich in spirits. Her Diosa hadn't chosen to show her many of them, which, for the most part, Elena appreciated. The spirits in Grady's old lands were noisy, but they seemed content hiding in their thick forest.

"The intent of the study is simply to report." Jo was continuing a conversation Elena thought had ended many miles ago. *Her spirit struggles so, my Mother,* she told her Goddess. "There are some anomalies in the interview between Pat and members of this family that Chambliss wants us to document."

Grady stirred beside Elena, her hand warm in hers. It was good to be among people who accepted such things. "You said this entire family believes they're cursed by a Windigo?"

"Correct, that's what I said." Jo sounded impatient again, and Becca sighed.

If they knew her Grady better, they would know she was not mocking this family's fears. She always treated people who believed in other worlds with respect. Since Grady had met Elena, the poor woman had become one of them.

"Not strictly correct." Pat's voice was dry. "The Abequas believe only one person in their family, the oldest woman, has this Windigo curse. The rest are just scared of it."

"What kind of anomalies came up in your interview?" Grady asked Pat, but it was Jo who answered.

"The interview was recorded. We'll hear it once we're settled." Jo paused as Pat turned them up a rattling rattrap of a road, more a wide path through the dense trees that grew quickly steeper. "We're nearly there."

And Elena was starting to think it was a good thing, that they were nearly at this cabin. She was beginning to feel afraid.

She didn't think Becca could hear it anymore; she was leaning forward in her seat, talking quietly to Jo. Pat was driving, and Grady was lost in her notes.

They were not many voices, the ghosts howling out there in the dark. They were one voice.

It wasn't here yet, but it was coming.

The big truck actually shuddered with its blasting scream.

"Damn, those winds are picking up." Grady knuckled a circle of steam from her side window.

"Yes, precursor to the storm," Jo replied. "It's not due to hit until tomorrow night."

"How big are we talking?" Grady asked.

"Don't worry, Doctor—Grady. Pat's vehicle has traction tires and chains in the trunk."

Elena squeezed her eyes shut, trying to block out that terrible noise, that lost and evil roaring. *Sweet Goddess, You who created every creature, living and dead, what have You done? What is this beast?*

A spirit of the lonely places does not help me. I do not know what that is. Please, my Mother, speak again, don't fade away as You do sometimes when I most need You.

"Hey." Grady's voice was low, her breath warm on Elena's hair. "You all right?"

She was getting there. The wind was the same, but the terrible, unnatural life in it was fading. The voice was falling silent.

"Elena?"

"Sí, I'm fine." She opened her eyes and patted Grady's hand. Her pulse was returning to normal. The darkness around them receded, and it wasn't haunted midnight anymore, just windy dusk.

Grady's smile was shy and sweet. "It's going to be all right," she whispered.

Elena knew Grady thought she was feeling sorry they wouldn't be alone together on this vacation. *Always, mi Diosa, Grady considers my heart.*

Then they pulled to a stop on a gravel circle and Elena looked up and *ay*! They were in Disneyland! Only better than Disneyland, where Elena had never been. Here was a castle, and all for them. This "cabin" that belonged to Jo was two stories high. It was huge, all paneled glass and rich honeyed wood.

And Sweet Goddess, was that a hot tub?

CHAPTER TWO

Jo glared up at the high ceiling, resenting the noise the two women made settling in, grudgingly aware that their rustling was muffled and faint. Sturdy construction helped immensely, and Jo needed thick walls in any abode she shared, even temporarily, with others.

"I hope they understand the upper level is entirely self-contained." Jo was unpacking the electronics while Becca handled their more personal possessions. Pat was taking her sweet time fetching firewood. "There's even a small kitchen up there. No reason at all to spend a lot of time together, except when we're working."

"Come on, I like them." Becca set the small framed photos she insisted on carrying with them everywhere on the mantel of the large fireplace. "Grady has a good smile, and it's cool that Elena's familiar with spiritual lore. She might prove helpful in this study."

"Chambliss hired an anthropologist for this study, not her girlfriend." Jo tuned the synthesizer carefully into the speakers. "She'll probably want to throw in a lot of primitive superstition. We don't need her mixing in Hispanic folk myths when this is a purely Native American phen—"

Becca's arms sliding around her waist from behind silenced her. "Dearest, do you plan to be in this mood throughout the upcoming blizzard? Because if you are, I'm moving directly to the dumping you outside in the slush option, and I'll spend the night in here making s'mores with Grady and Elena and Pat."

Jo smiled reluctantly and turned in Becca's arms. She sifted the softness of her hair in her fingers. Becca's tone had been light, but there was a weariness in her gaze that made Jo uneasy. She quickly reviewed everything she had said to the other three women on the drive here. She had just answered their questions, hadn't she? She hadn't been rude.

"I'll cheer up. I promise." Jo glanced up the wide staircase to check their privacy, then lowered her head and kissed Becca gently. "We brought plenty of groceries. If you like, we can make them a nice dinner."

Becca accepted her peace offering with a second kiss, a light brushing of lips that never failed to thrill Jo. "Uh, neither of us cook all that well, ace. Unless you brought lots of good deli stash…"

"I did."

"Cold cuts it is. And s'mores. Thank you, honey."

"You're welcome." Jo heard voices on the stairs and released Becca. Grady and Elena had changed out of their traveling clothes and they looked inordinately refreshed as they joined them. Jo remembered the quiet rustling upstairs and surmised they had not spent the entire time unpacking, but that was none of her business.

Jo wondered if Elena was the reason Grady Wrenn seemed lighter, somehow, than she remembered. She recalled a younger Grady's disposition as rather somber. She had taken her studies seriously as a doctoral student, and Chambliss said she had been equally diligent and accomplished in her career. Grady hadn't mentioned the class she took from Jo years ago, and she was grateful. Becca didn't need to hear another account of her infamous social inadequacy. At least Grady hadn't been among the cruelest of her students.

"Our capitol building in Santa Fe is maybe this grand, but maybe not!" Elena turned in a circle, taking in the spacious living room. Jo hardly noticed the luxury of the cabin anymore, and it was interesting to see it through fresh eyes.

She noted that Grady moved directly to the framed tapestries on the white walls, intrigued by their designs. She expected Elena to check out the large flat-screen television and other recreational amenities, but she focused instead on the photographs Becca had set on the mantel.

"Such nice faces. Are these your parents, Becca?"

"Yep, my mom and dad." Becca smiled. Jo knew any mention of Becca's lost parents pleased her now more than saddened her, and she was glad for that.

"I see the resemblance. And these laughing women, these are your friends?"

"Yeah, that's me and Jo and our buddies at the Rose, a great place in town. Maybe we can take you there, after we stuff you with salmon at Ivar's."

Jo wished Becca would stop promising these strangers social engagements, but she didn't really mind. Not with Becca looking at her with a simple affection and pride that warmed her to her core. It was Becca's reference to "our buddies" which she had spoken so naturally. She knew how hard Jo had worked to open herself to the friends Becca loved so much. How she had struggled to earn her place in their circle, and how pleased they both were that she'd won them over at last.

"And this beautiful painting of Mount Rainier." Elena stepped back to admire the large framed oil above the mantel. "Do you know the artist, Jo?"

"Yes, Pat's grandmother painted that. She was quite talented. I'm about set up here, Grady, if you're ready to hear that interview," Jo said in a friendly and welcoming tone.

"Sandwiches first, then interview." Becca headed toward the kitchen. "Somebody call Pat. I can also put cocoa on. That's an inspired call. I'll put cocoa on."

"I'm glad to help." Grady followed her, and Jo sighed. She would have much preferred to review the protocol for this study with Grady than make small talk with her girlfriend. She just hoped Grady remembered to wash her hands.

To her relief, the "spiritual healer" didn't seem inclined toward aimless chatter. Elena circled the room with her hands clasped behind her, studying the rich leather furniture in oak frames, the sumptuous Pendleton throw rug warming the hardwood floor before the hearth. Soft laughter emerged from the kitchen and, thank goodness, the sound of running water.

"I wouldn't even know what to call many of these things." Elena was standing beside Jo, her tone diffident, looking at the bank of computers and speakers lining the shelves. "You use these to speak to the dead, Jo?"

At least with this woman, Jo didn't have to deal with skepticism about survival beyond death, as she often encountered in the public. "Reliable communication with afterlife entities hasn't been established yet, I'm afraid." She remembered who she was speaking to and simplified. "We really can't talk to the dead at will. We're lucky if we can catch recordings of random messages. I've captured a few intriguing ones, though."

"Yes, me too." Elena's eyes crinkled warmly. "Do you ever hear from that old bat grandmother from Albuquerque? The one who keeps calling her son-in-law a *pinche* little bitch?"

It took Jo a moment to realize Elena was joking. After long years of study, she was adept at reading faces, but humor still often eluded her. She chuckled stiffly, and wished Pat would show up to fill the hearth.

They stood silently together, listening to the faint laughter from the kitchen. Elena's easiness with the quiet, paradoxically, made it easier for Jo to converse. "It's fascinating, though, trying to learn why these communications happen. Why ghosts, for lack of a better term, would make the effort to contact the living."

"They want us so badly." Elena rested her shoulder against the mantel. "Our ghosts are lonely for us. They are bonded so strongly to the people they left behind, they cannot bear the silence."

Elena couldn't know she had just described the guiding mystery of Jo's life—the possibility of such vital human connection, such love. It was why she had gone into this field, why she listened to the dead, to try to grasp the strength of that bond. She had only recently begun to understand it, and the reason was in the kitchen making sub sandwiches.

"But not every spirit is a harmless one." Elena seemed somber now, and she stood very still. "They do not always come back for benevolent reasons."

"Oh, I don't know." Jo smiled indulgently. "I've recorded voices that sounded angry or bitter. But I feel the portrayal of evil, bloodthirsty ghosts is largely a pop culture phenomenon. Something more likely to sell movie tickets than evident in the research—"

She broke off as Grady stepped down into the living room, carrying a heaping platter of thin-sliced meat and soft rolls. Becca followed with a tray of steaming mugs, her cheeks flushed prettily, apparently from the steam.

"Grady tells me they make grilled bananas with rum ice cream and Mexican hot chocolate sauce in Mesilla, Jo," Becca said. "Jo, we're moving to this Mesilla."

Jo helped her settle the tray on the table and entered carefully into the spirit of banter. "Well, we have gourmet chocolate truffles here in Seattle."

"I think you're missing the nuances of dessert, dearest, but I'll never sneeze at a chocolate truffle." Becca settled into a chair at the table and brushed her hands together greedily. The relish with which Becca consumed any food that was not unduly healthy still charmed Jo. She looked up as the broad front door opened. "Oh good, Pat! Just in time for chow. Join us."

Pat was carrying a double armload of kindling from the tarped stack she kept fully stocked out back. She grunted something courteous at Becca as she hustled the wood down the flagstone steps to the fireplace. "That's okay. I've got groceries in my trailer. Let me get a fire going here, then I—"

"Then you will join us for dinner, please," Becca said. "You guys want any of this? I'd be quick."

Apparently, Elena shared Becca's appreciation of fine cuisine. She plunked down next to Becca and dug in, leaving Jo and Grady to do an awkward two-step around the table to find chairs. They smiled at each other woodenly as they sat.

"You've got a pretty forested spread up here, Jo. Off the beaten track." Grady lifted a roll and split it open. "It seems nice and secluded."

"Yes, my family purchased the property many years ago." Jo glanced over her shoulder at Pat, who was striking a match to ignite the firewood. She saw no need to get into the specifics of their shared history. "I had this cabin renovated more recently. Thank you," she added.

"It's beautiful up here, but easier to imagine our cannibal monster in these snowy woods." Becca bit deeply into her sandwich and still managed to talk around it gracefully. "With those tall trees pressing in and a storm coming on, this place is perfect for Windigo ghost stories."

"Strictly speaking, the Windigo isn't a ghost." Jo hesitated, then deferred to Grady, more the expert when it came to such myths, and hoped Becca noticed her graciousness. "Isn't that correct?"

Her mouth full, Grady shrugged, nodded, then shrugged again. Elena laughed and dabbed a smudge of mustard from the side of Grady's mouth with her finger.

"Right," Grady said finally. "I know more about southwestern tribes than those who live in the north, but I believe the Windigo was never a living human being. It was a malevolent spirit that possessed humans and turned them into cannibals."

Pat approached the table, brushing wood dust off her palms, her blunt features ruddy from the cold. Becca smiled a welcome and scooted her chair to make room for her, then turned back to Grady. "That's the Windigo's entire résumé? That's all it did? Boo, you're a cannibal, go eat someone?"

Grady grinned, but Elena was listening carefully. "Well, it was a pretty handy spook to have around. The northern tribes had to endure some terrible winters. Awful famines. Cannibalism was a tremendous taboo among the Chippewa because it was a very real prospect when people got desperate enough. Investing a lot of fear in a Windigo helped keep the social order."

"What a sad necessity." Becca looked at the lavish spread of food before them. "There's a miracle that rarely occurs to me. That none of us will probably ever know hunger like that."

"Gracias a Diosa," Elena murmured.

Jo helped herself to potato salad and studied Pat, unable to read her face. Jo had once been incapable of reading most facial expression or body language, but she had made a thorough and careful study of human micro expressions. Now she could write texts on interpreting them. She wondered if Pat's guarded look was due to some offense she was taking at their conversation. Perhaps some politically incorrect insensitivity? "Are you familiar with this particular Native legend, Pat? I doubt that the Chippewa have much in common with your Makah tribe."

"No. I don't know anything about the Windigo." Pat accepted a sandwich from Grady with a nod of thanks.

Jo sighed. Perhaps Pat's frown was due to Jo's comment about purchasing the property that had belonged to Pat's family for generations. It was amazing how long some people could hold a grudge. Jo had been all of five years old when her parents bought this land; she could hardly be blamed if Pat's people were disenfranchised. She had been more than generous, trying to atone. She scowled at her. Pat was strong as an ox, but she was looking a little thin. She lived alone now. There was no one around to make sure she was taking good care of herself. Jo pushed the bowl of potato salad toward Pat sternly and then heard faint chiming music.

Becca peered around. "Is that 'Season of the Witch'?"

"We just sat down to eat, of course it is our witch." Elena rolled her eyes at Grady and rummaged in the pocket of her jeans. "Grady set my cell to play this whenever my mother calls. Grady is going to hell. Would you excuse me for a moment? I won't be long, believe me." She stood and walked off toward the kitchen, murmuring into her phone.

"Elena's mother," Grady explained. "She's a little—attentive. So, this Chippewa family that traveled out here, Jo. They think the oldest among them has been cursed by a Windigo? That she might become a cannibal?"

"Correct, the grandmother of the clan." Jo touched her napkin to her lips and got up. "This recording I mentioned is of the interview between Pat and the grandmother. It took place in the family home, not far from here. A few weeks ago, Pat?"

"Two weeks." Pat hadn't touched her sandwich, or the potato salad Jo had offered her.

"Do we know if there's any history of mental illness, Pat?" Becca asked. "In the grandmother, or other family?"

Jo answered her. "The possibility that some kind of culture-bound psychopathology might be at work is the reason Grady was asked to join this study." She went to the computer and clicked on the program containing the recording. "This interview is why our intrepid ranger here called me. You tell me what you think."

A subtle electronic purr filled the large room, followed by the crackling of an inferior recording device. Pat's low voice issued from the speakers.

❖

"*Okay. It's what, the third of January, about ten a.m. I'm Deputy Marshall Patricia Daka. I'm here with members of the Abequa family.*"

Pat's faint nausea returned at the prospect of hearing this. She would have to start smoking again if Jo insisted on playing this thing all weekend. She fingered the smooth prayer stick in her pocket, then slid out a toothpick to clamp in her teeth. Becca and Grady probably had no idea what they were getting into, but they were about to get a hint, and she felt a twinge of sympathy for them. Her own oddly flat voice continued.

"*I'm here about a report that the Abequas, a pretty large family, have been living on Lot Two-Four-Seven-Seven without a permit. But you're telling me you're all hiding here, hoping to escape someone, sir? Someone's out to get your family?*"

More rustling, then a man's gruff voice. "*No. Not someone.*"

"*That's Frank Abequa. I'm in the home Mr. Abequa shares with his grandmother, Selly Abequa, who's also present. Not someone, then—but what did you call whatever's chasing you, sir?*"

"*Witiko.*"

Becca leaned forward, intent on this pronunciation. Grady was listening quietly beside her. Jo crossed her arms and leaned back against the wall, watching them.

"*We call it Witiko. It's also called Windigo, or Wendigo,*" the man continued.

Pat remembered the deep circles beneath his eyes, his pallor, his weak chin. According to his Minnesota driver's license, Frank Abequa was fifty, but he looked twenty years older.

"*My grandmother thinks it followed her here. She's afraid it's going to hurt us.*"

"*A Windigo?*" *Pat sounded puzzled.* "*Can you say—*"

Abequa broke in, impatient. "*You should talk to Margaret. She deals with you people. She'll be here in a few days.*"

"I'm fine with talking with this person in a few days, but I do need more information today. Ma'am? Mrs. Abequa, your grandson mentioned a Windigo. Would you like to tell me about this?"

A sighing sound came over the speakers, as if this woman was so old she could no longer summon a voice, so ancient she could only moan in pain.

"Maybe you're right, I won't be able to help," Pat said. "But I'd like to give it a try."

The sighing sound was heard again.

"And when was this?" Pat asked.

"She's not picking up very well," Becca murmured. "I'm not hearing what the grandmother says."

"Keep listening," Jo said.

Pat's voice. "I see. This is when you lived back in Minnesota?"

That strangely unnerving gust again, a long, unbroken exhalation of breath.

Both Becca and Grady looked at Pat, puzzled.

"Pat's voice," Jo said quietly, "and the voice of Frank Abequa, came through clearly on this recording. But whenever the grandmother speaks, all that registered was this."

Becca shuddered visibly as the low moaning filled the room.

"Pat, you weren't hearing that?" Grady's eyes were large, and Jo smiled as if she were rather enjoying her reaction. "No one's saying anything about that wind, and you sound like the grandmother's answering you."

"Selly Abequa responded to all my questions very clearly." Pat raised her voice slightly to be heard over the discordant tone. "She told me the story we all know so far, about her family being chased by a Windigo. And she was calm and lucid through the whole thing. That's why this shook me a little."

"Listen." Jo nodded toward the speakers.

On the recording, Pat was asking more gentle questions, but her voice was fading. The wind was taking over. The sigh had become an eerie blast, and the powerful speakers sent it whistling around them.

There were atonal chords within this wind, a grating, animalistic growl that lifted the hair on the back of Pat's neck. And it grew in volume, filling their fire-warmed space with a nerve-jangling roar. Both Grady and Becca blanched, and Pat bit her toothpick in half.

A fleeting image of Pat's dream coasted through her mind. The Native woman racing in terror through a haunted night, chased by the unearthly howling of that same wind. She shivered, hard.

"That's what we needed to hear." Jo moved quickly to shut down the computer. "That sound continues for another three minutes, unbroken, and then stops. End of recording."

Becca had her hand pressed to her waist, and she reached over to lay trembling fingers on Grady's arm. "I might throw up on you, Grady. Sorry in advance if I do. Jesus, Pat, no wonder you were shaken."

Grady swallowed visibly. "I've never heard anything like that."

"I have, earlier today."

Pat hadn't seen Elena return to the room. She regarded them quietly, sliding her cell into her pocket.

"That's the voice of the demon who travels on the winds of this mountain," Elena said. "I heard it on the drive here. It hasn't arrived yet, but it's coming."

CHAPTER THREE

G rady loved field work and truly enjoyed the winds of the desert plains and the whistle of the breeze through high pine. This wind, tonight, she wasn't so nuts about. Frowning, she let the fabric of the heavy drape slip between her fingers across the dark window and turned to survey the expansive room.

The bedroom on the upper level of Joanne Call's cabin was larger than Grady's entire house in Mesilla. Through necessity, Elena still lived with her mother above her shop, but she spent as much time as possible at Grady's house. Her small, cramped house.

A gust battered the window behind Grady, and she flinched. The memory of the ghostly gale on that recording still had her spooked, and this late night wind echoed it too well.

Her highly sensitive wife, however, seemed unaffected by the sound. Elena's full figure was spread-eagled in the middle of the huge bed, the thick sea-green comforter extending a good two feet on all sides of her languid limbs. Grady didn't know how many thousand-thread counts those pricey sheets and pillowcases contained, but for Elena's sake she appreciated Jo sparing no expense in outfitting this place.

"We are buying a plane ticket for this *fabuloso* bed. It is coming home with us." Elena's chin was lifted, her eyes closed, her voice a dreamy purr. "Are you going to lurk over there by the window all night, like your Scottish banshee?"

Grady took three strides and hopped nimbly on top of the high bed. Elena giggled as she stepped around her and wrestled the comforter back. They both scrambled beneath the fleece sheets and assumed their natural spoon, Grady cuddling Elena's curves warmly from behind. She would have preferred to be spooning a naked wife, but the winter chill of the night outside justified Elena's worn cotton nightgown.

Grady buried her nose in Elena's curls and breathed in the safety of home. The cavernous room was dark, save for the subtle red glow of a nightlight low on the wall in one corner. The stately cabin was settling into a nest of snow and sleep around them, and Grady heard nothing from the lower level; Jo and Becca must have turned in too. And Pat, the ranger—had Becca said she lived on the property? Grady hoped the presence of law enforcement might keep her from throttling Jo Call before the end of the weekend.

"You know, I didn't pick up on them being a couple until we were halfway to Rainier." Grady lipped a tendril of Elena's dark hair out of her mouth. "I never would have figured Joanne Call capable of a relationship. And with someone like Becca Healy? Becca seems so normal."

Grady wasn't usually inclined to gossip, or to unkind character assessments, but Elena wouldn't judge her and she was still too cranked from that damn recording to sleep.

"Yes, Becca is very nice. And educated. You can tell she's had a lot of college."

Grady wondered a little at the wistfulness in Elena's tone.

"It must have been a surprise to you, to see your old teacher again. Was Jo a terrible teacher when you knew her years ago?" Elena asked. "Is that why you dislike her?"

"Not terrible." Grady sighed. "Just pretty obnoxious. Condescending and clumsy socially. Some of the jerkier guys in the class made fun of her, to her face. She doesn't even remember me. But it's good she's with Becca. I remember thinking she had to be a lonely woman."

"We can be happy they found each other." Elena turned in her arms and rested her head on Grady's shoulder, which had been designed precisely for this purpose. "Pat Daka is a lonely person, but the love between Becca and Jo feels strong to me, Grady. And look at the life they have ahead, protected by so much money."

Yes, definitely a wistfulness in Elena, but no trace of resentment. Elena and her maddening mother struggled constantly to pay bills, but she seemed to consider this their lot in life. She accepted Grady's frequent offers of help only rarely. One of the strengths of their young marriage was refusing to let money be an issue. This palace of a cabin had to be a dazzling new world to Elena.

"Well, you deserve a taste of how the two percent lives." Grady rested her lips on Elena's brow. "Even in a shared cabin. More power to the wealthy Dr. Call. The girl needs some perks in her favor."

Like all of Jo's students, Grady had known she was very wealthy. She didn't know the origin of her fortunes; she doubted afterlife communication provided that lucrative a living. But perhaps it brought more than a professor in a small college in southern New Mexico made. Grady would never be able to buy them a bed like this.

"Money will not protect our new friends, any of us, from this Windigo, Grady." Elena seemed stronger in her arms, still loving and tender, but she was holding a curandera now. "This family faces a terrible enemy, and I don't know how we can help them."

"Help them?" Grady stroked her hair. "I'm afraid we won't be able to help them, babe. We're here to listen to their story, document it for a journal."

"Well. My Goddess will direct us as She will."

Elena lay still for a while, and Grady could feel her gazing into the dark.

"You heard a voice in the wind today," Grady said finally. "And your goddess spoke to you about it?"

"I tried to explain downstairs," Elena said. "I didn't do a very good job of it. But yes, my Mother told me this is the Spirit of the Lonely Places. And tonight, in the wind howling out of those speakers, She whispered to me that its heart is encased in ice."

"Its heart is encased in ice?" Grady actually hadn't heard that whisper, and she was rather sorry Elena had remembered to bring it up now. An ugly image, this ravening monster pumping frost through its veins. "Did She happen to mention if this Lonely Places spirit is going to try to eat us?"

Elena laughed softly and snuggled back into her. "Mi Diosa doesn't warn me away from disasters, heathen *esposa* of mine. Otherwise She would have stopped me from buying my used Toyota."

"Elena. I'm still getting used to the notion that your Diosa talks to you, period." Grady lifted her head, but it was too dark to see her face. "The creator of all things, the omniscient and all-powerful, and She speaks to you, personally."

Elena murmured something light and teasing, letting Grady dwell on this. She rarely felt the need to explain her faith, and she was indulgent toward Grady's doubts. Grady wasn't even sure she could describe herself as a heathen anymore, since knowing Elena. Her curendera's world was too filled with spirits, some of whom Grady had seen at work in her own life, to comfortably accommodate her lifelong agnosticism now.

She grumbled into Elena's hair, not wanting to ponder the divine, or ice-hearted demons, or insufferable rich women. These were really nice sheets.

"We traveled a long way today," Elena purred into her throat. "How sleepy are you, *cara mia*?"

"You know *cara mia* is Italian, right?" Grady yawned. "In Spanish, I think you just called me 'my face.'"

"Hey, I am multilingual now, in the language of hot monkey sex." Elena snickered warmly against her skin, and Grady felt a thrill of a different warmth course pleasantly through a lower region of her anatomy. "And all of you is mine, Grady."

Really nice sheets, and they put them to good use.

❖

Grady trotted down the stairs before dawn, leaving Elena in a blissful and softly snoring sprawl across the bed. She was gratified to note the door to the master bedroom was still firmly closed. After Jo's crack yesterday about hoping Grady was accustomed to rising early, it was nice to have beaten their host out of the sack. A heavenly aroma of bacon was wafting from the kitchen, and she trailed it like a bloodhound.

"Morning, Grady." Immaculate in her freshly pressed uniform, Pat stood at the hooded range of the oven, nursing a large skillet of fragrantly crackling bacon. Pat reminded Grady of some of her students, the serious ones; she carried a sense of calm purpose, turning the bacon with a sure hand, but she offered a brief smile of greeting that softened her.

"You're my new best friend." Grady eyed the pan of scrambled eggs bubbling on another burner greedily. "Can I help?"

"Sure. Want to make us some OJ?" Pat nodded toward a paneled cupboard. "Jo keeps a juicer in there."

"Eh, let's go old school." Grady preferred the small hand press she spotted on a recessed shelf. She selected a knife from a drawer and halved a few oranges, then twisted them in the press. Another sublime fragrance reached her as Pat poured steaming coffee into a large mug and set it before her.

"It is the way of my people," Pat said quietly. "To sing the song of the sacred coffee bean in thanks to the rising sun."

Grady squinted at her, and a grin flickered around Pat's lips. They chuckled together, a companionable sound in the large kitchen. Perhaps Grady had passed some test last night in Pat's guarded eyes. Pat had seemed professional and distant when they first met, but an evening of sharing hideous ghost-winds must have bonded them.

Grady leaned against the hexagonal marble island that dominated the kitchen and sipped an excellent brew, pondering the meager light seeping through the high windows. "Ah, you Pacific Northwest types have New Mexico beat as far as coffee goes, but you still don't know how to do dawn worth a damn out here."

"The sun rises prettier over New Mexico?"

"It does over our piece of it." With a sentimental pang that surprised her, Grady pictured the stunning sunrise of the Mesilla Valley. Here, soggy cloud cover over the mountain didn't allow much vibrancy in the transition from darkness to light, more just a general lessening of gloom. Probably a fitting gothic backdrop to the day's mission.

"You sound homesick." Pat lay out strips of crisp bacon on a waiting plate.

"I am, a little. I guess New Mexico is home now. And you've always lived up here?"

Pat flicked her a glance. "I've always lived in the camper in the back of the lot. No one lives in this cabin except Jo, for a few weeks every summer."

Grady knew to abide the warning in that shuttered look. "You take great care of the place. It's beautiful here."

"Thank you." Pat's shy smile was back. "It is beautiful."

By the time they emerged from the kitchen carrying loaded trays, it had gotten light enough for the immense paneled windows in the living room to showcase the snow-spangled trees outside.

Grady whistled admiration of their glistening beauty, then saw Becca shuffling into the room in an oversized sweatshirt and sweatpants, grinning at them.

"I know, women are driven mad with lust when I dress like this." Becca yawned and blew her tousled hair out of her eyes, scratching her belly in mock seduction.

Grady laughed. "I wasn't whistling at you, but those slippers alone rate a warm round of applause."

"Aren't these da bomb?" Becca's face lit up and she extended one for Grady's inspection, a comically shaggy bear paw complete with black plastic claws. "I'd wear them to formal dinners if I could. They're so me, somehow."

"They are," Pat agreed.

Grady thought so too. The warmth and playfulness of the bear claws suited Becca, and Grady liked her for eschewing the fancier, more stylish slippers she surely could have afforded. She tweaked one of the plastic claws gravely in two fingers. "Wear them for our interview today. If the Windigo attacks, Pat and I can throw you at it feet first."

Becca laughed, sharing her bravado about a legend that was actually starting to creep them out more than a little, and it was in this odd pose, Grady tweaking Becca's slippered toe, that Jo walked in on them.

Dressed in tailored but practical wear designed for cold weather, Jo looked more crisply fresh than Grady would be able to manage without more coffee. She arched one eyebrow at them and stepped briskly to the table, then stopped short when she saw the plates of steaming eggs and bacon on it.

"But I was planning to make breakfast for us, Pat." Jo frowned. "I was going to make eggs Benedict."

"Breakfast?" Becca came to the table, clasping her hands reverently. "This looks wonderful, Pat." She smiled quizzically at Jo. "Honey, you never make breakfast. I didn't think you knew how."

"Poaching an egg isn't that difficult, Rebecca." Jo folded the cuffs of her thick sweater. "I Googled it."

The poor sap, Grady thought, doesn't even know when she delivers a laugh line.

Pat shrugged, apparently indifferent to Jo's lack of enthusiasm. "There are plenty of eggs for tomorrow, Jo. You had me buy lots of provisions."

"And our thanks to the fixers of this feast." Becca looked pointedly at Jo, then settled at the table as Elena's voice drifted down the stairs.

"You have one pistol and a shotgun, Mamá. I'm not going to tell Cesar to go buy you a crossbow. Now have a good day. Te amo." Elena looked startled to see all of them watching her, and she folded her cell with a bright smile. "Just the usual daily conversation every daughter has with her mother. Good morning, everybody."

"Hey, you." Becca lifted the pot of coffee invitingly. "Did you sleep well?"

"Oh, like a big mossy rock I slept." Elena ran her hands through her tumbling hair, wet from the shower, her breasts lifting with the motion, and Grady smiled dreamily. "You guys made such a comfortable home for us. I want to go to bed now, all over again."

Grady did too, given Elena's cleavage, but they had to prepare for the day. "Try some of this coffee first. Jo's cupboard had a mean French roast."

"Okay, just six cups, to be a polite guest." Elena held out her mug. "Pat, stop hovering like a dragonfly and sit down." Pat obliged, pinching her khaki slacks at the knees as she lowered herself gracefully into a chair.

Grady poured, waiting for Jo to alight. She was aware that she was probably sucking up to her ex-prof, but she felt a little sorry for her. For a moment, before Jo looked annoyed when she saw their breakfast, she had seemed honestly crestfallen. She had wanted to do something nice for them, and Grady regretted stealing her thunder.

"I'll have time to calibrate my recorder later." Jo seemed to consider this carefully before joining them to eat, but at last she deigned to do so. "I've checked the satellite radio, and there wasn't much snow in the foothills. The worst of it is headed our way tonight. But we'll still need time to get to the Abequas'. I'll want to be on the road in an hour."

Yas'm. Grady saluted mentally. *We'll trundle along with you, if that's all right.* She passed Elena a platter of bacon. "How's Inez this morning?"

"As always. As *mi madre* ages, she grows more and more herself." Elena spoke a world of wisdom with her usual offhand sweetness.

"I rarely talk to my parents," Jo said. "Grady, you've read the latest literature on culture-specific syndromes, correct?"

"Sure." Grady didn't get why any anthropologist working in a multicultural setting wouldn't have. "I understand more than one model might apply here."

Jo nodded. She raised her glass of juice and examined it, then replaced it on the table as if finding it lacking. "I'd appreciate it if you would step back for the interview itself and let me take the lead. I'm hoping to recapture the wind sounds we heard last night on a far superior device, and I have specific questions for the Abequas. Take copious notes on what the grandmother actually says."

Grady blinked, and she saw Pat's eyebrows shoot into her hairline. Even on more coffee, she would be unable to conceive of a less promising plan. "Jo, we might want to rethink that. We're dealing with a Chippewa family under a lot of stress. There are certain cultural influences you might not be aware—"

"I'll trust you or Pat to give me a high sign, if I misstep on the whole cultural thing. Becca, I'll want you to focus on assessing Selly Abequa's mental status, particularly signs of dementia."

"Pull up," Grady said politely. She laid her napkin aside. "Jo, it's not a good idea for you to conduct this interview. Trust me on this. Let me take the lead in speaking to this family, or let Pat do it. You and Elena can ask any follow-up—"

"Elena will not be asking questions, period. There's no need for her to come with us."

"I'm sorry?" Grady and Elena exchanged puzzled looks. "Elena has background in interpreting folklore. I told Jack Chambliss that I'd like her take on this study, and he had no objection."

"We don't even know that they'll provide an interview room large enough for four of us." Jo sighed and consulted the watch on her wrist. "I want Becca along because of her training in mental disorders. Elena's presence isn't necessary. She wouldn't bring anything of use to the table."

Grady glanced at Becca, but there was no help there; she was watching Jo with troubled eyes.

"Look." Grady was pleased at her even tone. "Jack Chambliss hired me for this study, Joanne, just as he did you. He didn't make any mention of you leading this team, so I assume no leader was assigned. We need to agree on this before we set foot out the door. Elena is going with us, and you're not steering this interview. We're not subjecting a First Nations family in crisis to insensitive questioning by a scientist."

Now Jo blinked. She probably wasn't accustomed to pushback, in any form. Grady felt Elena's foot touch hers beneath the table, but she ignored it. Pat was watching them all in bemused silence, sipping her juice.

"Science is all we have going for us in this study, Dr. Wrenn." Jo rallied. "We're here to document the mystery of that recording, not the dysfunction of a Chippewa fam—"

"*And,* that's breakfast for Becca." Becca rose smoothly and unhurriedly to her feet. "No, Becca's taking her bacon." She took two strips from her plate, then walked to the front door.

"Becca?" Jo called after her. "Where are you going?"

"I'm taking my bacon, and I'm going for a walk." Becca looked down at her slippered feet. "But not in these." She kicked them off, then stepped into one of the pairs of boots left at the door.

"Now?" Jo got to her feet, sounding suddenly plaintive. "You're taking a walk now?"

"Correct."

Grady could see how angry Becca was in her terse pronunciation of Jo's favorite word.

"I'm taking my bacon, and I'm taking Elena, who *is* coming along on this interview, and we're going for a walk." Becca snapped her fingers at Elena, and at another time and place, that might have felt rude, but now it seemed merely expedient. Elena got up, smiled fleetingly at Grady, and went to remove her parka from the row of maple pegs near the door.

Pat scrambled to her feet too, brushing crumbs from her palms. "I'd better chain up those tires."

Jo glanced uneasily at Grady. "But, Becca, by the time the three of you get back…"

"By the time we three get back, you two will have worked all this out." Becca slung a scarf around her neck and pulled open the front door. "Together, working in tandem, you and Dr. Wrenn will pull down your little-girl pants and remove whatever barbells, professional or personal, you have up your respective buttocks. 'Kay?"

Becca swept Elena and Pat out the door in front of her, then closed it firmly behind them.

The sound reverberated through the silent living room.

Grady stared openmouthed at Jo, who stared back at her.

"She can be a little fierce," Jo stammered.

Grady nodded. "So can mine."

It was the first faint moment of kinship between them, and Grady knew she had to build on it.

"Look, Jo." She scratched her head. "I know you don't remember this, but I took a class from you a long time ago…"

❖

Snow was novel enough in Seattle to make its crunch beneath Becca's boots a welcome distraction. She wasn't sure how often it snowed in New Mexico, but Elena seemed surefooted beside her, matching a pace Becca hadn't intended to set so fast. They waved at Pat as she disappeared behind the cabin.

"Sorry." Becca folded her arms against the chill and slowed down enough to qualify this as a stroll, as opposed to an escape. "I just thought we should get out of there. They didn't need an audience for their drama."

If Elena was upset by the scene at the table, she wasn't showing it. Crystals of snow drifted down from a branch high above their path, and she caught them on her tongue like a child.

"By 'they,' I mean Jo." Becca sighed. "Grady wasn't much out of line."

"Oh, Grady's real capable of stomping a line into the dust." Elena tramped cheerfully in the snow, as if to illustrate. "Not too often, though, and not if I'm stomping one myself. That's a good thing we've learned in this marriage. Only one of us has to be a sane person at a time."

Becca was glad to focus on something other than her clueless and abrasive partner. "How long have you guys been together?"

"Grady came into my life a year and a half ago." Elena extended her hand toward Becca, and her smile turned shy. "She just had these made for us for Christmas, and I love to show mine off. I can't with many, back home."

"I noticed these before. Grady wears one just like it." Becca clasped Elena's fingers and took in the delicate swirl of silver on her finger, encircling an irregular drop of deep turquoise. "It's beautiful, Elena. Classy and tender at the same time."

"Yes. Like her. Thank you."

Becca gave Elena's hand a brisk warming rub and released it, wishing she'd given her time to find gloves. Their breath frosted on the air before them, but the cold wasn't too bitter. And it was lovely out here; Becca had forgotten the picturesque charm of Jo's land. Carpeted in snow, it was even more beautiful in winter than summer, the only time she'd seen it. The six inches of new snowpack made walking cumbersome but rewarding.

They high-stepped to the deep metal trough that still stood at the edge of Jo's lot. It was a quaint throwback to an earlier age of grazing livestock, but apparently, Pat kept it in good repair. Becca remembered Jo mentioning this trough in one of her rare stories of her childhood—coming out here at dawn as a young girl in summer, scattering corn in this feeder, hiding in the brush to watch the near-tame deer gather for breakfast. Becca's throat constricted, and she closed her eyes. Her Jo had been that sweet kid, happy to feed her friends breakfast. Always alone, Becca knew.

Then she remembered something else Jo told her about this trough, and she grinned and put a hand on Elena's arm to stop her. A brief, nigh miraculous sun had broken through the clouds to wash them in gold morning light. This would be fun.

"Want to see something pretty?" Becca asked Elena.

"Always."

"Look back." They turned, and Becca did a double take. Jo had mentioned this trough marked a nice view of Mt. Rainier, but then Jo was an idiot of understatement. This vista of the mountain, shrouded in mist at its base but a shining testament to sheer cliffs to its tapered peak, took her breath away.

"*Ay.*" Elena sighed, and neither of them felt a need to elaborate. They sat back against the rough edge of the trough and drank in the mountain, and Becca appreciated their companionable silence. She wasn't sure why she decided to break it, except she found Elena so damn easy to talk to.

"My parents' ashes are scattered in a field of wildflowers not far from here." She nodded toward Paradise, a lovely, aptly named tract of land just around the bend of the mountain. "It was the first place I brought Jo, last summer. The first place we visited together, once we realized we *were* together."

"That must have been an honor for Jo. That you would share this field of wildflowers with her, that is so important to you."

"You're right. It was an honor." Becca was pleased that Elena understood, pleased to her core that Jo had too, and warmed by the memory. "It was a gift I gave her, and she knew it. Jo helped me heal from losing my folks in so many ways, Elena. I wish you and Grady could know that side of her."

"Ah, mi amiga, we've seen that side." Elena smiled at her around the hood of her parka. "Just in the way Jo looks at you, we can see she's capable of gentleness, and she has so much love for you."

Becca nodded, her brimming eyes on Rainier. "It's just a lot of work."

"Yes?"

"Sometimes I think if Jo and I could just build a big fortress and live it in together, shut out the world, we'd be fine. We'd be happy. Because with me, she's so fine, so much of the time. But we can't always be alone." Becca sighed. "I'm always going to need friends in my life. She's come a long way, but mornings like this remind me how hard being around people is for her."

Elena didn't offer easy assurance, letting the beauty around them soak into their skin and bring its own comfort.

"I know Jo faces some special challenges, Becca," Elena said finally. "And I know that you will always help her with them."

"The doctors who examined her as a child said she had a character disorder." Becca shook her head. "Then a learning disorder. Jo's had a dozen clinical labels slapped on her. None of them are even really accurate—"

"That's not what I mean." Elena was watching her. "I think there's danger up here, and Jo might be especially vulnerable to it."

"I promise I won't let her cook for us." Becca smiled uncertainly. "Um, can you say any more about this?"

"I wish I could, but that's all I'm sure of right now." A line appeared between Elena's brows. "It's just a feeling, like my feeling that our friend Pat is also a part of this. But I'm worried for Jo, and I know she's going to need your help."

Elena was not a flamboyant person, and she wasn't making this pronouncement with any scary-eyed claim to otherworldly knowledge. She just looked scared.

Becca shivered. "Okay."

Elena reached over and took Becca's hand and held it on her knee. "But I promise you one thing, *chica*, you guys aren't alone with this. Pat and Grady and I are here too, and we'll help you all we can."

This promise seemed to allow the sun to linger for a while, but it couldn't last. They watched the mountain until the clouds closed over it again, encasing them in snowy shadows.

CHAPTER FOUR

Jo was gratified when they pulled away from the cabin close to schedule. She noted Becca climbed silently into the back seat next to Grady, so she was not yet forgiven entirely for the silly clash at breakfast.

"Where is this family living?" Grady was peering out the window at the white forest aligning the narrow road. At least she was being sensible; they both considered the argument resolved and forgotten.

"About a mile south of Paradise. I guess that's an unfortunate way to put it." Jo caught Becca's eye, and they shared a slight smile. "The Abequas are no longer squatting on this land, Pat, correct?"

"Right." Pat steered the heavy vehicle down the slick drive with an expert hand, the frost crackling under the chained tires. "Frank Abequa tells me they've managed to rent this little compound of homes off a side road. It's not tribal land, any tribe, but it's the only housing they can afford. We're supposed to speak to this Margaret Abequa this morning, Jo, the woman Frank mentioned. Must be some kind of family matriarch."

"They've traveled such a long way." In the seat beside Becca, Elena was also gazing up at the snow-blanketed trees they trundled slowly past. "All the way across the continent, to try to escape this demon."

"Or a psychiatric disorder, which would have come with them," Grady said. "We have to keep that possibility in mind too." She turned to Becca. "Are you familiar at all with Windigo Psychosis?"

Becca lifted her eyebrows. "No, but you have my complete attention. There is such a thing?"

Grady nodded. "It's a culture-specific syndrome, an accepted diagnosis, though not without controversy."

"And a culture-specific syndrome is a disorder that's only seen in a given community?" Becca was looking at Grady with fascination, the way she looked at Jo while she tried to explain other worlds.

"Exactly. Windigo Psychosis doesn't exist outside the Algonquin tribes, such as the Chippewa, but many societies have their own examples. Another culture-bound syndrome is *la mala hora,* in New Mexico—the legend of the woman who appears at a crossroads to those who are doomed to die soon. Some folks in Hispanic communities have seen a frightening woman at a crossroads, and they quickly sicken and die, from no known physical cause."

"*La mala hora* is more than this syndrome, *querida,*" Elena said mildly. "But please go on."

"A person suffering from Windigo Psychosis believes they've been possessed by the spirit of a Windigo," Grady continued. "They're consumed with a craving for human flesh, even when other food is available. Some have actually begged to be executed, because they fear they're going to harm their families." Grady paused. "Some have harmed their families."

"Yeah?" Becca was sitting quite close to Grady on the wide back seat, Jo noted. "It's gone that far?"

"The most notorious case was Swift Runner, a Cree trapper up near Alberta, Canada. His family was very isolated during a brutal winter in eighteen seventy-eight. The oldest son died."

"And this Swift Runner ate his son?" Becca asked.

"And butchered his wife, and his five remaining children, and ate them too. He was arrested and executed at Fort Saskatchewan."

"Jesus," Jo whispered, and heard Elena softly invoke some other deity at the same time. Pat released a long, low whistle.

She wouldn't admit it aloud, but Jo was starting to be glad she had agreed to let Grady take the lead this morning. She was beginning to feel completely at sea in this quagmire of folklore and pathology. Give her the quantifiable energy of human existence beyond death, something she could measure with the right instruments, and she was on solid ground. The intricacies of normal minds in the living were difficult enough to fathom, forget cultural delusions and psychoses. It chaffed her to accept it, but those were much more Grady's purview, and Becca's clinical training in social work.

Even Elena Montalvo's background in a kind of Hispanic witchcraft was more suitable to this study than Jo's science, in some ways. Elena was sitting quietly, with a stillness Jo was coming to recognize as her natural state. She remembered her easy dismissal of Elena at the breakfast table, and reminded herself that she had to learn to think before she spoke.

She turned to look at Becca again and saw only her profile intent on Grady, the two of them talking quietly. Becca rested her hand on Grady's wrist as she spoke, and Jo frowned. She felt Elena's gaze on her, oddly searching, and she gave her a puzzled smile as Pat steered them down the path to the Abequa family's compound.

❖

Maggie lifted the panel in the bedroom window and peered out, seeing their new home through the judging eyes of these strangers.

The generational poverty of the Abequas had followed them here, reflected in the ramshackle cabins that composed the compound. Little more than shacks, the cabins formed a scattered half-circle around an open parking area. A few rusted trucks listed hubcap-deep in snow, all the transport available to the more than thirty people milling close to their doorsteps. A few mangy-looking dogs trotted through the muddy slush, collarless and forlorn.

Maggie's great-grandmother muttered something behind her in the cramped bedroom, something low in the old language, which Maggie didn't speak and had no intention of learning. She muttered something back and continued glaring out the hinged window.

Her tribe had gathered en masse this morning to greet these interlopers. Dark-haired uncles, aunts, greats, and cousins, shrouded in heavy coats, silently watched the women climb out of their truck. The family resemblance was evident not only in their features but in their sullen expressions. Small puffs of steam plumed from their faces as they waited. Maggie didn't like the look of her kin in the harsh morning light. They were too frightened these days.

Finally, all five of the women stood in the snow beside their ridiculously expensive vehicle. Maggie could have bought four new cars for her family for the price of that tank, with some to spare. Peachy. These were very rich women, and they'd brought the cop with them. She eyed the uniformed officer standing apart from the others, her hands clasped behind her back. Maggie's father had told her about this cop.

She clenched her teeth to bite back a yawn she was far too tense to enjoy. That damned dream last night, clutching a screaming baby, running from a man who was more spider than human, had shattered her sleep again. Rested or not, it was time to take charge.

Maggie gripped the ragged window ledge for a moment, then pushed off it and strode past the muttering Selly and out of the cabin. She slapped open the door and stalked out just as one of the white women stepped up the three stairs to the deck. The woman stopped abruptly and blinked up at Maggie through her glasses. Maggie planted her feet at the top of the stairs, and the woman backed down two of them, conceding space.

"Hello. My name is Grady Wrenn. I think you're expecting us. We've been told to speak to a Margaret Abequa?"

"Yeah, I'm Maggie Abequa. You can speak to me." Maggie tried to curb the knee-jerk hostility in her voice. This person was being perfectly respectful. Except she looked insultingly startled that Maggie was the speaker for her family, being so young. They all looked startled, except for the cop, who was staring at her hard. Maggie jerked her chin toward the others. "Tell me who they are."

She listened carefully to the tedious introductions that followed, studying these strangers. The cop continued to stand apart, but the other four turned slightly toward each other as couples, protective under the grim watch of the crowd. Wonderful. A nest of lesbians. She'd heard everyone in Seattle was a lesbian, but that was no real draw as far as she was concerned. If Maggie had wanted to find her own kind, she had no problem doing that in Minnesota. Lesbians were rare, but they were there.

But now that Maggie was here, she had no choice about that. It was time to do her job. She shook her head as Grady Wrenn droned on about the strange tall brunette's credentials. "I need to speak to the cop."

Grady stopped mid-word, her mouth hanging open, and the strangers all looked at each other. The officer, however, did not hesitate. Her hands still clasped behind her, she walked through the snow to the steps, then ascended them with slow calm. Maggie was standing at the top of the stairs, but the cop didn't hesitate, her dark gaze locked on Maggie as she rose to her level. It was either back up or have physical contact, and to Maggie's astonishment, she was the one to give ground.

The woman didn't press her advantage. She stepped onto the deck and stayed a careful three feet from Maggie, standing sideways as if she knew not to block her view of the other strangers. She waited for Maggie to speak.

"You're the cop who talked to Selly?" Maggie struggled not to cross her arms. She had been interrogated by police more than once in her twenty-two years, and she didn't like them. She didn't like the faint heat rising in her as she looked at this one, either.

"My name is Pat Daka. I'm a ranger with the Mount Rainier National Park Service." This Native was used to her title commanding respect. In Maggie's eyes, she was a cop. North, west, Native or white, they were all the same. This one had a voice like melted caramel. "Yes, I interviewed Selly Abequa. Are you related to her?"

"She's my great-grandmother." Maggie dug folded papers from the back pocket of her jeans. "I have a certified rental agreement for this property. We're living here legally now. There's no reason for the Park Service to be involved with us."

"I understand that." Pat Daka still held her in place with that oddly searching gaze, but her tone was courteous and professional. She glanced briefly at the papers, then Maggie returned them to her pocket. "I spoke to Frank Abequa when I was here two weeks ago. He's your father?"

"He's not here today," Maggie lied. Her worthless father was standing at the edge of the sullen crowd, and the ranger flicked a glance right at him. "You don't need my father. You can deal with me. I'm Selly's legal guardian."

"Are you out of high school, Miss Abequa?" Pat's voice still held that polite detachment, but Maggie felt her face flush with color.

She knew how young she looked. She also understood the impact her beauty had on men, and certain women. But when Maggie jabbed her fingertip into the ranger's broad shoulder, she knew it was her fierceness that made her finally take a step back. "I'm old enough to know my family's rights, officer. What you need to understand is this. Selly wants to meet with you, and that's the only reason you're here today. You and your friends can come inside. But my great-grandmother isn't well. If you do anything to upset her, you'll be escorted off our property."

Maggie nodded toward her family, and just for a moment, she saw warriors flicker in a few of them. She turned back to Pat, saw her lifted eyebrows, the new respect in her eyes. "Forcibly, if we have to. Okay?"

"All right," Pat said. "We know we're your guests here, and we'll behave accordingly."

Maggie scowled up at her. Maybe she was wrong, and Native cops were different. At least Native women cops, out here. She had no idea what local tribe this ranger belonged to—Maggie knew little enough about the tribes of her home state—but at least she had manners. She nodded brusquely. "Come with me."

She felt Pat's gaze follow her to the front door, and a brief sway took her hips. It was instinctive and irrepressible, that moment of dance, as natural as drawing breath, but Maggie cursed herself for it. She could fantasize all she wanted tonight about this stranger, in the privacy of her bed. This was Selly's time, maybe one of her last times, and Maggie had to keep her safe as long as she could.

❖

The windows in the small cabin were shuttered and dark. Grady followed the witchily beautiful Maggie Abequa down a narrow hallway, the others behind her, single file. Grady had crawled through cave dwellings and was on rational terms with claustrophobia, but fifteen seconds in this little house and the walls were already swaying in on her. She heard Jo speak softly into her recorder, and frowned at her over her shoulder.

Maggie stopped in front of a door that featured several good-sized padlocks, all hanging open from their hasps. Grady frowned at the locks, which looked newly installed. "This is Mrs. Abequa's room?"

"Yeah. This is where she stays now. She wants to protect us." Maggie opened the door without knocking, and a draft of old smoke hit Grady squarely in the face.

The confines of the house were already stale and dank, but the cloud emanating from the back bedroom was outright stifling. Grady had to brace herself physically as she entered the room, and she reached back automatically for Elena, who gave her hand a quick press.

It was ostensibly a bedroom, as one narrow bed was the only furniture the room possessed. The lone window had been boarded up with a sheet of plywood, except for one hinged panel, and weak light streamed around its splintered edges. Upon the bed sat one very old, very frail woman, draped loosely in a shawl and smoking a large pipe.

Selly Abequa had not left this room in days, perhaps weeks. That was Grady's first, certain impression from the smell of the place, and her second was they might need to get her to a hospital. As was her habit now in any state of alarm, Grady turned to Elena, who was regarding Selly with equal concern. This was tantamount to elder abuse. Before she could stop herself, Grady threw an accusing look at Maggie; hadn't she said she was Selly's guardian? Maggie returned her look with implacable disdain.

Maggie closed the door firmly, sealing seven people inside a very small space. The miasma of smoke was explained by the pipe, which Selly drew on steadily, her withered cheeks billowing with each exhale. Beady eyes studied them by the dim glow of the small lamp on the floor next to her bed.

"Mrs. Abequa." Grady knew they were towering over the bed, but there were no chairs. She lowered herself to sit back on her heels, a position that came naturally to her; her work entailed a lot of listening. She introduced each of them briefly, then addressed their most pressing concern, tactless but necessary. "Ma'am, you don't look very well. Do you need to see a doctor?"

"I've seen doctors." Selly Abequa's voice was both thready and gruff, but at least it wasn't the horrible moaning heard in the recording. Her ancient appearance brought that sound to mind, but if anything like that howling had emerged from her throat, Grady wouldn't have been able to stay in this room. She jutted her chin toward Maggie. "That young one took me to doctors back home many times. She took me again when she finally got her ass out here last week, after they sprung her from the drunk tank." She seemed to consider that matter settled, and pulled hard on her pipe again. "And my name is Selly, not missus anything."

Selly was all but hairless and a skeleton, or as near to one as anyone could be and still draw breath. Her skin hung in slack sheets around her gaunt face, and what Grady could see of her body through the shawl was rail-thin, dying thin. Grady had had the unhappy experience of witnessing deadly malnutrition in some destitute encampments, and she was seeing it again here, but she had to accept her subject's indifference, for now.

Grady was in no hurry to push Selly into speech, and she took in the cramped room. Food was featured prominently—groceries were neatly stacked against one wall. Loaves of packaged bread were in danger of being crushed by Jo's large boot. Bowls of fresh fruit. Several jars of peanut butter, unopened. A brimming sack of mixed nuts. Bottles of juice. All untouched. Grady saw Becca note these details, then return her gaze uneasily.

"Selly, we've come to ask you about the Windigo," Grady said finally.

"Huh." The old woman rocked slightly on the bed. "At least you call the bitch by its name. We've never seen it, not this generation of us. We knew it was coming, though, eh, Margaret?"

Maggie didn't respond. Selly held a sputtering plastic lighter to her pipe, and Grady waited for her to elaborate. She heard Jo whisper into her recorder again.

"It was seven generations back," Selly said finally. "The Windigo came one winter, when there was no food. One of our great-greats, our ancestor, was the only one of our family to survive its attack. He was just a baby then. His name is forgotten now. Maybe his whole misbegotten line should have been."

Grady straightened slightly. Frailty aside, there was a malign energy lingering in Selly Abequa, bitterness rising in her gimlet eyes.

"He lived to have little ones, whose hearts were frozen by the Windigo. Children who did shit harm to no one, but who grew up to want nothing but flesh. Usually, they would go off into the forest in the snow to freeze to death, to save the rest of us." She lifted one bird-boned shoulder dismissively. "But me, I'm selfish. I worked hard. I sacrificed for this family. They need to take care of me, now I'm old."

Selly seemed to direct this last to Maggie, who was wedged in one corner, her eyes impassive. Pat stood near her, her thumbs linked into her belt, listening silently.

"So we ran here."

Grady felt her eyes water in the sting of the smoke. There was something cloying in the tobacco Selly consumed in slow, methodical draws, if tobacco it was. Elena sometimes sipped the smoke of a variety of herbs in the course of healing sessions, but Grady had never detected this particular, slightly unpleasant odor before.

Almost as if realizing Grady's discomfort and relishing it, Selly blew the next cloud directly into her face, and up into Elena's, who stood close behind her. Grady's nostrils flared like a horse's, and she turned her head and snorted like one. She heard Elena's muffled cough.

"Selly!" Maggie's tone was unexpectedly sharp.

The old woman chuckled, a sandpaper sound. "Don't worry; it's not here yet. It hasn't found us yet."

Grady heard shifting behind her and tried to imagine how Jo was coping with the close confines of this room. Jo inched closer to the bed ahead of them, extending the recorder, but she stayed discreetly against the wall—for Jo, she was showing restraint. At least she wasn't barking out rude questions.

Then again, Grady couldn't think of a more intelligent one. "Selly, do you believe you're possessed by the spirit of the Windigo?"

"Do you believe you have any hope of understanding my family?" Selly spat. She breathed more smoke in Jo's direction, then in Becca's, behind her, and again Grady heard Maggie hiss in reprimand. Outside of kiva ritual, this was a rude and insulting act in any culture. "Big city college people. Unless you have money to pay us for this talk, you should go away. I've told our story enough. I'm sick and I'm old and I have no more fucking patience for—"

"If you're not possessed by a demon, stop behaving like one," Elena said, and Grady was shocked by the coldness in her tone. "Being old and sick is no excuse for such meanness, *abuela*. Answer our questions, and we'll leave you in peace."

Selly was blinking rapidly, and Grady realized she was blinking rapidly herself. When it came to infirm elders, Elena was imbued to her marrow with a kind of old-school courtesy, and she had never heard her address any patient, of any age, so bluntly. Becca glanced at Maggie apologetically and started to speak, but Grady lifted a subtle hand to still her. Selly Abequa's bald head was starting to tremble with some palsy, and they had to cut to the chase.

"Selly, what will happen when the Windigo finds you?" Grady wasn't sure the old woman would respond, but she finally pulled her sullen gaze away from Elena.

"When the bitch comes, it comes. We're not running anymore. I'm too tired. My family will be safe. The locks on this door are strong, and I'm not strong. My family never sleeps." Selly gave that almost childish shrug of one thin shoulder again. "When the Witiko comes, I'll die in this room, and they'll scatter my bones on this mountain. Very far from home."

Grady felt a hand on her shoulder. It was Becca, an insistent clasp, and she nodded. The old woman looked gray and spent, and there were entirely too many bodies in this room. At least Jo had made her own recording. That was enough for the day. "Selly, we should let you get some rest. Thank you for your time. We might want to speak with you again, so I'm going to leave my card with Mag—"

"So long as you leave," Selly muttered, plucking at her shawl with twig-like fingers. All the macabre bravado had drained out of her, and she looked sadly depleted. Her midsection emitted a mournful gurgling sound.

It was a disciplined stampede out of the fogged bedroom, but a stampede nonetheless. Grady slipped Maggie her card, and Elena paused in the dark living room to speak to her, but Grady didn't wait to eavesdrop; she just wanted out of there.

❖

A blessed blast of cold, fresh air hit Pat's face as she followed the others out onto the porch. She couldn't pull in the clean oxygen deeply enough. Their silent audience of Abequas still waited in front of their sagging cabins.

"Are you all right?" Becca touched Jo's face with concern. "You went scary pale in there—"

"I'm fine." Jo shook her off and straightened, but she was clenching the rickety railing of the porch with both hands. "Grady, all my sound checks were normal, so our recording should be—"

"Great." Grady turned as Elena emerged from the cabin and took her arm. "What say we make tracks?"

"Sounds good to me." Becca clasped Jo's hand insistently, and they went to the stairs.

Pat started to follow, but a none too gentle touch suddenly gripped her forearm. Maggie Abequa's eyes were glittering and hard as she watched them leave the porch. For an astounding moment, Pat's breath left her lungs.

She lived like a monk. She was rarely moved by physical beauty, unless it involved mountain vistas or azure lakes. But this woman was the most sensual, alluring human being she had ever seen. And Pat was on the job. She had no time for this.

"Something happened." Maggie's voice was strained, and her fingers stayed clenched around Pat's arm. "Something happened."

"What is it, Maggie? What are you talking about?"

"I don't k-know!" Maggie stammered. "Some banshee, voodoo Indian bullshit!"

"Can you be more specific?" Pat asked politely. Then she frowned. "Maggie, you look scared."

"Maybe *you* should be scared!" Maggie balled her fist and smacked Pat's chest, rather hard, and then flashed a hand toward the women waiting at the truck. "Do you care about any of them? Then *you* be scared."

Maggie's fierceness faltered. She rested her palm on Pat's chest, where she'd struck her, and looked up at her with sudden uncertainty. Pat heard muffled laughter from the crowd of Abequas, but she didn't know what had amused them and she didn't care; she was lost in the light of those eyes.

"Listen to that Mexican girl," Maggie whispered. "Now, go look after your friend." She nodded, and Pat followed her gaze.

Alarm sluiced through her. Jo was on her hands and knees in the snow, the others clustered around her. Pat strode to the stairs, but Elena lifted a quick hand in reassurance.

"She's all right, Pat," Elena called. She was kneeling in the slush next to Jo, and Becca and Grady were starting to lift Jo to her feet. "Just a dizzy spell. Let's get her home, okay?"

A clumsy snowball plopped six inches from Jo's foot, and Pat heard that sly, rumbling laughter again. The watching crowd of Abequas was mocking the fallen stranger. Mocking Jo. Two other children were stooping to form more snowballs.

Pat heard Maggie's sharp cry of rebuke to her family, and then her gasp as Pat vaulted the rail of the deck, dropped several feet, and landed hard but walking. The laughter sputtered off as Pat stepped directly into the half-moon opening in the throng of the crowd. She didn't draw her weapon. She didn't raise her arms from her sides, because it wasn't necessary. She just stood there.

Apparently, the fire in her eyes was enough. The ragged children let their half-formed snowballs drop to the ground. The last of the chuckles faded, and the men and women stared at Pat in sullen silence. Pat waited, to be sure it would hold. Then she turned and walked toward the truck, her indifference in exposing her back to them proof of their weakness.

She made the mistake of looking up at Maggie, and came to a dead halt. She wasn't Maggie anymore. For one heartbeat, she was someone else, someone equally beautiful but foreign, someone from Pat's dreams.

And then she was Maggie again, her lips parting, her lovely eyes widening as she looked down at Pat.

"Pat?" Grady had to reach out the window and slap the door sharply to jar her attention from Maggie. "Yo! I think we're ready to roll, here."

Pat swallowed and made herself move quickly to the Outback. She ducked behind the wheel and keyed the engine. In the back seat, Elena and Becca were on either side of Jo, who was white as chalk but at least sitting erect, her eyes closed as if in deep thought.

Becca's brow was still creased with worry. "I'd like to get her out of here quickly, Pat."

"I hear that." Pat cranked the wheel, and the heavy tires ground free of their ruts and carried them out of the compound.

CHAPTER FIVE

L *a mala hora.* The bad hour.

Lulled by the rocking of the truck, Elena closed her eyes and prayed. *Why do You keep singing these words to me, Diosa, but You bring me no other helpful instruction? Yes, I remember the sad history of the desert towns, the sighting of the woman at the crossroads. The many who have seen her frightening face, and knew they were destined for an early grave.*

And I remember Becca pointing out the memorial at the side of the intersection yesterday, the shrine to the murdered ranger, which bore her portrait. Jo saw that sweet image, and called it gruesome.

Elena was afraid the others, not even Grady, understood that it was already too late. They could leave this mountain now; Becca and Jo could return to the tall buildings of Seattle, Grady and Elena to the peace of their desert valley, and it would follow them. *La mala hora* was a moment in time, not space. Whatever this was, it would find them now, wherever they went.

"This is payback for you turning up your nose at the breakfast Pat made for us." Becca was talking to Jo. "You didn't eat much dinner last night, either. No wonder you got light-headed, in that smoky little closet. How are you feeling?"

"Again, I'm fine now." Jo sounded curt, more herself. She seemed restored, sitting tall and straight on the long seat, but

Becca sat protectively close against her. "And my head was never all that light. What's your take on Selly Abequa, Grady? Cancer? Some other wasting illness?"

"I think she's starving to death." Grady lifted one shoulder slightly, a sign of her tension, and Elena slid her hand to the back of her neck to rub the stiffness from her muscles. "She claims she's been checked out by doctors. If there's no medical cause for her emaciation, this might be a conscious decision. She's choosing to die."

"Deliberate self-starvation." Becca didn't look convinced. "That would take a tremendous act of will, Grady. Maggie seems to be taking good care of Selly physically. Her family has surrounded her with groceries. It would be an almost inhuman effort for someone who was starving to deny herself food that's readily available."

"Then she's insane?" Jo asked Becca. "This Windigo Psychosis?"

"You know, I don't think she's psychotic." Becca's intelligence was so clear on her expressive face, and she was right in this. "She tracked what we were saying pretty well. Her responses were certainly odd, but she seemed lucid to me. She's reality-based, even if her reality is very different from ours."

The food the old woman craved was all around her, yes, but there was enough humanity left in her that she dared not eat. *Sometimes I wonder at the cruelty of Your more mysterious creations, my Goddess. You sculpted the beautiful mountain Becca showed me this morning, and the lush forest on either side of this path, and the love I share with Grady. Yet You also created a spirit so malevolent it has haunted this family for generations, so deadly it has infected an old woman with the terrible selfishness I witnessed this morning.*

Pat's eyes met Elena's in the rearview mirror, and again she wondered about her. What was this lonely ranger's role in all this? And the new girl, Maggie, younger even than Elena. Both of them were a part of this journey. *That's helpful to know, Diosa, but I have spoken to You several times about being more specific.*

As for Selly Abequa? I leave her to Your mercy, for I have none for her.

"We should have asked the great-granddaughter about Selly's mental health history, but we were too busy trying to breathe." Grady sighed, her shoulder loosening beneath Elena's fingers. "Maggie seems pretty hostile. I'm not sure how rock solid any of the Abequas are. The whole clan creeped me out a bit."

"I'm with you on that." Becca huddled against Jo in the back seat. The powerful heater blew welcome warmth over Elena, and the windows begin to steam.

Pat flicked on a switch to defrost them, then studied Jo in her mirror, making sure she was all right. Elena remembered Pat's frightening stance before the Abequas, almost daring them to come through her to get to Jo. She realized there was love between them. And Elena was filled with relief that this warrior woman would protect Jo from her heart, not only out of duty. She was afraid Jo might need protection, badly.

Sweet Mother, here is your Elena riding in this expensive car with all these graduate degrees. Both Grady and Jo have the title of doctor. Becca's degree is probably very advanced too. She has had many years of college. I'm smart, but I have community college and a nursing certificate, that's it.

Sometimes I'm too proud of the knowledge I've earned in my work with You, Diosa. I know this. Help me listen to these more educated minds. Don't let me shut out any real solutions Grady and Pat and Jo and Becca might have for us. But You and I know they are not on the right track yet.

And none of them, not even Grady, has asked me for my opinion.

"What is the Windigo supposed to look like, Grady?" Becca asked.

"Well, let's see. I found some images on the Net, but I was surprised there weren't more of them. A few consistencies stood out."

Elena closed her eyes and pictured their enemy as Grady's rich voice painted it for them.

"The Windigo is huge, always portrayed as a towering creature, three stories high. It's animalistic, more beast than human, often featuring bony antlers. But it's almost spider-like, so thin it's all but skeletal, with sharp, grasping talons. And all the stories mention its howling, like a fierce wind. Basically, the Windigo is death by starvation, made visible."

"I don't understand." Becca lay one hand on the headrest of Grady's seat. "Is this thing supposed to be a mutant animal, then? Something like our Bigfoot? Or is it a kind of demon? Selly Abequa said the children of her line had been possessed by the Windigo—as in demonic possession?"

"She said their hearts were frozen by the Windigo," Pat corrected her, and she was right. Elena remembered Selly's words very well, and Grady met her eyes.

She shared Becca's wish to know the nature of this beast better. *Ay, Madre, are the witches and malevolent spirits of my desert valley not enough to entertain You? Must You ask me to cope with the strange ghostly evils of a Native tribe whose roots are way up north? I know nothing about their ways. I've never been north of Hatch.*

"The Chippewa have only called the Windigo a spirit. The Spirit of the Lonely Places," Grady said, and Elena remembered Grady always listened to her.

"But you said last night that this isn't a spirit in the way we usually refer to one," Becca said. "As in, the surviving energy of a human being who's passed on?"

"Right, the Windigo was never a living creature. But from the oral history, I believe it was a kind of malignant spiritual energy," Grady said. "It was a monster generated by the mass agony of a dying village. When starvation hit isolated tribes in winter blizzards, the suffering must have been unimaginable. There was literally nothing to eat. The Windigo was created in the minds, and around the story fires, of a desperate people who faced the very real possibility of cannibalism."

"So the Windigo was the product of a kind of mass hysteria." Becca looked thoughtful. "But there was a rationale to this hysteria. The legend kept the tribe from breaking a strict taboo."

"Or it gave them a rationale for breaking it." Jo was watching the scenery pass out the window, and her tone was bland. "You can't really be blamed for eating your cousin if you were possessed by a huge monster with grasping talons that forced you to do it."

Elena closed her eyes again. *The blood of the cannibal Swift Runner's six murdered children cries out to me, my Goddess. I don't entirely understand what happened to Jo this morning, or what she is now. But I hope You find a way to explain this to me soon. The sky closes over us.*

A storm is coming.

❖

The day certainly began oddly, but Becca would call no day that ended with a soak in a hot tub a bad day.

She had survived the deaths of her parents and an adolescent fling with alcoholism, and she had eaten Jo's cooking. Becca knew she was made of tough stuff. She wasn't going to let a tragic old woman and her own obstinate lifemate distract her from the pleasure of this glorious physical indulgence.

"I'm a noodle now. I'm noodlic? It happened just since dinner." Grady's head was resting against the padded lip of the tub, her eyes closed. The planes of her face seemed more chiseled without her glasses. "This even beats the Gila Hot Springs, Elena."

"No argument from Elena." Elena reclined across the tub from Becca, her dark hair a floating cloud around her face. She had been quiet since supper.

Jo had been quiet too, and she hadn't joined them out here for this nocturnal soak. Becca craned her neck, but she couldn't see Jo through the large front windows of the brightly lit cabin. She must still be by her console of speakers, dissecting the recording of their disturbing interview with Selly Abequa. They had hardly been able to coax her away to eat, but at least she had inhaled the excellent dinner Pat prepared for them, making up for her earlier scant meals.

Pat emerged from the house and slid the glass doors shut behind her. Becca had insisted she allow them to share the after-dinner cleanup, but Pat seemed programmed to make herself useful in Jo's luxurious mini-mansion. She had probably been in there remodeling the kitchen while they lolled in this blissful tub.

"And here I had you pegged as an intelligent woman," Becca called to Pat. "Anyone who turns down a soak in this thing, after the day we've had, has the mind of a mollusk."

Pat was expressionless as she tossed a white cloth over her shoulder. "It is not the way of my people, Becca," she said quietly, "to have sex with a bunch of white girls in a hot tub, unless we are well paid for it."

Grady sputtered on the water and laughed. She slapped the side of her hand across the surface and doused Pat with a satisfying splash. Pat stepped back, grinning, and Becca was delighted. This was the first time she'd heard Pat crack a joke, and that rakish grin transformed her briefly back into a friendly, handsome rogue of a Lone Ranger.

"Come on." Becca waved a lazy finger at one of the chaise chairs adjoining the tub. "At least sit with us for a while."

"Thanks, but I need to check the generator out back, in case we need it after the storm hits. Then I'll want to turn in." Pat bobbed her head. "I'll wish you guys a good night."

"Sleep well, mi amiga." Elena watched Pat saunter out of their circle of light toward the darkness of the back lot, as if she shared Becca's wistfulness at seeing her go. There was something forlorn in Pat, some note of sadness that Becca was only beginning to sense.

"Elena, did you forget to take your cell out of your pocket before you got in?" Grady sounded hopeful.

Elena craned her neck toward the slatted shelf adjoining the tub, the cell phone resting on it. "Sorry, no such luck."

At least Elena's mother was leaving them in peace tonight. Becca just wished Jo was here to share the quiet, which was broken only by the sweet gurgling of hot water sluicing around their semi-submerged bodies. Their semi-clothed bodies. Becca chuckled into the bubbles at her chin. What other three lesbians in the continental U.S. would partake of a dip in a top-of-the-line hot tub in T-shirts and shorts? Any three married lesbians, she decided.

"Maybe this snowfall will be really impressive." Grady's attractive features were illuminated by the recessed lights in the sides of the tub. "Maybe it'll dump so hard and fast we won't be able to get out of this thing until roughly April."

"Jo can cook eggs Benedict every morning, and bring them out to us on a snowshoe." Becca looked at Elena with feigned dread, but Elena's answering smile was tepid. Becca wondered if she was worried about the blizzard coming tonight, which did threaten to be formidable. The solid cloudbank reflected only the faint glimmering of the field of snow, lending an eerie silver sheen to the night. At least the winds seemed to have abated, which suited Becca right down to her pruney toes. She winked reassurance at Elena.

"Ay. Now, of course, I can think of nothing but my mother." Elena sighed and rolled over in the water, then pushed herself to her feet. "I'd best call her before it gets too late there, Grady. I said I would."

"Well, if you gotta." Grady rose with muted splashing, and gallantly took Elena's hand to help her over the edge of the tub. "Give Inez my best. And put on that robe, please."

"*Si, Mamácita,* I would surely have forgotten my robe up here in the Arctic." Elena's tone was teasing as she slid her arms into one of several lush terrycloth robes they had draped next to the tub. "Would you sit down before you freeze to death? I'll be right back."

Grady lowered herself into the steaming water. Becca could see her clearly, her appreciative longing as she watched Elena walk up the stone steps to the cabin. Grady's thin T-shirt clung to her neat breasts, and for a moment, Becca could see her nipples just as clearly as her face. She averted her gaze.

Jo looked at Becca with that same longing often, but only when they were alone. She would never reveal such emotion in the presence of others, even their friends.

Their lovemaking the night before had been thin and unsatisfying. They had both been shaken by that terrible recording of the wind. Becca's preferred remedy for this angst would have been to lie quietly curled together beneath the plush comforter. Jo had opted for quick sex and then hours of brooding aloud about the Abequas.

She had serviced Becca well, of course, before the brooding. For a scientist painfully impaired by social awkwardness, Jo was quite an adept lover. She had made a thorough and skillful study of Becca's body—the kinds of touch that aroused her, the best use of breath and lips and tongue. And lordy, had that research paid off, even last night. But orgasm had not been what Becca needed last night. She'd wanted comfort, emotional connection, not fireworks.

The scenic glories of this mountain retreat aside, she wouldn't bet on that connection improving much this weekend. If Jo was distracted the night before, now she was focused like a laser on this macabre project.

Becca decided to look at Grady again, because avoiding looking her way so as not to see her nipples was starting to feel sixth grade. Grady's face was half-submerged in the rushing water, only her dark-lashed eyes peering above the surface. She was watching the surrounding trees with an owlish intensity. She caught Becca's look, snickered into the water, and sat up.

"Sorry. We just can't let this forest go unwatched for long. Not at night. The Windigo always hid in the forest, and it always attacked at night."

"Well, look who turned out to be as mean as a junkyard rat." Becca frowned. "Don't you go invoking that creature out here. Not with me floating boob-deep in a hot tub and unable to run."

"It skulked among the trees." Grady waggled her eyebrows. "It blew down on them through the rattling branches on the gales of the—"

Becca splashed Grady full in the face, and they both snorted laughter. In fact, Grady almost giggled, and she did not seem to be a woman who giggled, so Becca knew they were both literally laughing in the dark. If the Windigo amused them, it wouldn't be able to eat them. Becca loved this logic.

"Elena only picked at Pat's delectable chicken stir-fry tonight." Becca stretched her arms along the lip of the tub. "Just when I thought I'd met a woman who shared my good instincts for fine food. You think she's all right?"

"Not sure. There's something off with her." A shadow dimmed Grady's face. "This hasn't turned out to be the peaceful vacation I promised Elena. But it's had its good points." She smiled again. "She's enjoying getting to know you guys. I am too. And that was the best chicken stir-fry ever to hit a plate."

"Right? Thank God Pat can cook. At least we enjoyed the few pieces we were able to wrest away from Jo." Becca tuned her tone to casual. "Elena told me this morning that she's worried about her. She said Jo might need my help this weekend. Just a feeling she had. And this was before the whole Jo fainting in the snow thing."

"Well." Grady's expression was somber, disconcertingly so. "Elena's feelings skew toward being right, most of the time. Not always. But if she's worried about Jo, I think we should listen to that. Let's keep an eye on her."

Elena had offered similar support on their morning walk. Becca allowed herself another moment of simple relief that hers were not the only eyeballs looking out for Joanne Call, for once. She felt a fleeting regret, probably not for the last time, that Grady and Elena lived so far away. She would miss them both.

Grady stretched luxuriously in the roiling water, rested her head against the padded wood, and closed her eyes. Becca stared openly at her long, languid form, blurred by bubbles, her bare, muscled arms and shoulders, her graceful, strong legs. Becca felt a distinct and pleasant subterranean stirring in her sex.

And she wasn't looking at Jo.

❖

At least she had made Becca happy last night. Jo rubbed her burning eyes and clicked back to the key section of the recording. She might be neglecting Becca right now, but last night in bed she had made very sure to meet all her needs.

Besides, she was out there lounging comfortably in a hot tub, enjoying Grady Wrenn's company. She could hardly complain of being too put-upon.

Jo heard an unwelcome murmuring and turned, annoyed at the interruption. Elena was passing through the living room, her ever-present cell pressed to her ear. She met Jo's gaze and smiled. Then her smile faded. She whispered into her cell and closed it.

"You're still troubled by Selly Abequa's voice, Jo?"

"I'm hardly troubled by it." Jo checked the console's settings, hoping Elena would move on. "I just can't figure out why she suddenly becomes audible. It would be nice if your girlfriend was in here working on this with me, but she's otherwise engaged."

Jo sent the sounds of the interview coursing through the room again. She had tuned the filters so that abysmal, howling wind wasn't so harrowing.

Just as in Selly Abequa's initial talk with Pat, that wind had sounded whenever she answered Grady's questions. Except at the point the howling suddenly stopped, and Selly's voice was heard quite clearly.

"—city college people. Unless you have money to pay us for this talk, you should go away. I've told our story enough. I'm sick and I'm old and I have no more fucking patience for—"

Jo snapped the recording off impatiently before Elena's rude voice could be heard again, interrupting the old woman.

"Yes, I remember that moment in our talk this morning."

Jo sighed. She had all but forgotten Elena was there. She had stepped down into the living room and was coming closer, looking at Jo in an odd way. And Becca thought she had to remind Jo all the time about staring at people.

"Are you hungry, Jo?"

Jo was certain the mild growling in her gut had not been all that loud, so she didn't understand why Elena asked. She had witnessed Jo consume more than her fair share of their evening meal, so she had to know she couldn't possibly be hungry. Perhaps Elena was just being snide about being shorted on the chicken. Jo opted not to answer her, but she simply wouldn't go away.

"Do you remember what happened this morning, Jo, just before we hear the old woman's voice at last?"

"Yes, I remember the interview, Elena. I was there." Jo was irritated at whatever spiritual implications Elena was groping toward, whatever superstitious interpretation she wanted to affix to the sudden emergence of Abequa's voice. "Look, it might be best if we left this study to the empirical analysis of data. That means measurements we can track and observe, look at. It's not that I don't value your background in folk myths, or whatever, but as I've said, Grady can offer any cultural—"

"Listen to me." Elena was suddenly standing very close. She reached up and took Jo's chin in her fingers, and her grip was not gentle. In Jo's brief acquaintance with Elena, her eyes had always been friendly and mild. They were neither now. "You have no idea who you're speaking to, Dr. *Mujer.* Little Elenita is on to you. I would remember that, before you toss out my background in *folk myths* like it was trash. I might be your best hope, Joanne. I've been places you will never see, and maybe you should be grateful for this."

It was easily the longest speech Jo had ever heard Elena make, and she struggled to digest it through the murk rising in her mind. Looking down at the suddenly fierce Elena, Jo was nearly afraid of her. Then she was swept by a thoroughly unexpected sensation of regret and almost childlike hurt feelings.

"Elena," Jo whispered. "I was very rude. I apologize."

Elena did not ease her iron-fingered grip on her chin. Her glare was infused with the strangest kind of authority, rendering her somehow taller and older and wiser than Jo, but then her aura of certainty began to fade. For a moment, Elena looked as confused as Jo felt. Her touch grew more gentle.

"Ah, Jo. That's all right. We've all had such a long day." Elena rested her palm lightly against Jo's cheek. "Try to get some rest soon, okay?"

"Okay. Good night."

Elena patted her face, her touch contrite now.

Jo watched Elena until she disappeared up the stairs to the second level.

She thought of Becca and Grady outside, alone in the hot tub, out of her sight. She started to go out to them. Her stomach rumbled again.

Jo turned back toward the kitchen. Pat and Grady may have cooked all the bacon that morning, making their gratuitous breakfast, but if not, Jo was frying the rest of it.

❖

Elena's knees were shaking as she climbed the carpeted stairs. Faint music chimed in the pocket of her robe. She made it to the landing, well out of the hearing of the alien creature below, before she opened her cell.

"You left your heathen gringa wife outside in a bathtub with another heathen gringa?" Her mother hissed. "And then you tell me this, and then you hang up the phone! On your *madre*. I did not raise you to be so disrespectful, or to be so *estupida* as to leave your naked *esposa* alone in the night with a naked gringa!"

"They're not naked." Elena rested her head against the wall and closed her eyes, comforted by her mother's voice. "Grady sends her best to you."

"*Pah.* Tell her I made six batches of *empanadas* today and stuffed them all down my maw, saving not one for her. She will get none of them, because she stole my only daughter." The querulous tone, as much a part of her mother as her faint moustache, was draining from her voice. "What is it, *niña*? You sound so far away from me."

"I feel far away, Mamá."

Inez Montalvo was only rarely able to summon the genuinely selfless maternal concern Elena heard clearly now. "Tell me what worries you."

"I'm going to be tested up here, it turns out. I don't know that I'm equal to this test." Elena thumped her head softly against the wall. "And the stakes are enormous, Mamá. I'm a little scared."

"What is this test?"

"It's a long story. I'll tell you later. Just not tonight. I'm pretty tired."

"*Ay, Dios.*" Her mother was thoughtfully silent a moment. "But have you prayed on this burden, my Elena?"

"Yes, I have. Often."

"With every breath?"

"With every breath." Elena smiled through the tears in her eyes. "Just as you taught me."

"My good girl. And the gringa, she is helping you with this test?"

"Yes, as much as she can."

"Grady is a good person, Elena. A strong person. You let her help you. This is not always easy for you, as you are pig-headed. Yes?"

"Yes," Elena agreed.

"Okay."

"Okay. Thank you, Mamá. Sweet dreams to you."

"And you *will call me* in the morning."

"Sí, I will. Good night."

"Te amo, Elenita. Take good care of my daughter."

CHAPTER SIX

Maggie would have sworn an oath she remembered no Chippewa words from her childhood, but she was wrong. She spewed every foul obscenity ever born in two languages as she staggered through the snow.

"Bastards," she gasped. Oh, her slimy coward of a father. Let him slink smugly home to Minnesota now. Let the whole sorry clan go with him. She wanted nothing more to do with any of them.

Maggie stopped and leaned against a tree because she had to. She bent over and rested her hands on her knees and pulled in air, her nose and eyes dripping. "How the hell far…are you?" she wheezed. She meant the dark woman, Pat, and the four others who had come with her that morning. She had only the vaguest notion where any of them lived. "A mansion," and "that way," were little fucking help, but that was the only direction her family would give her. They were already packing as she slammed out the door and into the night.

Every single Abequa had flatly refused to come with her. To Maggie's incredulity, they also refused to let her use one of their dilapidated junk heap cars to find the women, or even to drive her to them.

"We're headed the other way," her father had said. "The highway is east of here."

"But you said it was less than two miles!" Maggie protested. "Just help me find them and drop me off!"

"Let them take care of their own." Her father had shrugged. "We always have."

She pushed off the tree and plowed on, grateful for the faint tire tracks she could see in the road, made by Pat's vehicle only that morning, and now filling with fresh snow. They were like Pat's footsteps, leading back to her.

The storm had begun, but it hadn't hit in full yet. A determined, steady snow had been falling for almost an hour, and she had to churn through it with each step. Luckily, Maggie's people knew cold and snow, and the bitter chill of the night air didn't faze her.

She didn't know how far she had walked, only that it had been miles, or how late it was, only that it was after midnight. An uneasy sense of déjà vu crept over her, and she shook off the false memory impatiently. To her knowledge, she had never before risked a fucking heart attack by running through a blizzard in the middle of the night, so she had no time for lying illusions.

Gold lights. Very far up a steep side road, but the fading tire tracks turned that way. Maggie drew breath into her aching lungs and began the climb. When she finally reached the top of the icy drive, she stopped short. Pat's big truck was parked at the side of the house, but what was a park ranger doing living in a place as grand as this? Did she actually *live* with the rich white women?

She couldn't even find the damn entrance! Maggie staggered around the side of the huge house, hoping she wouldn't be jumped by guard dogs, then back toward what had to be the front door. The moon was supposedly full but so scudded by cloud cover the night was almost fully dark. And the tasteful, recessed lights dotted here and there were no help—

Fury streaked through Maggie's exhaustion, her fear and her grief, and she snatched up a good-sized rock from the yard. She hurled it at one of the windows and screeched, as loud and long as her breathlessness would allow.

The rock smacked against one of the high windows, but the richness of the thick pane held; of course, these people could afford thick windows. Enraged, Maggie screamed again and searched the ground. She found a bigger rock beneath the snow, and she pitched it at a front window as hard as she could.

This one smashed through, a soul-satisfying explosion of sound.

Maggie tried to form words but found she had none. All she could do was shriek them awake. High in the house, at last, another low light flickered on. She backed up a few steps in the slush, trying to see the upper floor.

And then Maggie was hit so hard, so solidly, she flew off her feet and crashed into the snow. What little air she'd had was gone gone gone, and all she could do was grapple with the gorilla holding her down.

"Park security." The voice was recognizably Pat Daka's, maddeningly calm in spite of the strength of her grip flipping Maggie onto her back. "Lie still."

Maggie had no choice. Pat's face emerged above her, inches above her. Her fierce eyes studied Maggie in the dim light, and then recognition seeped in.

"Maggie?"

They were both motionless, Maggie on her back in the snow, Pat clenching her arms, holding her down. That intense déjà vu again.

"Pat?" Another voice, faint, from the entry. More irritated than afraid. "What the hell's going on out there?"

"It's all right, Jo." Pat stared down at Maggie. "Just go back in the…" Her words trailed off and her eyes widened.

Terror like Maggie had never known closed her throat, and the world went dark.

❖

Elena seemed to know what she was doing. Pat told herself this for the third time and struggled to keep her distance from the deep sofa where Maggie lay, still unconscious. Elena was some kind of healer, she had looked after Jo earlier, and she assured them Maggie would be fine soon. But Pat thought she'd been out a rather long time.

"Did she really *walk* here?" Becca must have shared Pat's worry because she kept hovering behind the sofa. "Grady gave Maggie her card. Surely she knew she could call and we'd pick her up—"

"But then she would have had no excuse to break my window." Jo frowned at the mess of broken glass in one corner, and Pat hated her for a moment. Jo seemed to hear her own callousness. She scowled and plucked a blanket from the back of another couch and draped it over Maggie, who was already swaddled in two others.

Pat started to speak, but Elena lifted one finger to silence her. Wrapped in a flannel nightgown, she was seated on the sofa beside Maggie, measuring her pulse at the throat.

Elena nodded. "She's calming down. Her heart rate is almost normal now. I don't see any signs of hypothermia or other injury. And Maggie is young and strong; we just need to give her time to rest and warm up."

"I hit her pretty hard." Pat heard the plaintive note in her voice and silenced it. Her job was protecting Jo Call, her friends, this property, and all of this national park. She'd had no way of knowing this screaming, rock-throwing lunatic was Maggie Abequa. "Any chance she smacked her head, maybe a concussion?"

Elena slipped her hand beneath Maggie's tumbling curls and probed the back of her scalp again. "I still feel no swelling, Pat, and her pupils are equal and reactive. If she doesn't wake up in the next several minutes, we'll run her to the nearest hospital. But for now, I'm not too worried."

"Pat, would you build a fire." Jo hadn't asked a question; she had issued an order, but she looked grudgingly concerned. "Please. It's rather cold in here, and this girl's still trembling."

Pat was relieved to have something to do. She went to the wide hearth and lifted the heavy iron fire screens in one motion, still galvanized by a sick rush of adrenaline. Her knees were shaking, and it was a relief to crouch away from the others and pile wood high on the grate.

"Something happened," Maggie had told her that morning, before Jo passed out. Pat remembered the dismay in her eyes. It was nothing compared to the fear that had consumed Maggie as Pat knelt over her in the snow a few minutes ago.

Maggie hadn't passed out because Pat tackled her, or because of her long, chilling hike through a mountain blizzard. She had fainted from soul-shriveling horror. Pat had seen that reaction once before, when she had to tell a mother that her beloved son had died hiking on Rainier. It wasn't an expression you could forget, and Pat had witnessed it again tonight.

And before tonight, she realized, and not just in that bereaved mother. The Native woman in Pat's dream, the one who thrashed beneath her murderous lover's hands. Every night now, in Pat's fevered sleep, she looked up at her killer with the same raw terror.

"Hey."

Pat recognized Becca's shaggy bear slippers coming up beside her and had to smile at this small welcome note of levity. She finished lighting the fire and got to her feet, and Becca helped her replace the screen.

"Are we feeling all right tonight, ace?" Becca spoke quietly, with a note of older sister solicitation. "You're looking a little shook."

Pat was usually adept at keeping her emotions to herself, but apparently, Becca was unusually adept at picking up on them anyway. She shook off the dream's lingering creepiness. "I'm all right, thanks. Just startled out of a deep sleep when I heard that yelling."

"We were too. Scared me to death. Listen." Becca rested a hand on Pat's wrist. "It didn't escape my notice this morning that you were willing to take on a whole mob of angry Abequas after Jo passed out. You were Xenic, Pat."

Pat was puzzled. "I was what?"

Becca sighed. "You were very impressive. Thank you for looking out for Jo."

"You're welcome, Becca." Pat responded with automatic courtesy. She studied her grandmother's painting over the mantel to avoid Becca's discerning gaze.

Pat figured Becca knew that she was, for all practical purposes, Jo's employee. Jo paid her to look after the property, to cook for her when she was up here. Becca might even know that Jo's grandparents bought the land that had been in Pat's family for generations. What she might not understand was Pat had loved Joanne Call like a sister since she was a very little girl, and no one on earth could threaten or mock her in her presence.

But Maggie was her concern now, and Pat started to turn back to the sofa to check on her. Then she hesitated. Something about her grandmother's painting nagged at her. The fire was beginning to catch, and red and gold light flickered at the base of the framed canvass.

"Pat?" Becca's hand was still on her wrist. "What's—"

"I'm just worried about our guest." Pat turned, and Becca's fingers slid off her arm. She offered her a rueful smile and walked toward the sofa.

Pat refused to succumb to the chill working up her back. In the painting, Mt. Rainier looked swathed in gray shadows. Someone had been smoking a lot in here, or something was wrong with the fireplace. There was nothing supernatural in the slight darkening of the pigment of the painting. It must have been damaged by smoke recently, and the damage was slight. No one else had even noticed it.

"Ah," Elena was saying. "It looks like our friend is—"

Maggie came to in a galvanic rush, and immediately began thrashing beneath the blankets.

"Hey, Maggie, it's all right. You're safe." Elena rested her hand on her brow, but Maggie snapped her head away from her.

"Get me out of this thing," she snarled. Pat thought she still sounded afraid.

"You shouldn't move too quickly, chica. It's okay, you're—"

"Let me up, I said!"

Elena nodded. "Okay, you got it." She helped Maggie disentangle herself from the blankets.

Maggie flailed to her feet, and Elena rose with her. She looked around the large room wildly, and settled on Pat.

"So, I knew it!" Maggie hissed. "I *was* jumped by a guard dog! Where the fuck do you get off, Smokey Bear…"

Maggie closed her eyes, and if possible, went even more pale. Elena sighed and placed the tip of her finger on Maggie's chest. She pushed gently, and Maggie collapsed bonelessly back into the sofa. Elena sat beside her again and lifted her wrist to check her pulse.

"*Bueno*. Are we through with our tantrum? Now maybe you will listen to Dr. Elena. Who is only a nurse, but a good nurse." Elena smiled at Pat, who was clenching the back of a chair. "You'll be fine, Maggie. Just sit for a moment. Ah, here's Grady."

Grady emerged from the kitchen, holding a steaming cup. After Pat had carried Maggie in here, Elena had dispatched Grady up to their room to retrieve some kind of tea. She yawned, looking younger and sleepy without her glasses, and handed the cup to Elena. "Sip this slowly, please." Elena wrapped Maggie's hand around the cup. "We need to warm you up inside too."

"What is it?" Maggie grumbled, blinking into the steam.

"A wonderful blend of leaves from the Chihuahuan Desert, near my home. I'm also an herbalist, and this tea should help you feel more yourself soon."

Pat thought Elena's soothing voice would help ground Maggie as much as any tea; at least it was helping Pat.

Maggie allowed Elena to drape the blankets across her shoulders again as she sipped the tea, still trembling visibly. Her tumbling hair was damp from the snow, and the way she held herself reminded Pat of a roe paused in mid-flight. The cavernous room was silent except for the crackling of the fire.

Grady finally stirred and started to speak, but Elena reached over and touched her arm. Elena shook her head, and then looked at Becca. Becca was watching Maggie with her usual friendly interest and compassion, as was Jo, with her usual detachment. Then Elena looked at Pat and nodded. She patted the cushion of the sofa to beckon to her and got up.

Pat came around the sofa and sat carefully next to Maggie. "Tell us why you're here, please. Does this have to do with Selly?"

"Not anymore." Without warning, Maggie's arm flashed out and she hurled the empty cup across the room. It shattered against the flagstone of the hearth. They all jumped, but that seemed to be it. That was all the violence Maggie had in her, and she slumped back into the cushions. "Selly's dead."

"What?" Becca whispered.

"I found her a few hours ago. She tore a blanket into strips and hanged herself in her room. And why not?" Maggie was so young, so cynical, and she sounded so lost. "Her job is finished."

The fading blue tattoo of the labrys on the back of Maggie's shoulder had been the scandal and gossip of her clan, once they understood its meaning. Inexpertly done, she'd had it etched into her skin the day she turned twelve, shortly before she ran away the first time. Maggie pulled down the neck of her sweatshirt and rubbed the two-headed axe with her finger, waiting for Deputy Dog to get the hell out of her bedroom.

Pat was shaking a very thick pillow into a fresh pillowcase to add to the one already on the bed. It would take three Abequa pillows to match the size of either of these plush cushions. Maggie lifted one and cradled it in her lap.

"Are you about through?" she snapped at Pat.

Pat ignored her and dropped the pillow at the head of the bed. She shook out a rich comforter and draped it across the fleece sheets.

Maggie knew she was being churlish. She couldn't help it; she was so tired. Thank God Elena, the nurse, made everyone stop grilling her so she could get some sleep. She looked around the "guestroom," as Becca called this spacious suite. Maggie had lived in cramped rooms she shared with a dozen cousins, in detox, and in cells in juvie lockups. That about covered it. She'd never slept on a bed as grand as this. She was willing to toss Pat Daka through a window if it meant she could try it out soon.

"So are you their maid too?" The moment the words were out, Maggie was appalled at herself, but she couldn't take them back. She knew she'd struck home by the way Pat's face filled with color.

"I work for Joanne Call. I live in a trailer out back." Pat checked the window on the far wall to be sure it was tightly latched. "You said tonight that Selly's job is finished, Maggie. And this morning, you told me something happened when we were with her. Are you ready to clarify either of those statements?"

Maggie slumped on the mattress and closed her eyes. This was her punishment for the maid crack. "I don't know. Don't ask me what I meant."

"I'm afraid that's not good enough."

"Look, I *don't know* what's happening." Maggie just wanted to be young. Would she never be allowed to be young? "I know what that crazy old woman believed. I know what my inbred, two-steps-from-the-tepee family believes. And it's all a bunch of fucking ghost stories used to scare little kids."

"Then why did you come?"

Maggie squeezed the thick pillow to her chest, angry at the tears filling her eyes, angrier still at her own cowardice. She was more like her yellow father than she would ever admit. "I'm afraid here, Pat."

After a long moment, Pat sat on the bed next to her. Apparently, she slept in T-shirts, tight white T-shirts. She rested her elbows on her knees, the hard, rounded muscle of her shoulder an inch from Maggie's. The gold light of the lamp beside the bed bathed her austere features in a muted glow. Maggie breathed in the silence between them, and it calmed her.

"Don't you feel it?" Maggie asked softly. "In this huge house? It feels exactly like Selly's room now."

Pat started, then appraised her with sterner eyes. Maggie saw a war going on behind them, the same war raging in Maggie's mind. But whatever Pat saw when she looked at her allowed her to reveal a flicker of her own fear. Her own acknowledgement that Maggie was telling the truth. Maybe it was being Native, maybe only the two of them could feel it, but at least Maggie wasn't alone in this.

There was some weird, odorless pollution here tonight, beneath this vast and splendid roof. Maggie had never set foot in the place, she had no idea what the mansion had been like before, but she doubted it felt like this.

"After my mother ran out," Maggie said, "I was brought up by that old wretch you met this morning. And I grew up sick with fear, all the time, from her stories. So I got away, as soon as I could. But they needed me too much, see? I kept coming back."

Maggie turned her head, cursing herself, and swiped a hand across her eyes. She sounded about eight years old. "I came here to warn you guys. Something bad is happening. It's been happening for a long time, for whole generations. But now it's going to happen to *you*, all of you. And honest to God, Pat, that's all I know. Please, can I just be alone for a while?"

Maggie gave in to her impulse, though she gave in to many of her impulses and lived to regret it. She rested her forehead briefly on the top of that warm, broad shoulder. Then she sat up.

Pat's face was blurred through the tears in Maggie's eyes. Pat brushed the flat of her thumb very gently across the high crest of her cheek, lightly, the touch of a feather on her skin, catching a tear. Then she cleared her throat, a muted rattle of a sound, and stood up.

"I'll let you get some rest. The others will sleep in too. Count on lunch, rather than breakfast." Pat hesitated at the door and turned back to her. She hitched her thumbs in the belt loops of her jeans and regarded Maggie thoughtfully. "I like all of these women, Maggie. They're good people. And they were only trying to help your family. They deserve your help now too. Right?"

"Yeah." A deep sigh escaped Maggie, and she nodded miserably. "You're right."

"Okay." Pat smiled at her, a small sun breaking through the pervasive gloom. "Sleep well, *sewa*."

Maggie frowned. "Who?"

Pat looked puzzled. "I'm sorry?"

"Never mind." Maggie didn't know who Sewa was and she didn't care. She was asleep before she folded her legs onto that soft, sweet bed.

CHAPTER SEVEN

Jo dreamed.

Her hands were curled beneath her chin, Becca's mild scent still on her fingers, which usually made for pleasant dreaming. Not so tonight. Jo's sleeping self tried to make sense of this.

Could that be the faintest trace of blood she smelled, along with the warm familiarity of Becca's scent? Impossible. Neither of them were menstruating. But in memory—or was Jo hearing it now, in the quiet of their shared bed, that hitch in Becca's breath that indicated tears?

First, Jo remembered quickly, Becca rarely hid her tears from her, so if there was something wrong, surely she would have said so, before they slept? Their lovemaking had been unusually passionate, quite excitingly so. Jo was sure of this.

But Becca had stopped her. For the first time since their very earliest gropings, when poor Becca was training a forty-year-old virgin in the art of lesbian lovemaking. She had pushed her away, ordered her to stop, and the shame of that swept Jo. She curled more tightly on her side.

Damn it. She couldn't be too badly hurt. Becca was a sexual free spirit to a degree that had always amazed and intrigued Jo. A little rough foreplay was not all that new to them, nor was harmless domination fantasy. Jo continued to dissect this in an analytic sense, to drown out her humiliation and sorrow. She had hurt Becca.

Her mind turned methodically to her dream, the scarcely remembered and disquieting fragments of it. Then she was...

Following through cold night skies.

Sharp talons stretched wide. Howling gusts billowing out withered cheeks. Her withered cheeks.

Flying fast on wind, soaring, spinning. Rattle-whistle-rattle of wind through bony ribs.

Then even these fragments faded, and Jo slept.

❖

"Look, Seattle dykes are a bunch of complete whackos." Maggie craned over her shoulder and frowned at the far-off yelp of Elena's laughter. "Are they all in menopause or something?"

"It wouldn't surprise me," Pat grumbled. She had no real quarrel with Maggie's assessment; she'd decided Jo and her friends were crazy as loons too. The loaded bag of sandwiches almost toppled off the bend of her arm, but Maggie's quick grab saved it. She perched the sack, with the rest of their hastily packed lunch, on the deep snow filling the steel trough.

Why Becca insisted they eat way out here, this far from the house, was beyond Pat. Why they had to tramp through this fresh snowpack, and why in the world four mature women were now *sledding down a hill on inner tubes*, was more than Pat could fathom on little sleep.

She and Maggie worked side by side in the grudging silence of two servants preparing lunch for their rich mistresses. But it was tough to hold on to that illusion; Becca had all but twisted Pat's arm off, and Maggie's too, trying to get them to join in.

"Come on," she'd taunted, a wicked sparkle in her green eyes. "You guys aren't going to let us punk you youngsters? Scared of a wee hill like this?"

"Uh, no, you go on and enjoy yourselves." Pat eyed the black rubber tube Becca had slung over one shoulder. It was almost as big as Becca. "We'll set up."

"Why do these two get to stay down here with the turkey loaf," Grady complained, "while you drag the rest of us off a cliff?" Her words were muffled by the scarf wrapped around her face. Blinking in the high noon glare coming off the snow, Grady's spectacles made her look like a more feminine and martyred Harry Potter.

"Enough bitching, Wrenn." Becca gave Grady a gentle smack on the butt with her foot. "Heft that tube, climb that hill…"

Elena's laugh was light music as she took Grady's arm to steady her, and Pat began to wonder if Becca had the right idea. Even Jo cracked a smile as Grady pretended to slip again so she could drape herself over Elena. Jo took the tube Becca carried and slid it gallantly onto her own shoulder, then offered Becca her arm. The crystal beauty of the day, the cloudless blue bowl of sky overhead, began to filter through Pat's sullen sleepiness.

Judging from the shouts and laughter sounding from the rise behind them, Becca's enthusiasm had won out; they were obviously having fun up there. A lot of fun. Pat sighed. Maybe she would sneak back here with a tube later, if things were quiet. She hadn't been tubing in years, and she used to love it.

"Becca's nobody's dumb blonde, you know?"

To Pat's surprise, Maggie seemed to track her thoughts.

"I'm glad she herded us out of that house." Maggie hugged herself against the brisk chill and leaned back against the trough. "It's really pretty out here today. Reminds me of the best of home."

A dimple appeared in Maggie's cheek, a glimpse of the still-girlish sweetness she couldn't always hide. To Pat's relief, she seemed none the worse for her rough tackling the night before, or at least not visibly bruised. The lines of Maggie's body were supple and relaxed as she lounged against the trough, sensual even in the rare moments she wasn't trying to project sensuality. Watching her, Pat felt a small warmth pulse at the crest of her shoulder, where Maggie's forehead had rested so briefly the night before.

The silence between them stretched long, but it was the almost pleasant, tingling silence Pat remembered from intense high school flirtations. It had been that long, that many years since she felt such pure attraction to another woman. She had never experienced a human connection that seemed almost cellular, bred in the bone, and it frankly scared her spitless.

Low, whooping laughter echoed close by, and Pat turned to see two dark tubes stuffed with four women sliding toward them at precarious speed. It might have been a race, and if so, Becca and Jo were winning, the tube they rode gliding over the snow like a hockey puck across glazed ice.

Pat stared at Jo's face, and two thoughts hit her in the same moment. The first was a memory—the only other time she had ever seen Jo look happy. Pat had been four years old, Jo in her early twenties. There was an old photograph of the two of them sledding down this same hill, a bundled little Pat cradled in Jo's lap, her long arms around her. The cheap camera caught Pat's delighted toddler grin, and this same expression on Jo's face— unguarded. Purely happy.

Pat's second thought brought unashamed tears to her eyes. Jo had found Becca, and Becca brought Jo that happiness now. Not just a rare, adrenaline-charged moment of it, but maybe for the rest of her difficult life. Pat had never dared hope for this, that Jo would escape her loneliness, and the gentleness and protectiveness of her arms around Becca told her she had. The truth of it sank in, and Pat grinned at them broadly and rested one boot on their tube as it slowed to a stop at her feet.

Then she was startled by a truly amazing stream of curses ringing through the air. They were in Spanish, but there was no doubt they were profane, and they were gushing from Elena in an unbroken howl. She had toppled onto her back in Grady's lap, her boots flapping in the air, and their tube was still going great guns. Grady couldn't stop laughing long enough to help her screaming wife; she was too busy holding them both on the streaking tube.

Pat started to laugh too, until she saw the trajectory the tube was taking, and she lunged for Maggie a second too late. The side of the tube smacked heavily into her ankles and Maggie went airborne, then crashed into a snowbank on her back.

"Oh, gosh!" Grady steadied Elena and peered over at Maggie anxiously as their tube spun to a halt. "Maggie! Sorry about that. You all right?"

"What the fuckity-fuck *is* it with you people?" Maggie screamed from the snowbank. "This is *twice* I've been knocked on my ass since I met you!"

Pat chuckled and crunched her way over to her, waving reassurance to the others. At least Maggie had chosen a deep bank. She was pretty well buried. Pat grasped one flailing hand and pulled carefully, and a sputtering Maggie emerged, white flakes showering from her dark hair. Maggie was laughing, that distinctive cackle that tickled Pat as she helped her step free of the slush. She realized she had done this before, more than once, helped this laughing woman to her feet after a fall in the snow. A mild wave of dizziness swept Pat, and for the space of a second, Maggie's face was more angular, her hair darker and down to her waist. Then she was Maggie again. Pat shook her head hard to clear the static from her thoughts.

"You let them beat us, Grady!" Elena's cursing had stilled while they waited to see if Maggie was okay, but now it resumed, a colorful muttering as Grady hoisted her up. "My mamá is right about you, you useless gringa. I want a divorce now!"

"We creamed you guys good, Elena. Not even close." Becca heaved out of the center of the tube with a helpful push from Jo. Her cheeks were flushed with high color, and all of them looked more lively than they had in the past two days.

Grady unsnapped the breast pocket of her windbreaker and took out a silver ring, the duplicate of the one she wore, and handed it to Elena. Elena lifted it to her lips before slipping it on her own finger. Apparently, Elena entrusted her ring to Grady before they embarked on dangerous quests like sled runs, and accepting its return must signal her grudging forgiveness for their defeat. She gave Grady's cheek a quick smacking kiss.

"Perhaps we should turn to business now." Jo sounded almost reluctant, but she was eyeing the spread of food hungrily.

"Alas, perhaps you're right." Becca snapped out a blanket and spread it over the snow by the trough. "Here, this'll soak through, but we'll be dry long enough to eat. Man, you sure were scared up there, Elena. You shrieked like a little baby girl. Don't they have any hills at all in New Mexico?"

"We live in the desert, *pendeja*. Not a lot of snow or hills there." Elena settled cheerfully on the blanket next to Becca and blew on her hands to warm them. "We're very sorry that Becca and Jo plowed you down like that, Maggie."

"Honey, I believe we're the ones who did that." Grady brushed some snow off Maggie's shoulder apologetically. "It was an accident."

"Yes, that was you." Maggie slapped Grady's hand away playfully. "You and Elena take the turkey loaf sandwiches. I think I spit in both of them, but it was an *accident*."

Becca handed around sandwiches, smiling, but Pat saw her shoulders slump in apparent relief at shedding her cheerleading role. She understood that Becca had been working hard this morning at her trade, some kind of social work. She had brought them together as a cohesive group, laughing now under a harmless blue sky, and last night Pat would have thought such a feat was impossible. But Becca was obviously tired. There were shadows beneath her eyes.

Jo didn't seem to notice Becca's weariness, or anything other than the food before her. She dug in with a joyless determination, chewing silently, her eyes lowered.

Grady took the lead with the natural authority that must come easily to a college professor. She didn't sound superior as she spoke to Maggie, though. She just sounded kind. "Maggie, I want to tell you again I'm real sorry about Selly's death. That must have been a bad shock."

"And you found her, chica?" Elena asked the question gently, and Pat winced, imagining that gruesome discovery.

Maggie shrugged. "Of course I found her. Who else would find her? I'm the one who cut her down too." She started to say more, then just shrugged again and bit deeply into an apple.

Elena rested her hand on Maggie's hair. She was only a few years older than Maggie, but in that brief moment she was her mother, the mother she should have had.

"We'll get you home as soon as we can today," Grady said. "You probably want to be with your family."

"Huh, there's no home here," Maggie snorted. "My family is driving those ramshackle heaps back to Minnesota right now. Those stinking little hovels up the road are deserted. There's nothing there except the body of an old woman with a broken neck, wrapped in a blanket because the ground's too frozen to dig…"

Maggie trailed off, and sat still beneath Elena's touch caressing her hair.

"You've been through a lot." Grady was quiet for a moment. "Pat can help you make arrangements for Selly, Maggie. We'll help all we can."

"Of course," Pat murmured.

"I keep wanting to thank you, and I'm not even sure why." Grady rested her elbow on her knee. "You trekked all the way out here last night in the middle of a blizzard. You took a big risk, because you wanted to warn us that we're in danger. Maggie… what danger?"

Maggie sighed. Pat watched the child drain out of her, and the woman sat straighter. "Selly told you 'what danger,' yesterday. The Spirit of the Lonely Places. The Cannibal Beast."

They waited. Jo ate stolidly, but Pat and the others had lost interest in lunch.

"Selly told you that one of our ancestors was possessed by the Windigo," Maggie continued. "Like, two hundred years ago. This guy killed and ate his wife, but their baby lived to grow up and spawn its own kids. Kids like those charming brats who threw snowballs at her yesterday." Maggie jutted her chin at Jo. "My whole sorry family has been convinced forever that we're cursed. That the Windigo will come back someday to finish the job on us, because of that baby who lived. Selly made us run all the way out here to escape it. The Windigo has a heart of ice, she told us, and it doesn't like being robbed of a kill."

Becca shivered and pulled the collar of her jacket closer around her neck. "Do you believe in this curse too, Maggie?"

"Of course not." Maggie turned haughty. "Do I look like an idiot to you?"

"Well, kind of, honey." Becca didn't miss a beat. "You just stood right in the path of a speeding inner tube. Just saying."

Pat winced, but Becca had hit the right note. Maggie smiled at her reluctantly, and her shoulders relaxed.

"Okay, granted. I'm an idiot. I ran through a blizzard to warn you about a curse I think is bullshit. But someone had to, and no one else volunteered."

Grady unscrewed the top of a thermos and poured steaming coffee into their cups. "I guess I don't get it yet, Maggie, any of it. Why Selly did what she did, why your family left so suddenly, why you're worried about us."

"The smoke, Grady." Elena dipped her head at Maggie. "I'm sorry. I don't presume to know about the rituals your family practice. But don't many Native American tribes smoke herbs as part of their ceremonies? As Selly did yesterday."

"I can't be your token expert on Native American rituals." Maggie glanced at Jo uneasily. "But yeah, Selly blew smoke in your faces yesterday. And yes, I think she believed she was getting rid of the curse. My family bought it too, so they ran for home the moment they thought they were free. The Abequas believe they aren't cursed anymore, because the curse has been passed on to you."

"On to us? Into us?" Grady probed. "All of us?"

"If my family could have foisted this nightmare onto just any white person, I promise you, we would have done it a century ago." Maggie's tone was dull. "Selly was looking for someone who was vulnerable. Undefended, I guess. Maybe she thought she found someone."

Silence fell over the snowy meadow, and they all looked at Jo. Jo, who had the most brilliant mind Pat had ever encountered. Who seemed to think nothing of the fact that her grandparents had ruined Pat's family, but she put Pat through college and refused all thanks. Jo was her older sister in every way but blood. Pat loved and hated her, and she was scared for her now.

Alone among them, Jo was eating steadily, without pleasure, but her chewing slowed as the silence continued. She seemed puzzled, and her gaze lingered longest on Becca's face. "I'm sorry. Did I miss something?"

"Jo, you felt ill yesterday, right after you left Selly's room." Elena leaned closer to Jo, as if she shared Pat's protectiveness.

"Yes. Briefly. The closeness of that tiny room got to me." Jo tore off the corner of another sandwich with her fingers, her brow furrowed. "But I've been fine since. Entirely myself."

"Have you?" Becca rested her hand on Jo's leg and searched her face. "Were you entirely yourself last night, honey?"

Jo frowned. "What are you talking about?"

Becca lowered her voice. "You've never been so rough with me before, Jo. It scared me a little."

Guilt flickered across Jo's features as clearly as shadows across snow. She averted her eyes and tossed the remnants of her sandwich into the snow-filled trough. "Please. Can we return to some semblance of reality here? Are we thinking I've been possessed by a Windigo?"

"We're just trying to make sense of this, Jo." Grady rubbed Elena's hands in her own to warm them. "The power of suggestion in ritual can be very strong. I'm wondering, if Selly made you believe on some level, even unconsciously—"

"I'm not sure how Selly could have convinced me of anything." Jo was regaining her imperious air. "For one thing, I didn't realize she was trying to breathe the curse of the Windigo into me, along with all that noxious smoke. I just thought she was an extraordinarily rude old woman. Secondly, had she been truly amoral and succeeded in infecting me, why am I feasting on all these fine cold cuts, instead of on one of you?" She looked at Grady pointedly. "Wasn't Selly Abequa starving herself? Why would I be—"

"Say what you want about my great-grandmother, all of you." Maggie rose to her feet, her cheeks flushed. "She did what she thought she had to do to save our family. And that rude old woman, who had no morals, killed herself because she understood that someone who would do such a thing to another person has no right to live in this world. You people enjoy your nice lunch. I've warned you. I've told you all I know. Pat, I've earned a ride into Seattle. I'm sure there are shelters there."

Maggie turned and left them, moving back toward the house with the grace of a woman used to walking in deep snow. Pat stared after her, an amazing pang of loss singing through her heart.

Elena started to get up, but Jo sighed harshly.

"Ah, no. I've done it again." Jo balled her fist on the lip of the trough. "Becca, I'm sorry. We can't let her run off like this. Let me apologize. At least I'm getting lots of practice at that."

Jo unwound her long limbs and stepped around the trough to follow Maggie. Pat made herself study the breathtaking vista of the mountain so she wouldn't have to watch Maggie getting smaller in the distance. As always, the beauty of a sunlit Rainier brought her comfort, but it was meager and fleeting this morning. *Don't go, sewa,* she pleaded silently.

In the quiet that followed, Grady lifted a container of coleslaw and set it before Elena. "Here. Try to eat something. You didn't have much dinner last night."

Elena lifted a plastic fork without enthusiasm, and Pat saw a strange expression cross Becca's face. She was looking at Grady almost wistfully, with an odd yearning.

"To be honest, I'm not sure where we should go from here." Grady slipped off her glasses and rubbed her eyes. "Clearly, there's nothing more we can do for the Abequa family. Without Selly, our study's at a standstill. Jo and I will just have to write up what we have before we drive back tonight. I don't want to see that young woman disappear into the shelters of Seattle, though. Pat, is there any possibility Maggie could stay here, just until she decides what she—"

"Absolutely," Pat said quickly. "I'm sure Jo would be fine with her staying at the cabin."

"What about everything Maggie just told us?" Elena was picking at the coleslaw. "What about Jo?"

"It might be worth it to have Jo's doctor in town check her out, Becca," Grady said. "Are you worried?"

"I'm always worried about Jo," Becca said quietly. She started packing up their lunch. "But I guess I can't go as far as worrying that she needs an exorcist."

"Becca." Elena's tone was even. "I warned you about all this. Have you forgotten so quickly? I tried to tell you Jo would be in danger this weekend."

Becca blinked. "But, honey, neither of us believes in demonic possession. We aren't Catholic. Jo may not be cursed by an evil spirit, but there's something definitely not right with—"

"And what about you?" Elena snapped at Pat. She tossed down the container of salad as if at the end of her patience. "You're not Catholic, Pat. You're not a member of Maggie's tribe. Are you as blind to what's happening as the rest of these educated gringas?"

"Hey, easy," Grady murmured.

"You're supposed to protect people. That's your job." Elena searched Pat's face. "Are you, too, going to deny the nature of our enemy until it's too late to help our sister?"

Pat closed her eyes unwillingly.

"Elena, please, look at me." Becca sounded contrite. "I'm so sorry, I didn't mean to discount your…um. Jesus. P-Pat? Is this normal up here?"

Pat opened her eyes again and saw Becca gaping at the sky to the north. She started to turn, but Rainier caught her gaze and she froze in astonishment. A heavy blanket of darkness was creeping up the mountain, cutting off the sunlight bathing its foothills. Pat shot to her feet.

"Wow." Grady's voice was faint. "There wasn't anything in the forecast about another blizzard."

An immense black cloudbank had appeared on the horizon and it was moving fast. Incredibly fast. Its deep shadow spread like liquid, swallowing the sunlight that hit the mountain at high noon.

"No." Pat couldn't tear her gaze from the threatening sky. "That is not normal up here."

The temperature dropped ten degrees in seconds. It had been a sunny and quiet morning, but now the peace of the day vanished in the growing moan of the winds.

Pat looked down at Elena. "Are we already too late?"

Elena was pale and her voice trembled. "I don't know, Pat."

A frigid gust of air slapped across Pat's face, jarring her into action.

"Come on." She took Becca's arm and pulled her to her feet. "Don't stop to take anything. We have to get inside."

CHAPTER EIGHT

The women roamed the lower level of the cabin like caged animals as the squall roared overhead. Maggie paced angrily, as incapable as any of them of settling into one of the deep sofas. Not with Pat still out there. She was going to have to commandeer a search party soon, if—

The heavy front door swung open and they all whirled toward it.

"How stupid *are* the Indians out here?" Maggie stalked to Pat, who was shaking off a heavy layer of snow in the entry. "Didn't anyone ever teach you *not* to wander around outside in a gale force blizzard? I've known idiots like you who vanished in a heartbeat!"

"Everything's battened down out back." Pat ignored Maggie, which pissed her off no end, and reported directly to Jo. "The windows are bolted."

"Are you all right?" Jo asked gruffly.

"Christ, Jo, of course I'm all right. I grew up on this mountain." Pat clenched the tip of her glove in her white teeth and yanked it off. "How about upstairs?"

"Becca and I fastened every latch we could find up there." Grady gave Pat's shoulder a companionable slap. "Come and sit by the fire. I'm getting frostbite just looking at you."

Maggie's pulse was slowly resuming a less painful cadence. Since everyone was finally sitting down, she deliberately chose an armchair across the wide room from Pat. She scowled to see she was still shaking with cold and drawing air in deep pants.

"I grew up in this area too." Grady tipped the heavy screen guarding the roaring fire to drop in another stick of kindling. "I never saw a storm like this, or even heard of one. Ouch."

"What?" Becca asked.

"Just a splinter." Grady frowned at the side of her hand. "Were you able to call out, Jo?"

"No reception," Jo muttered. "I'll try again later. Elena, do you plan to join us?"

Elena still moved restlessly around the perimeter of the large living room, her arms folded in a shawl. "I'm right here, Jo."

"Grady's right. This isn't normal." Pat's face was brooding as she held her hands near the flames. "That sky. This wind. I know every mood Rainier has, every season." She looked at Maggie. "This is not natural."

"You may have to change some of the ways you see nature." Maggie's bones knew this. Her mind had tried to deny it all her life, was denying it still, but the tempest above them compelled her to tell the truth. "No, your mountain has never seen a storm like this. No one alive has."

"At least we're well stocked with flashlights and candles if the power fails." Grady, doctoral degree or not, was clueless, still focused on practical matters. Maggie kept hoping Elena would join their circle. She found her presence oddly comforting, and her eyes seemed more open than the others did.

"I guess it's safe to assume no one will be driving into Seattle in the immediate future." Becca sounded cheerful, even relaxed, and Maggie sighed. She recognized a social worker in crisis control mode when she saw one; they constantly meddled with her family. She would be no help.

"Which is fine, as far as I'm concerned," Becca continued. "We can all…" Her voice faded as an ominous, growling thunder rolled over the house, but then she brightened again. "We can all have a slumber party right shucky-damn down here, I was going to say. If *that* goes on all night, I want you Amazons sleeping around me. Grady, please stop picking at that before we have to amputate."

Becca went over to sit next to Grady and cradled her palm in her hand. She tipped it toward the light of a small lamp. "Oh, for heaven's sake, I can hardly see this tiny fleck. You were grimacing like you had a spike in your hand."

"That is a spike." Grady frowned. "Ow."

"Hold still. This is why God invented fingernails."

"Jo, those two snowmobiles are in the back shed." Apparently, Pat still thought they could just run away from this. "Once it calms down out there, I might be able to get them going."

"Why waste your time?" Jo looked away from Becca and Grady and stood abruptly. "Once the storm lets up, a plow will come through to clear the roads."

"All the way up here, off the main drag?" Grady nodded her thanks to Becca and shook out her hand. "No offense, Pat, but unless the Park Service is much faster than it used to be—"

"I can pay enough to make it worth their while. We'll be out of here tomorrow." Jo headed toward the kitchen. "Did we leave all of the cold cuts out by the trough?"

"I think there's still…" Becca peered around at Jo. "Honey, surely you can't be hungry. We just ate. Are you feeling all right?"

"Can we declare a moratorium on asking me how I feel, Becca? I feel fine." There was no malice in Jo's tone. She seemed almost bored, but there was a rigid set to her shoulders that disturbed Maggie. "However, if we're going to be here an extra night, and we have an extra guest to feed, perhaps it would be wise to check our provisions." She didn't look at any of them as she left the room.

Becca eased back against the sofa cushions, her shadowed eyes on the flames. "I'd apologize for her, but I'm actually reassured. That was pretty vintage Jo. Maybe she really is fine."

Grady gave Becca a gentle tap under the chin with one finger, and Becca smiled at her warmly. Maggie looked from one to the other, and then at Pat, who was still glowering at the fire. She was surprised Pat wasn't picking up on this. Did she really not notice the outright flirtation that had developed between these two? Jo had sure as hell noticed it, and she hadn't looked pleased.

Something quivered in the back of Maggie's memory, something triggered by the odd frisson of romance she'd just witnessed. Selly had always warned them to watch each other. She said the Witiko would change the rest of the family as well, when it came to take Selly. It always changed the loved ones too, to enrage the cursed into killing them. Maggie blinked, willing Selly's cracked voice out of her head.

"How do you know when someone is having a heart attack?" Elena asked suddenly. She was standing in the far corner of the room, gazing out an ice-glazed window.

"What's that, honey?" Becca asked.

"The first symptom of a heart attack. It happens every time." Elena traced a form on the glass with the tip of her finger, but Maggie couldn't see its shape. "*Ay*, that's right. None of you gringas are certified nurses. You probably wouldn't know this. The first symptom is not chest pains or breathlessness; it's denial. The first sure sign that a person is having a heart attack is they insist they are not having a heart attack."

"Elena," Grady said. She sounded almost testy. "Are you going somewhere with this?"

"It's true. Denial is the most reliable symptom. Look it up." Elena shrugged. "But we all believe Jo when she tells us she is fine."

And with theatrical timing, the lights went out. Gloom swept through the large room, held at bay only by the crackling fire.

They had been talking about this possibility for the last hour, but dismay gripped Maggie nonetheless, a childish fear of the dark.

"Ah, peachy!" Becca still sounded relaxed as the wind punched at the house. "We have no power and Jo thinks she's cooking tonight. It's getting dire around here."

"What the hell?" Grady shook the flashlight she held and clicked it again. "I just checked all these lights, not half an hour ago. This can't be out."

"Hey, Jo?" Becca called to the kitchen. "Any extra flashlights in there?"

"One," Jo's reply drifted back. "I believe Grady was supposed to check it, but the batteries are dead."

"It's two o'clock in the afternoon." Pat said this reasonably, an adult pointing out the obvious to a pack of unruly children. The room quieted.

Maggie turned automatically to the windows, disoriented. Pat was right. Not two hours had elapsed since their sunlit picnic in the meadow. It was full night outside.

Pat stood up. "Grady, light the candles on the mantel, please. Becca, Maggie, find matches and light the candles on the tables around the room. Be sure they're safely placed."

Her voice was music, a low melody of quiet authority. Pat was changing before her eyes, or becoming more what she had always been; Maggie didn't know how else to explain it. She was becoming deeply familiar, and Maggie didn't know how to explain that at all.

"Sounds like a good plan." Grady turned to the hearth, and instead of cowering together in the unnatural night, Pat had them sparking lights to push back its shadows.

Maggie held a match to one of the candles and saw Pat cross to Elena. Elena still stood in the corner watching them, not offering to help. Pat spoke quietly to her, and Maggie had to shift subtly closer to eavesdrop.

"Elena." Pat held out her hand, and waited until Elena rested hers in it. "I want you to stop calling us gringas. The way you're using the word now it's an insult, a racial slur. It sets you apart from us, and we have to be together tonight. Do you agree?" Pat's larger hand was gentle, holding Elena's fingers. She was much taller and could have loomed over her, but she kept a respectful distance.

After a long moment, Elena's shoulders lifted with her breath. "I do agree, mi amiga," she murmured. "Thank you."

Pat smiled at her and released her hand.

Maggie started as Jo elbowed her way through the kitchen door. She was carrying a large bowl overflowing with corn chips and picked her way carefully around the furniture.

"Jesus, it's dark in here," Jo grumbled. "Do none of these flashlights work?" She paused next to Becca and took a small plastic container from atop the bowl of chips. "French onion dip." She handed it to Becca. "I believe you're very fond of French onion dip. Correct?"

Maggie registered this gesture even through her anxiety. Seattle lesbians had weird courting rituals; that's what this was. Or maybe an apology. Maggie didn't know Jo well enough to be sure. The worst storm in two centuries, and she'd been scavenging through a dark kitchen trying to find a treat to make her girlfriend smile. Maggie's heart warmed to Jo a little.

"I do love me my French onion dip." The sweetness of Becca's expression told Maggie she was right. She accepted the container and rose to her toes to kiss Jo's cheek. "And my sweet dip of a scientist."

"Good," Jo said softly. She straightened and then gasped.

"What?" Becca asked quickly. She turned and followed Jo's gaze to the fireplace, and then dropped the container to the floor, white dip spattering over her feet.

"What is it?" Maggie couldn't see anything alarming in the crackling flames.

"Pat?" Jo barked, and Maggie realized she and Becca weren't staring at the hearth, but at the large oil painting mounted above it.

Grady had lit the tall candles that stood in ornate holders on either end of the mantel. Whickering gold light flooded across the painting, which was damned ugly in Maggie's opinion, but she couldn't see why—

Pat inhaled sharply and crossed the room to the fireplace in three long strides.

"What's happened to it?" Grady blinked up at the canvass. "That's not the same painting that was here yesterday, is it?"

"It's the same." A muscle in Pat's jaw stood out. "My grandmother painted this. She gave it to Jo on her eighteenth birthday."

"The mountain is smaller." Elena's words was hushed. "And, Grady, look at the sky."

It was an odd landscape. Maggie could see that. She hadn't even noticed this painting the night before, what with being tackled by a butch moose and all. It disquieted her now. A distant but recognizable outline of Mt. Rainier beneath muddy, churning clouds, forbidding and cold.

"My grandmother's signature is still right there." Pat's hand hovered over the bottom left corner of the frame.

"What do you think you're doing?"

There was a sudden, intense wariness in Jo's voice. She took a few steps away from all of them, even Becca, and stared at them as if they were strangers.

"What do all of you think you're doing?"

One long hour later, Grady adjusted the trio of tapered candles on top of the dresser in their bedroom upstairs, convinced she was going to burn the mansion down around their ears. How else could this bizarre weekend end but in disaster? Grady hoped with unabashed selfishness that she wouldn't be the one to bring any fresh calamity on their heads. It was bad enough not knowing how to keep Elena safe.

The ceiling of the room they shared was so high, the candles did little to illuminate the echoing space. Elena sat quietly on the wide bed as Grady did what she could to beat back this strange night. A light scent of piñon drifted on the air from the powdered incense Elena had burning on a side table, and Grady found it soothing.

"I'm not hearing anything from downstairs." Grady meant the large bedroom off the main floor. "Maybe Becca talked Jo into resting for a while. The valerian you gave her must have kicked in. That was really strange down there, Elena."

Elena shrugged, which made her look like Maggie, young and faux indifferent.

That frightened glittering in Jo's eyes. Spittle had actually flown from her lips as she hissed at them, accused them. Becca had been struck silent, everyone else immobilized by Jo's sudden venom, her bared teeth.

"Hey, Jo, I think you should calm down." Pat spoke to her with the professional calm of a ranger confronting a belligerent drunk. "No one here is trying to pull anything over on you. We're all as confused about this as—"

"Shut your mouth, Patricia." Jo's voice was ice-cold. "Your grandmother loved me. She loved me." Her arm flashed toward the macabre painting over the hearth. "She would never have given me that."

"She seemed to come around after a few minutes." Grady wanted to reassure herself as much as Elena. "That weird paranoia hit Jo very suddenly, but it didn't last long. She responded to reason, eventually. Becca was able to calm her down."

"You mean we were able to convince Jo that we didn't mess with her painting, that we're not trying to drive her crazy? And so she is fine again, now." Elena spoke with a weary cynicism that was utterly unlike her, at least when they were alone together.

"Hey." Grady felt a pang of misgiving, an uneasy flutter beneath her breastbone. She sat beside Elena on the bed, careful not to jar her, close enough that their shoulders touched. "Tell me what's going on with you."

"I don't know, Grady." Elena rubbed her forehead with the heels of her hands. "I still don't know how to help these people."

"Okay." Grady rested her elbows on her knees and studied her in the faint light from the candles. "I've seen you tackle frustration before. Times when you've been worried, when you haven't known how to help. It's never made you like this."

"Like what?" Elena snapped.

"Snappish." Grady waited, and finally Elena cracked a smile, a rueful acknowledgement that made her Elena again.

"I'm sorry, querida. I'm just scared." Elena laid her head on Grady's shoulder, on the tender spot reserved for no one else. "I've never felt so much at sea, so lost. And my Goddess has fallen silent, Grady, about this Windigo. That frightens me more than anything."

There was desolation in her voice as well as fear, and Grady rested her lips in Elena's hair. Grady still might not believe fully in any deity, but Elena had been strongly connected to hers from the day she was born. She must feel terribly alone. "How can I help you, babe?"

Elena was silent, fumbling with something she held in her lap, and then she relaxed against her side. "Like this, sí? Help me just like this. Hold me for the rest of this strange, dark day, and then hold me through the long night to come."

"I'll hold you through all our days, all our nights."

Elena lifted her head and their lips met, and a longing for home keened through Grady like a lost wind, the aroma of green chiles roasting, the royal sweep of the Rio Grande. She had to get Elena out of this suddenly alien place, get her home to their valley.

Elena looked better; her eyes were warm and clear again. Something nearly slid off Elena's lap and she grasped it, then held it up for Grady to see.

"Well, hey there, Inez." Grady lifted the little feathered Makah mask toward the candlelight. The small flames gleamed through the slitted eyeholes. "You haven't called for seven minutes. We've missed you terribly."

Elena chuckled, a welcome note of normality, of the home they had in each other whether they were surrounded by mountain pine or desert sage.

"Ay, I should call Mamá. She'll be worried." Elena opened her cell and flicked a finger at the dark screen. "Still no reception, and no wonder."

The storm howled around the cabin, the eerie, midday midnight still cloaked the mountain.

"Querida, I'm going to try to pray. You should go downstairs and show this mask to Pat. Ask her about this Makah legend. We might want to know more about how the children of her tribe defeated this Cannibal Woman."

"Not a bad idea." Grady tapped the mask against her fingers. "If you're sure you'll be okay for a while, I'll go talk to Pat. I'll check in on Jo and Becca too."

She planted another kiss on the top of Elena's head, then made her way through the shadowy room to the door. She almost had it closed behind her when she heard Elena's soft voice.

"Sí, by all means, Grady. Go check in on *Becca*."

❖

Becca thought she was navigating the dark stairs quite well, like a chubby panther running on steroids and jangled nerves. She could hear Pat and Maggie below, talking in the inky gloom of the living room. Pat would listen for any stirring in the far bedroom, any sign that Jo was awake.

She hadn't thought she'd need a candle for this brief trip, but she'd forgotten how immense Jo's frigging fortress was. She clenched the railing with one hand and groped the dark air with the other. Here was the hallway, so if she could remember if the door to the upstairs loft was the second on her right or the third—

Her cold fingers touched a cold face, and Becca gasped raggedly and shrank back against the wall. *"Who?"*

"B-Becca?" Grady sounded just as rattled.

"Jesus carpenter Christ on a crutch, Grady." Becca tried to keep her voice down, her hand pressed to her waist, and then she started giggling. It wasn't that funny. It was sheer nerves, but she couldn't help it.

Grady waited her out gallantly, chuckling a few times to keep her company. "I'm sorry, Becca. Didn't mean to scare you. Is everything quiet down there?"

"It's quiet as a tomb down there." Becca could make out the high planes of Grady's features now, by the dull white glow of the snow filtering through an upper window. "Actually, before you almost ended my young life by scaring the crap out of me, I was on my way to thank Elena for that tea. It put Jo out like a light, and I think rest is what she needs."

Grady murmured something noncommittal, and Becca would have preferred rousing agreement. "Elena's needing some private time right now, but I'll pass on your thanks."

"Good. Okay." There didn't seem to be anything more to say, in the dimness of this hushed hallway. Becca should head down the stairs and return to Jo.

"I was serious about that slumber party." Becca turned back to Grady. "We'll let Jo take a good long nap, but then I want us to pile sleeping bags in front of the fire. Everybody should be together the rest of the day."

"Day." The outline of Grady's handsome head lifted as she looked up at the window. "Only a real stretch of the imagination can call this daylight. And it's getting pretty cold in here, have you noticed?"

Grady's gaze was actually on her nipples. Becca could feel her hunger crawling greedily over her breasts, and her face flushed with heat. She stepped closer to her without thinking, then tried to summon rational thought. "Well, I'm not sure exactly what powers this house. Could be our heating is out, along with our lights."

"Pat will know. We might have to bundle up in—"

Becca surged against her, and Grady stumbled back and caught her. Becca clawed for the back of her neck and pulled her head down hard, and their mouths met with a clashing of teeth and lips. A cruel and delicious pleasure churned through Becca, and after a stunned moment, she heard Grady growl welcome into her open mouth.

They clutched each other feverishly, their hands roaming as the kiss grew almost savage, and then Grady pushed her back—a hard, abrupt shove. Becca staggered, then steadied herself. She heard Grady's harsh panting and tears sprang to her eyes, confusion and horror seeping into her every cell, where only blinding lust ruled a heartbeat ago.

"Oh n-no," Becca stammered. "Grady—forgive me. Please, I don't know what…"

"Becca." Grady's voice was hollow with shock. Becca tried to draw an even breath. "Listen to me. I'm going to go back to Elena now. And you're going to walk downstairs, and go back to Jo."

Becca closed her eyes and the brimming tears coursed down her cheeks. "Grady," she whispered, "that is *exactly* what we're going to do."

She wanted to apologize again, to explain, but she didn't know how the hell to explain why she had just betrayed a woman she cherished with her whole heart. Becca stumbled toward the staircase and focused on getting back to Jo without breaking her neck.

CHAPTER NINE

Pat lifted a candle and made her way to a side table in one corner of the dark living room. She picked up the small frame, scowling. She had never liked Jo's banishing this photo to an afterthought of a distant table. Becca had placed the framed pictures of people she loved on the mantel over the fireplace, where family portraits belonged, and that's where this one was going.

She returned to the hearth and put the little frame next to one of a smiling couple, perhaps Becca's parents. They were not Jo's parents, which was a good thing; Pat's grandmother wouldn't tolerate sitting close to Jo's parents. None of the Daka clan could abide any of the Call family. Jo was the only Call her grandmother would speak to, the only one she liked.

"No." Pat studied the three faces in the old photo by the lights of the side candles. "Jo was right. My grandmother loved her very much."

"Why?"

Pat remembered she wasn't alone in the echoing room. Maggie stood next to her, looking at the snapshot on the mantel.

"I mean, didn't you tell me Jo is your boss? Why would your grandmother love a white girl who grew up to be your...I'm not trying to be disrespectful." And she wasn't, for once; there was only friendly curiosity in Maggie's tone.

Pat shrugged. "I don't know. Jo came up here with her parents a lot when she was growing up. My grandmother was a kind person. Maybe she didn't like how mean the rest of my family was about Jo, behind her back, because she was different."

"You mean obnoxious?" Maggie's teasing was still gentle, and Pat smiled reluctantly.

"Yeah, my grandmother said Jo was always obnoxious, from the time she was my age here." Pat touched her own small face in the photo, taken by a cheap early-nineties camera. On the same day, the same camera had taken the picture that was framed in Pat's trailer, the one of Jo holding her on the inner tube.

Jo held four-year-old Pat protectively in her arms in this shot too, almost proudly, both of them bundled in windbreakers. Her grandmother stood beside them, wrapped in a thick shawl, her arm slung around Jo's shoulders, grinning broadly and toothlessly at the camera.

"Jo looks so young here. Almost gawky, kind of sweet." Maggie jutted her chin toward the room where Jo slept. "Hard to imagine her as anything but a rich scientist who snaps people's heads off. I like the way she can be with Becca, though."

"Me too." Pat touched her grandmother's image with one finger.

"You loved your grandmother a lot, didn't you?"

"Yeah. I loved her like crazy." There was such fun in the old woman's lined features, that gummy smile, such simple happiness in the day. "She was the one who brought me up, really. She was nicer to me than anyone in my family."

"Maybe she didn't like how mean the rest of your family was about you, behind your back, because you were different. Maybe they were even mean about you to your face."

Pat was startled by the longing in Maggie as she looked at her grandmother, the wistfulness in her tone. And she was dead right about the way Pat's family treated her when she was a teenager, the way they treated her to this day.

"That must be why you and Jo get along pretty well, right? You've both always known what it's like to be outcast."

"What are you talking about?" Pat knew damn well she hadn't told Maggie anything about her adolescence, never mind being "outcast."

"Oh, please." Maggie smiled at her dryly. "I'm not interested in jumping your bones, Smokey Bear, not today. Sorry, tonight. This might be the longest night of our lives, and I only want us to still be alive when the sun comes up. But it's not rocket science, guessing why your family is mean to you. Same reason mine is mean to me."

Maggie raked her fingers through her tumbling hair, her breasts lifting with the motion, and Pat averted her eyes. This kid was practically jailbait. And disclaimer aside, Maggie was flirting now. Sensuality oozed off her in palpable waves; she could turn it on and off like a light switch. Pat wasn't a stranger to rash sex, but she wasn't going to bed a vulnerable girl who seemed to know no other way to connect with the world. She slammed an inner door firmly shut on her own arousal.

"All I know is Jo looked out for me." Pat stepped away from Maggie, toward the recessed door that led to the bedroom where Jo slept. "She got me away from the others for a few hours, took me sledding, showed me how to leave corn in the trough for deer. Jo spent time with me."

"And she never tried to seduce you?" Maggie's air of disdain was back, as easily switched on as her eroticism. "Jo's what, twenty years older than you? She never took you out behind this mansion and put the moves on when you were a baby dyke? Is that what you mean by 'she looked out for me,' Pat?"

And Pat knew, because she understood every nuance of Maggie's body language, that she was stung by Pat's rejection, and that's where this fresh scorn was coming from. She didn't care, and it took effort to keep her tone even.

"Jo looked out for me by putting me through college after my grandmother died, Maggie. And a week after my Park Service jeep slid off an icy back road last winter, I came home to find that Outback parked by my trailer. Jo had it delivered, the keys and the title left in it, because she wants me to be safe. That's what I mean by looking out for me."

Pat stalked away from the hearth as Becca came down the stairs and into the living room. She gave them a brief smile, but went directly to the bedroom and let herself in quietly.

"Maggie, what's the matter with you?" Pat wanted an answer, because she knew Maggie wasn't just superficial or cruel. Why she knew all this, the subtleties of this near-stranger's expressions, the very nature of her character, mystified Pat, but for now, she'd settle for hearing Maggie's truth. "What happened to you to make you like this? Does everyone have to want something from you? Can't people just be loving, Maggie?"

"What happened to me?" Maggie seemed unfazed by Pat's intensity, and she no longer looked disdainful, just mildly sad and old beyond her years. "Well, for one thing, you were raised by this woman." She brushed one finger across the smiling image of Pat's grandmother. "I was raised by Selly Abequa."

Pat nodded.

Maggie helped her move the hearth screen to settle another log on the fire.

❖

Jo was dreaming again.

It must not have been a bad nightmare, she decided, as nightmares go. As with all her dreams lately, she couldn't remember a moment of it; only that it had been a rather disturbing one. Becca was curled against her back, deeply asleep; Jo's waking had not even been startling enough to disturb her.

Happily, Jo was not well versed in nightmares; until recently, poor Becca suffered more from them. Jo wondered how Becca's clinical training would interpret the fading remnants of these dreams, the ones she couldn't remember. Becca had mentioned once that she favored Jung. She liked his mysticism. What would she make of this onslaught of forgotten delusions?

Jo scrunched the pillow beneath her neck and tried to drop back to sleep. There was no telling what Elena Montalvo had put into her tea to make her dream such things. Jo knew what valerian was. It was a common enough herb, but whatever that brew had contained, it wasn't valerian. She was unable to fathom what Elena might be up to, couldn't begin to understand the thought processes of that devious little witch.

Jo closed her eyes on the harshness of that characterization, troubled all over again by her lack of generosity. She knew Becca genuinely liked Elena, was beginning to think of her as a friend. Becca made friends so easily, and she had an uncanny knack for seeing the good in others. Jo remembered the gentleness of Elena's hands as she tended Maggie last night, the concern in her eyes as she helped Jo at the Abequa compound, after she fainted.

Well, Jo amended, after she sat down so suddenly. She had not fainted. In any case, Elena deserved better than snobbish insults from a crazy woman.

And Jo had been crazy earlier, in the living room. Even held in Becca's arms beneath a warm comforter, she was chilled by a rush of shame, remembering her behavior. What had gotten into her, turning on the others like that, hurling ridiculous accusations? Her motives were as mysterious and elusive now as that forgotten dream.

Jo frowned into the darkness, wondering what time it was. At least the odd storm seemed to be abating; the high whistle of the wind had lessened. She had apparently slept through dinner and into full night. None of them had thought to call her to eat, which was annoying. Grady Wrenn had doubtless feasted well on Jo's groceries, on the dinner Becca had doubtless prepared for her.

Her stomach rumbled with hunger.

❖

You might be silent, sweet Goddess, but You are here.

Elena warmed the side of her face against Grady's sleeve as they carefully descended the stairs. Her Diosa was everywhere; how could she have forgotten that? Even if her weak mortal ears couldn't hear Her through the static flung up by this Windigo, her Mother still reached her somehow, to bring comfort and strength.

Elena was able to sense her Goddess, recall a more benevolent universe, through Grady's touch, her fingers inside her, her tongue. Their lovemaking had been so sweet, after that first fervent groping, so rich and satisfying. Her knees still wobbled as they stepped off the last riser together, and she heard a low chuckle near the crackling fire.

"What's so funny, officer?" Grady's tone was light as she spoke to Pat, and Elena was relieved to know she was refreshed and relaxed as well.

"You two do look a little like the holy family." Pat lifted a stoneware mug toward the shadows they cast on the wall, and Maggie laughed too.

Elena had to agree. The tall candle Grady held aloft outlined her taller form, wrapped in a blanket, her arm around Elena's shoulders. Close against Grady, Elena carried bundles of blankets, and together they resembled a lesbian Joseph and Mary picking their way down cobbled streets.

"Sheesh, I can almost see your breath." Maggie waved them closer, then lifted a kettle from the hearth. "It's colder than a witch's tit in here. Have some of this; we heated up some cocoa the old-school way."

"Thank you, both my tits are really cold." Elena accepted the mug of steaming cocoa gratefully and wrapped her chilled fingers around it. There was no sound from the master bedroom Jo and Becca shared, which was good news. It might be wise to keep Jo in a drugged sleep until she could figure out what to do. She would ask Jo to take more valerian later.

"A fine way to celebrate the passing of that dang storm." Grady settled cross-legged on the pine floor before the hearth and sipped from her mug. "I don't suppose there might be any brandy, Pat, lurking around in a drawer somewhere? I cheerfully admit I'd love to spike this chocolate."

"No, Jo had me..." Pat trailed off, and her features closed subtly, the quiet shutting of a door.

"It's all right, *hermana*." Elena respected Pat's instinct for privacy, but this was not the time to keep things from each other. "Finish what you were going to say."

The gold light of the flames flickered over Pat's face, and then she nodded. "Okay. Jo has always had liquor in the house. She never drinks much, but she likes a glass of wine at night, or a shot of really good bourbon. But before you all came up this weekend, she asked me to throw everything out." Pat shrugged. "I figure Becca's had a problem with drinking in the past. My sense is she's beaten it; she's just too smart to spend much time in a place with booze lying around."

"Yeah, Becca's smart there." Maggie lifted one of the blankets they brought down and wrapped it around her shoulders. "I've been in and out of rehab and drunk tanks since I was fourteen. I shouldn't be around the stuff either. I'm glad Jo had you throw out the bottles, Pat. None of us should be drinking this weekend."

Elena felt a niggling at the back of her mind and tried to grasp it, but it slithered away before it made sense. Maggie's face was so lovely in the firelight, and so pensive. She had been through much more than even Elena had suspected, brought up in that heartless family, beset by the demons of addiction.

Can't we do better than this, Diosa? Elena's Goddess might not answer her, but She still had to listen; that was their deal. *Shouldn't we women who love women do a better job of looking after our daughters? In these enlightened times, why did this beautiful girl have to go through her painful adolescence all alone?*

It was there for just a second, a light shimmering around Maggie's head, a sign that Elena had long recognized as a signal that the Goddess had bestowed a gift. She realized that this was Her gift to Maggie, their very presence together in this firelit room.

Maggie had been deserted by her family, threatened by a monster, and stranded in a freak blizzard, and yet in that moment of divine shimmering, she was revealed to Elena as safer than she had ever been in her young life. For the first time, Maggie was in the company of like-souled women, strong and loving friends. Short of finding a lifemate, the Mother could offer no greater blessing.

Pat knuckled steam off the pane of a side window. "Maybe it's calmed down enough out there that I can take a look at the generator out back. There isn't an excuse in the world for this place losing heat so fast, lines down or not."

Elena smiled, because Pat sounded so personally offended by the chill in this luxurious cabin. Then her smile faltered because she mustn't lose sight of the truth. No, their ordinary world held no excuse for this growing cold.

"Has it stopped snowing?" Grady asked.

"Yeah, and the wind's died down." Pat sighed and came back to them. "At least it's getting late enough in the day that it's supposed to be dark, this time of year."

"Well, if there's any wind at all, you won't be able to check a generator by candlelight, genius." Maggie tossed Pat a folded blanket. "Since none of these flashlights are—"

A sharp cry rang from the back bedroom, and alarm streaked through Elena. Pat was moving before the sound faded as the rest of them scrambled to their feet.

"Was that Becca?" Maggie ran after Pat.

The door to the bedroom slammed open just as Pat reached it, and Jo nearly knocked her off her feet. They were almost the same height, but Jo pushed past Pat aside as if she were a doll and lunged into the living room.

"See to her!" Jo hissed. She was white as chalk. She flashed a commanding hand toward the bedroom and then started for the front door. Elena dodged to one side or Jo would have plowed straight into her, and she struggled hard to gather her wits.

Pat ducked quickly into the bedroom, then emerged just as quickly as Jo threw open the cabin door and raced outside. She spoke with amazing calm. "Elena, talk to Becca. I'm going after Jo."

"We're going after Jo!" Maggie was already snatching jackets off the pegs on the wall. "The idiot is out there in shirtsleeves!"

Elena made herself move toward the bedroom; one running step, two.

The story Grady had told, of the Cree Indian Swift Runner's six cannibalized children, his wife. The shreds of their mangled remains strewn through a cabin in Canada's deep winter, their innocent blood frozen in rusty pools on the wood planks.

Elena shook her head fiercely to shake off the terrible vision; Becca needed her. But it wasn't until Grady gripped her hand that she was able to run with her to the master bedroom, breathing a prayer for the safety of the others.

Her first sight of Becca filled Elena with such relief she almost sagged against the doorway. Pat had seen at once that she wasn't badly hurt. She sat on the wide bed, the heavy comforter snarled around her waist. Her eyes were wide with shock, but Elena saw no blood, and Becca's chest lifted and fell with her gasping breath.

One of Becca's full breasts was exposed. Elena clenched her fingers hard around Grady's hand and bared her teeth in a sudden snarl. Grady was seeing this, the lush blue-veined swell of Becca's pale breast, capped by a tan nipple. And in the next heartbeat, with great effort, Elena reclaimed herself. She was a healer, a *curandera* of her people and her Goddess, and this was a frightened sister she was growing to love.

"No, no, sit still, please." Elena moved to the bed and sat beside Becca, keeping her from rising. "Let me take a look at you. Grady, would you bring that candle closer?"

"Elena, where is she?" Becca's voice shook, but she was visibly collecting herself. Her hair was tousled around her shoulders, her face still lined with sleep, and she pulled the torn neck of her T-shirt up over her breast. "Jesus, she was out of here before I could even wake up—"

"Don't worry about Jo. Pat and Maggie have gone after her." Grady held the candle so its faint wash of light touched Becca. "What the hell happened in here?"

"She pinched me. Or she…took a bite out of me." A half-laugh sputtered out of Becca and her fingers brushed her breast. "I don't know. I was sound asleep. It's not bad. It just hurt for a moment."

"Let me see. It's all right, *hija.*" Elena spoke to Becca with the same tenderness she would show a young child frightened of a vaccination. She rested her hand over Becca's fingers until she moved them and allowed Elena to uncover her breast again.

The candlelight revealed what she had not seen before—in that first moment when Elena had been so shamefully consumed with rage. The white curve of Becca's breast was marred with a perfect half-moon of deep red indentations. Jo's teeth had not broken the skin, but she had come close.

"Ay, this must have been painful." Elena brushed Becca's hair back gently. "But you're right, Becca. It isn't too bad. You can expect some bruising, but I have a salve upstairs that will help this heal quickly."

"What's happening to her, Elena?" Becca stared at them both. "Jo would rather jump off a cliff than harm a hair on my head. I promise you that."

"We believe you, amiga." Elena looked at Grady because she had to see her face. How terrible it must be, to fear for the life of the woman you loved. Becca may not yet understand how high the stakes of this battle were, but the darkness in her eyes meant she was beginning to grasp Jo's danger.

"Pat and Maggie will bring her back." Grady spoke to Becca kindly, as she would to a frightened family friend, and Elena cursed herself as a shrew and a fool to ever suspect otherwise. "When they do, we'll work on this together."

"Sí. And your color is better." Elena touched Becca's throat to measure her pulse. "But you are not getting off this bed until you can show me a slightly slower heart rate."

"Elena," Becca protested. "We need to—"

"Hush, you *pinche* little boob, I'm counting." Elena winked at Becca, because winking had become a friendly language between them, and she did use this brief silence to count her pulse. But mostly she prayed.

CHAPTER TEN

Maggie followed Pat blindly out of the cabin, gasping at the stunning bite of the night air. It was suddenly Minnesota cold out here, killing cold, and it might kill Jo if she got away from them. Maggie hefted the jackets higher in her arms and almost stumbled into Pat's broad back.

"There." Pat pointed, and then Maggie saw Jo too. Her distant figure stood knee-deep in snow at the top of the rise leading into the forest, her back to the house. Christ, the woman probably only had socks on her feet!

"Maggie?" Pat kept going.

"Right behind you!" Maggie slapped her back. They followed quickly and carefully in the deep holes Jo's feet had punched in the snow. They were both practiced at plowing their way through hard snowpack, but thankfully, this city dweller seemed less so. If Jo took off on another bat-crazy sprint, they'd be able to catch her.

"Joanne," Pat barked. "You wait right there!" Maggie figured this was Pat's Park Ranger tone, the one she used to order drunk teenagers out of their cars, and Maggie for one would have heeded it.

When they reached Jo, she was trembling spasmodically, her bare arms prickled with gooseflesh, her dark hair a tangled fury around her pale face. Pat slung a jacket over her shoulders at once, and Maggie tied the sleeves of a second around her waist.

Jo didn't resist their efforts, but she didn't help them. Her gaze was locked on the dark trees, and even in the faint light reflecting off the snow, Maggie could see the muscles in her jaw standing out.

"Becca?" Jo's voice was guttural.

"She's fine. Elena's with her." Pat took her arm. "Jo, you need to come back to the house. Right now."

"Listen to me." Jo looked at Pat, and Maggie shivered. Her eyes were coated with an odd silver sheen. "I take it your service pistol is in your trailer. I want you to get it and carry it with you at all times."

"All right. We can talk about this and walk at the same time." Pat tugged Jo's arm, and Maggie took her free one, but she didn't budge.

"Listen to me first. Get your gun and watch me carefully every minute until we get out of here. If you see me threaten Becca again—if I do anything, make any move that might harm her—put me down like a dog. I need your promise on that."

"This isn't the time for drama, Jo," Pat snapped. "I'll discuss anything with you, but not out here."

"You can't let me hurt her, Pat."

"Becca is fine!" The steam of Pat's breath plumed from her mouth in an angry burst. All three of them were shaking like aspens in the bitter chill, but even through her anxiety, Maggie wondered if Pat realized Jo's breath had been invisible. "You're no threat to her. Now move your—"

"Patricia." Jo's fingers closed over Pat's, and it struck Maggie that she hadn't seen this Jo before. She wasn't an imperious rich white woman issuing orders now, and she wasn't a crazy psycho possessed by a Windigo. She spoke to Pat quietly, as an equal and a sister. This must be the Jo both Pat and her grandmother loved. "Promise me you won't let me hurt her."

Pat closed her free hand over Jo's fingers. "Yes. You've got my promise."

Jo nodded. The night was eerily still around them, the heavy cloud cover oppressively low above their heads.

"Jo, seriously?" Maggie turned Jo toward the house. "You might lose some toes if you stay out here much longer." Actually, she was no longer certain Jo could freeze, but she and Pat sure could. "Come on back now."

"I'll go back." Jo extricated herself, slipping her arms free of their grip with an odd courtesy. "You two will go to Pat's trailer and get her gun before you join us."

Jo started toward the dark house at an awkward pace, lifting her knees high to step in the prints they'd left. Trembling, Maggie watched her go, resisting the image of the looming mansion as a black void against the white trees around it, preparing to swallow Jo whole again.

Maggie realized she was able to see with increasing clarity as a sick greenish light flooded the plain of snow. She turned and looked up into the dense bank of clouds and saw a near-perfect circular break drift open in them. She felt Pat's shoulder brush hers as they stared up at the strange moon.

It was full and recognizably the moon, but she doubted any orb like this had ever gleamed down on this mountain, bloated and fat and pulsing with a slick light that looked almost wet, circled by a nimbus of dull green.

"My grandmother taught me all the stages of the winter sky." Pat's voice was hollow next to her. "I've never seen a moon like this, Maggie."

"Me n-neither." Maggie's teeth were chattering hard. "I think maybe no one's seen a moon l-like this for—Pat, it's so fucking cold…"

"Let's get inside, *sewa*." Pat wrapped her arm around Maggie's shoulders, and she felt the immediate ease and rightness of that motion, the quiet click of their bodies fitting together. This was not the time to dwell on that, because they had to get under cover before the cold killed them.

And first they had to make their way to the trailer to pick up a gun, because Maggie knew Pat always kept her promises.

❖

What are you trying to tell me, old woman?

Pat still spoke to her dead grandmother on a regular basis. Not daily, but often. She always listened for a reply from her spirit too, and would for the rest of her life. That was a reasonable expectation to have of someone lucky enough to be mothered by Delores Daka.

Across the dark living room, her grandmother's signature was faintly visible in the corner of the painting over the hearth. Pat brooded over the sinister changes in the landscape again. If wise ancestors really spoke to the living from beyond the grave, as Jo claimed, she wished they would do so more clearly than just muddy up what had once been a truly nice painting. If her grandmother was sending her a message here, she couldn't dredge any wisdom from it.

They had settled in on the lower level for the night. In addition to the Glock .22 now safely concealed in Pat's belt holster, she and Maggie had brought armloads of fresh firewood in for this cold slumber party. The fire in the hearth was roaring, pushing back both the dark and the growing chill in the room for a precious few yards.

Becca had coaxed Jo down again, her long form stretched out on one of the deep sofas, warmed by thick blankets. Becca sat on the floor near her head, sifting her fingers through Jo's dark hair, her eyes on the flames. Elena and Grady were huddled closer to the hearth, heating more cocoa near the fire. One of them laughed softly. Maggie was making her way closer across the gloomy room, and Pat felt a small muscle between her shoulders relax at the sight of her, a welcome from her very sinew.

"It's warmer over there by the fire, Smokey Bear. I have to teach you everything." Maggie's eyes crinkled, but not in flirtation now, just friendly interest. "What are you doing all alone in the dark?"

Pat shrugged. "I like a little space, I guess. I'm not used to being around people twenty-four seven."

Maggie nodded. "Look at it this way. If we were over at my place, all of us would be stuck back in that terrible little bedroom."

"I'm counting my blessings." Pat did so literally, brushing her thumb over the prayer stick in her pocket.

"Hey." Maggie glanced over her shoulder at the others, then stepped closer. "What you told Jo out there. That you'd shoot her if she tried to hurt Becca again. Did you mean that?"

"I promised her. Sure, I meant it."

"But you really care about her." Maggie studied her. "How can you keep a promise like that to someone you care for?"

"Well." Pat watched Becca stroke Jo's hair lightly. "I've never had that, what they have together. Elena and Grady have it too. If I had it, if I loved someone that much, I'd like to think I'd do anything to keep them safe. I'd ask the same promise from Jo."

Becca looked over at them with a tired smile. She had efficiently organized their sleeping arrangements, but with none of the cheerleading brio she had shown that morning. Becca was quieter now. She teased them less. Pat missed it.

The wind outside had eased. It was no longer blowing in titanic bursts, but it still gusted around the cabin in sudden surges. That eerie moonlight was still shining through some portal in the clouds to bathe the snowfield outside in faint green light. Rainier was famous for the blue cast of the moonlight that washed its cliffs at night, but Pat had never seen this sickly green tinge.

She started to pull out her cell, then remembered it not only couldn't get a signal, the damn thing wouldn't even light up. "You got the time, Maggie?"

Maggie shook out the watch she wore on her wrist, a quaint relic but somehow in keeping with her eclectic style, and tilted it toward the fire. "Yeah, it's just after seven. Jesus, were we eating sandwiches out of that trough only this morning? It feels like weeks ago."

"Sure does." Pat smiled at Elena, who had left Grady by the hearth and was carrying steaming mugs over to them.

"Here, you two. You need to try hot chocolate, Mesilla style."

Maggie breathed in the steam. "What did you put in this? Is it anise?"

"No, not anise, but something like it. Also a whisper of cinnamon."

"Hm," Pat murmured. Chocolate and something like licorice and cinnamon. It sounded terrible, but one sip and she vowed she'd never drink cocoa any other way. "This is da bomb, as Becca would say."

She shifted to cup the mug in both hands to warm them and felt her prayer stick slip through her fingers. Maggie bent to retrieve the little twig, but Pat moved swiftly and picked it up first.

"Sorry. No touch but mine kind of thing." She hoped Maggie wouldn't take offense, but she just looked puzzled.

"Can I ask if this is your prayer stick, Pat?" Elena was smiling down at the twig in Pat's hand as if she were sharing a loved family photo, and Pat was surprised a Latina would recognize it.

"Yeah. My grandmother found it for me. Much less bulky than a crucifix." Pat slipped the stick back into her pocket. She used the crucifix line whenever one of the white men or women she worked with asked about the prayer stick, but Elena just chuckled understanding.

"Sí, much less." Elena slipped a delicate silver chain from around her neck. At its end was a small, smooth stick of petrified wood.

"Hey, you have one too?" Maggie studied it with interest, but kept her hands respectfully clasped around her mug.

"I do. Grady gave me this the day she asked me to marry her. She said a holy man from one of the tribes up here gave it to her as a gift during one of her field studies. A Cayuse tribe, Pat?"

"Right. The Cayuse are an Oregon tribe." Pat liked the way the polished wood shone in Elena's palm. She could imagine it resting cool and smooth against her skin.

"Grady told me that a Cayuse holy man breathed a prayer for her into this stick. She liked him, he was a nice old man, and she knew he would only wish a good thing. Grady thinks it was a prayer that she would find lasting love—that she would find me."

"Man." Maggie smiled at Elena with open admiration. "That's flat-out romantic, girl. Who knew college profs could be romantic? No wonder you married her."

"She's also incredibly hot in bed," Elena added, slipping the delicate chain back around her neck.

"Yeah?" Maggie sounded even more admiring. "She is? *Grady?* Well, she's really cute. But like, what kind of—"

"The Cayuse live at the base of the Blue Mountains, Elena," Pat interrupted. "That's near Pendleton, Oregon." She tried to think of more interesting facts about the Cayuse, but luckily, Jo chose that moment to stir.

"Hello, sunshine." Becca spoke quietly as if not wanting to startle Jo, and settled on the side of the sofa to look down at her.

"What time is it?" Jo mumbled, rubbing her face in her hands.

"Just after seven at night, Jo," Pat said. "You were out like a light for a couple of hours."

"I'm starting to really like Elena's tea." Becca helped Jo sit straighter, then folded the blanket back over her lap. "She promised to send some home with us so I can sleep through staff meetings. How goes it, ace?"

"I feel better." Jo turned her head carefully, as if loosening her neck, and she did look better to Pat. "More myself, anyway." She smiled at Becca and touched her face tentatively, and Becca held her fingers briefly against her cheek.

"Elena's tea can't hold a candle to Elena's cocoa." Grady was pouring a cup from the kettle near the fire. "Take a few swigs of this, Jo. It's about time we all put our heads together on how to get through the rest of the night."

Pat was grateful for Grady's calm summons; she might have been introducing a lecture on cave dwellings. Becca and Jo arranged themselves on the sofa, and Maggie drifted over to the cushioned armchair beside it. Pat watched her go, drawn by the subtle music of sensuality in Maggie's movements as she simply crossed a room.

"May I see your prayer stick again please, Pat?" Elena asked.

Puzzled, Pat pulled the stick from her pocket and cupped it in her palm. Elena glanced at Maggie, then up at Pat, and then folded Pat's fingers gently closed over the small twig. She whispered a few words in Spanish, too softly to be heard.

Elena nodded and patted Pat's hand. "Thank you. Okay, come join us, please."

Pat stared after her, confused by the ways of curanderas, but trusting Elena was kind. She followed her and settled into another armchair in the firelit circle.

"I have to admit, some of what's happened the last two days I think I understand, but so much of it just mystifies me." A good facilitator, Grady was turning them directly to the task. "I understand that freak storms can happen, and that power can go out. But the personality changes we're seeing around here— those worry me more."

Grady paused and looked at Becca, who didn't meet her gaze. No one rushed to fill the silence, but it was obvious to Pat that Grady was talking about Jo. Pat wasn't sure day turning into night and that creepy moon should be dismissed as a "freak storm," but she was willing to see where this was going.

Finally, Grady continued. "Maggie, we talked about a few things on the way over to interview Selly yesterday. One was a phenomenon that's linked to the legend of the Windigo, called Windigo Psychosis."

Pat felt the words thump home in the room. Becca looked at Jo, but Jo merely frowned into the mug she held.

"Are you familiar with it?" Grady asked Maggie. "It's a psychiatric disorder that's supposed to afflict some people who believe in the Windigo."

"You're being tactful." Maggie's tone made it clear she wasn't paying a compliment. "It's an excuse some crazy fuckers have used for killing and eating their families. Yeah, we're familiar with it."

Grady took Elena's hand and held it on her knee, but Elena was looking into the fire. "Jo, I think we need to talk again about the possibility that you're showing signs of this psychosis. I don't mean you're psychotic—you're obviously reality-based, right now. But earlier, when you were with Becca…"

"You must have been dreaming, honey." Becca inclined her head, as if trying to catch Jo's gaze. "When we were resting together. Some hell of a nightmare that made you lash out?"

"I don't remember my dreams, Becca. You know that." Jo sipped from her mug.

"What about the painting, Grady?" Maggie gestured toward the framed oil over the hearth. "Are you saying Jo went crazy and messed with that?"

Maggie sounded contemptuous, but Grady only shrugged, and with a start, Pat realized that's exactly what she thought.

"We all slept in this morning," Grady said. "This room was deserted for a few hours."

"And without waking Becca, I crept in here and used my stellar skills to paint *that*." Jo nodded curtly at the painting. "I have no artistic talent whatsoever, Grady. Look at it. That's an oil landscape, and it's clear as a photograph."

That was still true. Pat's grandmother had been a uniquely gifted artist, and her painting of Rainer had once been a sun-drenched splendor that enchanted the eye. Now it was an ominous mass of cliffs sheathed in dark clouds, the setting for a horror story, but it was still expertly rendered. There were no fresh brushstrokes on the canvas. The painting was more than two decades old, and there was no new shifting of color in it; it was a uniform blend of aged and murky oils.

"Then either I forgot about altering that painting, or I'm lying now about doing so," Jo continued. "Two rather large leaps, in my opinion."

Pat frowned. "If Jo changed the painting this morning, wouldn't we have noticed it? We were all in here before we went to the hill to sled."

Grady raised her eyebrows. "You might be right, Pat. Maybe we would have noticed. But do you remember specifically looking at that canvas this morning?"

Pat closed her eyes, struggling with an instinct to protect Jo from yet another cold, academic diagnosis, this time a truly damning one. She couldn't remember if she looked at her grandmother's painting before they left the cabin. She could only remember the storm closing over them, and asking Elena if they were already too late. "No. I wouldn't be able to testify in court that the painting was the same this morning."

"What about that wind, Grady?" Elena stirred finally. "The wind we all heard in the recording of the interview, our first night here? Were we all psychotic then?"

"Jo thinks there was something off with the instrument used to do that first interview, sweetheart." Grady rubbed Elena's fingers, as if they were cold. "Remember? Last night, she listened to the session we all had with Selly yesterday, and her voice came through just fine."

"Wait." Maggie frowned, the fire casting shifting red light across her features. "You have recordings of Selly's voice?"

"Yes," Becca said. "Pat recorded the first talk she had with Selly, two weeks ago. It was kind of…unpleasant to hear. Whenever your great-grandmother spoke, there was this terrible, howling wind."

"Yeah, I've heard that wind." Maggie sat back and crossed one leg over the other. "But now you're saying Selly's second interview came through clearly? Interesting. No one ever successfully recorded Selly's speaking voice before, not her entire miserable life."

"Oh," Becca said weakly.

"Maggie." Pat waited until she met her gaze. "Jo doesn't have any reason to lie about this. If she said she heard Selly's voice in the second recording, I believe her."

"I believe her too." Maggie was trying for a jaded air. Pat could see her fighting for it, but beneath it, she knew she was deeply unsettled. "Pat, the wind wasn't in Selly's voice anymore because the wind wasn't in Selly anymore."

Maggie looked at Jo with sadness, a regret that chilled Pat. "You want to hear that wind, Jo? If our electronic gadgets ever work again, you talk into that thing."

CHAPTER ELEVEN

G rady hadn't seen cold like this in the Pacific Northwest. The high desert of New Mexico could be cold in deep winter, but the mild nights of her home region had never been this bitter. Particularly not inside the comfortable confines of a lavishly appointed cabin.

"This is looking to be a pretty long night." Pat was muscular, but she looked puffed to superhero status inside a sturdy jacket and that long coat. They were all bundled up and staying close to the hearth. "It's just getting colder out there, and in here. But the winds have died down, so I want to go start the Outback and make sure its tank is full. If worse comes to worst, I guess we can pile into it, run the heater and stay warm enough to sleep."

"Yeah, it might come to that." Grady held her hands out to the fire. "We might need to look at putting some food together soon too."

"I'm still full of corn chips." Maggie was pacing restlessly in front of the hearth. She nodded toward the sofa, where Becca and Jo and Elena were talking quietly. "Jo didn't touch any of those chips. Did you notice?"

"No," Grady said flatly. Jo's food intake was not uppermost in her mind at the moment. "I'm sure there's enough in that fridge to get us through breakfast, though. Jo claimed she could pay someone to plow us out in the morning. You agree there's a good chance of us getting out of here then, Pat?"

Pat shrugged toward the side windows. "It's freezing up pretty solid. I'm not counting on any early road clearing rescue, no." She flicked a glance at Grady, a silent acknowledgement of what could be a grim reality. "I still don't understand why that generator out back hasn't kicked in. It's top of the line. I'll check that while I'm out there."

"I'll go with you, in case you get lost." Maggie sounded annoyed, but Grady was learning she often sounded annoyed when she was worried. "Maybe while we're out there we can *check* why none of the batteries in our flashlights work, either, or the batteries in your pricey computers."

Pat grimaced. "One thing at a time, Maggie." She hesitated and turned back to Grady. "Will you keep an eye on Jo?"

Grady's feelings toward Jo were still ambivalent at best, but she was touched by Pat's protectiveness. "Of course, pal." She hesitated. "Pat?"

"Yeah?"

"I know you're worried about Jo. We all are. But I'm not sure she's our only concern here."

"What do you mean?" Pat stepped closer to hear her.

Grady shook her head. "Nothing specific. We're just seeing some personality changes since our trip to the Abequas that really puzzle me. I have a feeling Jo's not alone in all this."

She wouldn't mention the fact that Becca hadn't looked her full in the face all night. Grady would follow her gut in terms of trusting Pat, but she couldn't confess that kiss.

"Do you need anything from me?" Pat was watching her closely.

"No. Just wanted to share that thought." Grady nudged her. "You two be careful, and come back quick."

Pat nodded, her brows furrowed, and followed Maggie to the back door.

The discussion between Elena and Jo and Becca seemed a little intense; they hardly looked up as Pat and Maggie slipped out of the cabin and into the night. Grady lifted a heavy brass poker from the rack by the fireplace and slipped it behind the screen to poke listlessly at the burning logs.

A familiar warmth settled between her shoulder blades as Elena rested her head there and slipped her arms around Grady's waist.

"Hey, you," Grady said.

"Hey, my Professor Gringa." Elena squeezed her gently. "This crazy storm. I like it, I've decided."

"Oh, you like it." Grady poked at the log. "Why is that?"

"Well, we don't understand why our cell phones won't work, but do you realize our chances of having hot monkey sex *without* being interrupted by a call from my mamá are much better right now?"

Grady chuckled. She set down the poker and turned in Elena's arms. "I guess being cut off from Inez is a mixed blessing. Are you fretting about her?"

Elena shook her head, and she was spookily beautiful in the gold light of the flames. "No, we left Mamá in good hands. I just know she worries about us."

"Yes, she does. I'm afraid she'll worry more if we can't reach her and we're not on that flight into El Paso in the morning." Grady sighed. "Meanwhile, our chances for hot monkey sex are slightly dimmed by our breathless audience around here."

Elena glanced back at Jo and Becca on the sofa and arched one dark eyebrow in a suggestive quirk. "Only slightly. The night is still young and maybe we'll all get bored. Or at least cold enough for a little group groping."

"We can hope." Grady rubbed Elena's arms briskly to warm her.

"*Cara mia*, 'my face.'" Elena brushed Grady's brow with her fingers. "I know this face. I know how burdened you are, querida, by what's happening to all of us. Will you let me help?"

"Of course, Elena."

"Listen, then." Elena stared at the flames for a moment. "I have come to accept that you will always approach mysteries from the world of the mind, Grady. Just as I will always approach them from the world of the spirit. And these are both good things, good ways of seeing, as long as we respect each other's worlds, sí?"

"Yes. I agree."

"Okay. Then for you, I will consider the possibility that Jo is in the grip of this terrible madness, this Windigo Psychosis, as you and Becca believe. And for me, you *must* consider the possibility that this Windigo is more than a legend. That it exists today, and its curse is real. And that this curse has passed into Jo, as Maggie and I believe."

Grady tried to buy time to form a reply. "You and Maggie?"

"Yes. Maggie is Native, and so is the Windigo. She doesn't need me to convince her of the truth. Pat is also Native, but the Windigo is a winter demon. It has never haunted her tribe, because the Makah live here, in a land without real winters. And Pat has a university degree, like the rest of you." A disquieting flicker of irritation passed over Elena's face. "I see her struggling with all this. And Becca and Jo are still so far from accepting what's happening. I might need your help to fend off this Windigo."

"Fend it *off?*" Grady hoped she would soon be able to do better than just repeat Elena's last few words. "How are you thinking you'll do this, sweetheart?"

"I haven't worked it all out yet." That annoyance again, so unlike Elena. "I'm just telling you I might need your support, Grady. If Becca and Jo, even Pat, fight me on this, you might need to step in and convince them to let me work. I don't care what they say. Don't let them stop me."

"Elena." Grady cupped her face in her hands. "Darling girl. I've listened to you. Are you listening now?"

"Of course," Elena whispered.

Grady closed her eyes, thinking hard. She'd never said anything like this to Elena, never had reason to. "Please be careful of pride, my love. You just said you value both our worlds, but you're telling me you're certain you're right about this; that your way of doing things will be the only way to go. I know you've had wonderful success in your dealings with the paranormal in the past, but there's just something off about you right—"

Elena stepped back, out of the circle of her arms. She looked up at Grady in a way she hadn't since the days right after they met, when Elena still considered her an ignorant gringa academic. "Okay, Grady. Thank you. I'll be careful of my pride. And now I should heat up some more cocoa for Maggie and Pat. They'll be cold when they get back."

Grady was cold too, and colder still as Elena moved silently past her and out of the firelight.

❖

"Jesus f-f-fricking…" Maggie was almost giggling as she and Pat scrambled into the front seats of the big truck, but it was laughter born of bone-deep chill and gnawing anxiety. Pat had had to use real force to yank the ice-frozen door open, only to admit them to a plushly interiored icebox. "Just w-what do you think will work in here that isn't w-working out there?"

"Well, the heater, for one thing." Pat fumbled with a ring of keys and finally inserted one into the ignition. "Jo needs to demand a refund on that damn dead generator. It's not even five years…"

Maggie's heart sank as Pat twisted the key again, the other keys on the ring jangling. Silence, except for their gasping breath. She hadn't expected the truck to start, just as she knew the generator wouldn't, but she could feel Pat's astonishment in a bleak wave.

"No," Pat murmured. She cranked the key again. "I keep this fucking thing tuned like a watch, Maggie."

"I'm sure you do." Maggie hoped their reality was sinking in at last. It was very dark inside the truck, and she struggled to make out the rugged outline of Pat's face. There was no artificial lighting, of course, and only that strange, thin green glow of the Snow Moon to beat back the night. She could see a faint reflection of the fire's glow inside the cabin through a side window. "I don't think any of our toys are going to work again until this is finally over, Pat."

Pat said nothing. Maggie heard her fumble with buttons on the dashboard. "Even the radio's out. Christ. I was counting on being able to call for backup if we need it."

"Look, it's just one night. We only have to make it until morning." Shivering, Maggie hunched and wrapped her arms around her knees. "All my family stories are real specific about the Windigo descending one t-terrible night. So if we can just hang on until the sun rises—"

"Maggie, you're getting all this from family stories? Seriously?" Pat sighed harshly. "What would your family say about all our technology going dead, then?"

"Hey, I don't have all the answers, okay?" Maggie snapped. "Selly told us the old stories. The last time this happened, the last time the Windigo came, there probably weren't computers and iPods around to go dead." She was shaking hard. "Could you ease up on me a little? I'm just as scared as you are."

She waited miserably, her face numb with cold. A silence fell between them and lingered. Maggie tried again to make out Pat's face. "What?" she asked.

❖

She's your sewa, right? So kiss her.

Pat heard her grandmother's voice clearly in the hushed darkness. Delores Daka had lost most of her teeth early in adulthood, and her speech held a lisping quality. Her tone was teasing and fond in Pat's mind, but very sure. It could be no one else.

Pat was stunned and freezing, and she couldn't see Maggie. But she had promised her grandmother that she would listen for her, all of her life. And these were pretty direct instructions. You walked your talk or you didn't, another of her grandmother's teachings.

"Maggie?" Pat cleared her throat, a gravelly rattle, and then she could think of nothing else to say, how to explain or ask permission. "Excuse me, all right?"

She reached out tentatively and touched Maggie's shoulder, which was suddenly all the navigation she needed. Her uncertainty vanished, and she slid her hand beneath Maggie's tumbling curls and cupped the back of her neck. She leaned toward her and their lips met smoothly, effortlessly, with a unique glide-click of homecoming.

The chill began to drain out of Pat.

❖

"You planning to avoid me until the glaciers melt?"

Becca heard the gentle teasing in Grady's voice, the lack of blame, and she made herself relax. She couldn't help glancing over her shoulder to be sure Jo couldn't hear them. Jo was dozing again on the sofa; Elena was sitting on the stone lip of the hearth, gazing moodily into the fire.

"That depends." Becca hesitated, then patted the seat of the cushion beside her and waited until Grady sat. It took some courage to meet her eyes, but Becca had never lacked courage. "Are you going to let me apologize again for jumping you like that?"

"Yes, I am. I'm sorry for my part in it too." Grady's simple acceptance was a balm to Becca's sore soul. "I know neither of us wanted that, Bec."

"Not when we're in our right minds." Becca shivered and lowered her voice, wishing they were closer to the heat of the fire. She felt a small twinge from the stinging half-moon of teeth marks on her breast. "Grady, what's happening to us? I would never do anything to make Jo doubt my love for her. Mind you, you're adorable and everything…" At this point, under any other circumstance, Becca would have touched Grady's wrist. When she spoke to friends she was a toucher, but now she refrained. "I'm attracted to you, Grady, but then I have a pulse. I'm attracted to lots of women, and I'm sure Jo is too. We would just never act on it. I acted, with you."

"I acted back." Grady looked at Elena, by the fire. "And believe me, it was as out of character for me as it was for you."

"Something you asked Jo this morning keeps coming back to me." Becca grasped this fragment of memory with a relief that felt desperate. "You brought up the power of ritual. You wondered if Selly's antics with the smoke might have convinced Jo, unconsciously, to believe in the Windigo legend. If her subconscious believes she's possessed, she might behave as if she's possessed. That's the theory, right? Well, you and I witnessed the same ritual, pal."

"We did. So did Elena." Grady was still watching Elena. "I've wondered that too, whether we're all getting caught up in a culture-bound syndrome."

"Is there anything in the Windigo legends about the entire family going as bonkers as the person who's cursed?" Becca was half kidding, but only half. She'd rather see this in terms of some group psychosis than the malevolence of a monster bleeding through an entire family.

"I just think we might be getting as vulnerable to suggestion as Jo," Grady said. "We might be affected in different ways and to different degrees, but we're each—hey, Jo."

Grady's tone was still pleasant, but Becca saw her eyes widen and she looked around quickly. Jo was rising from the sofa.

"Honey?" Becca's heart stammered in her chest.

Jo's face was a pale mask of rage as she lifted the iron poker from the rack by the fireplace.

❖

The chill began to drain out of Maggie, quite literally.

Their kiss was sweet and long, and a sensual heat was surely rising in her center, but some part of Maggie's mind remained rational enough to wonder at what was happening with the rest of her body. The truck itself was warming. The engine remained dead, but Maggie's shivering began to ease as a delicious comfort crept through the biting cold and banished it entirely.

She wrapped her fingers in the soft fleece of Pat's collar and pulled her gently back, sorry as hell to end the moment. "Are you feeling this?" she whispered.

"Yeah."

Maggie could see Pat pretty clearly now and not by the sick green light of that moon. Her features were illuminated in a mild gold glow. They stared at each other. Not even the sheer, visceral chemistry connecting them could account for that light, or the growing warmth in this truck.

Maggie made a conscious effort to cage her arousal. She could do that. She'd had practice controlling her urges when necessary. She was relaxing against the seat, her body surrendering the locked tension that comes with unrelenting chills. Maggie was suddenly sleepy and hungry and almost content.

"I don't understand this," Pat said softly.

"Me either," Maggie whispered. "Where in the hell is this light coming from, this—"

"Maggie." Pat touched her face again. "I don't understand *this.*"

And Maggie got it, this quiet woman's wonder at that unexpected kiss, how natural and beautiful their touch felt. She smiled and cupped Pat's palm against her cheek. "You sweet idiot. Right now, *this* is the only thing that makes perfect sense to me."

And then she was distracted by shadows darting against the side window of the cabin, and she ducked her head and tried to see inside. "What the hell is happening in there?"

She heard faint shouting.

❖

Pat kicked the front door wide-open with a resounding crash. Maggie was right behind her as she barreled into the cabin's deep living room, and the first thing Pat saw was the spark-strewn log that had burst from the fire grate and rolled across the wood floor. The glass-iron grate was half-shattered, shards scattered across the hearth.

Then Pat heard the grunting, gasping efforts of a dark knot of bodies thrashing at the foot of one of the sofas, and she leapt over it in an adrenaline-fueled burst of acrobatics.

"Hey! *Hey!*" she bellowed and grasped the first collar she could. It seemed all four of the women were in a tangle of arms and legs on the floor, but with some effort, Pat was able to haul Grady off of Jo. She tossed her onto the sofa then dropped to her knees, straddling Jo's sprawled form. Elena was trying to restrain one of Jo's arms, and Becca knelt on her other side, one knee across her shoulder.

"Let go," Becca shouted, and Pat saw she wasn't talking to her—Jo was clenching a fire poker across her chest, trying to wrench it free.

Pat took hold of the poker immediately and shifted it across Jo's throat. She bent over her, not pressing the iron into her skin but letting her feel it. Elena fell back at once, lifting her hands to make way for Pat, but Becca stayed with Jo, half-lying across her, all of them gasping for breath.

"Jo," Pat said clearly. "Drop your hands. Joanne! Drop it."

It took a moment for Jo to hear her; Pat could almost see her awareness seeping back, the blind rage in her features fading. She blinked and then gaped up at Pat, and slowly, her fingers unwrapped from either end of the poker and her hands fell from it.

Pat didn't budge. "Is she hurt?" she snapped at Becca.

"I don't th-think so," Becca stammered.

The smoke from the log that had toppled off the grate was stinging Pat's eyes. She lifted the poker from Jo's throat and extended it to Maggie, who stood transfixed behind the sofa. Maggie accepted the heavy iron with shaking hands.

"Jo, I'm turning you over." Pat leaned and took her weight on her left foot. She grasped Jo's elbow, and Jo offered no resistance to being turned onto her stomach. Pat held her wrists together at the base of her back with one hand, and fished through the pocket of her long coat with the other. She'd taken several plastic restraints from the back of the Outback before she and Maggie got into it, and she slid one now around Jo's wrists. "What happened in here?"

"She lost it, she just—" Becca broke off and stroked Jo's hair. "Honey, lie still. I'm here. Pat's here. You're okay."

"Grady, I think you're bleeding," Maggie said.

Elena scrambled to her feet. Grady was sprawled on the couch where Pat had thrown her, and blood was running freely down the side of her face. She touched her head and winced, but sat up straighter in the deep cushions.

"I'm okay, Elena." Grady was staring down at Jo, but Elena sat on the sofa beside her and turned her head carefully so she could see her brow.

"Becca?" Facedown on the floor, Jo's voice was precise and urgent. "Are you all right?"

"I'm fine, honey. Please, just hold still."

"Becca." Pat made sure the restraint was secure around Jo's wrists, grateful she wasn't fighting her. "Tell me what happened."

"We were talking." Becca was coming around, regaining composure, her touch on Jo's hair tender. "Grady and I were here. Elena was by the fire. I thought Jo was asleep. But suddenly she stood up and just...grabbed the poker."

"And she took a swing at Grady?"

"No," Becca whispered.

Pat's heart sank. "She attacked *you?*"

"No, not Becca," Elena said. She was examining Grady's bleeding forehead, but she glanced down at Jo with compassion. "Grady was injured when she stepped in to stop Jo. Jo came after me."

"Pat?" Maggie's voice was high and thin, and they all turned to her. She extended one trembling hand to the fireplace.

Pat looked at the hearth with its shattered screen, at the photo of her smiling grandmother above it, at the painting of Rainier over the mantel. It had changed again.

The mountain in the background was more distant still. The luxury cabin, built years after Delores Daka had created this painting, was now visible in the foreground. And the cheerful gold light that had originally bathed the image, the light that had turned murky and dark only that morning, had altered again.

The painting of Rainier was now illuminated by the bilious green glow of the full Snow Moon looming above it.

CHAPTER TWELVE

E lena stepped out onto the broad front porch and closed the door firmly after her. She wasn't sure why she took this precaution; the inside of the cabin was almost as cold as the air out here.

She grimaced as she swept snow off the railing and washed her bare hands with it. No power up here meant no running water, so snow would have to do. This was going to be real interesting later, with all that cocoa she'd been pouring into everyone; peeing off this porch would be fun.

She scrubbed her wrists, hissing at the icy sting but relieved when the last streak of Grady's blood washed away. The sight of it disturbed her beyond good sense. She knew Grady was all right. Jo's wildly swinging poker had only struck her head a glancing blow, thanks to the Goddess, but the cut had bled liberally.

It was eerily quiet out here, which she preferred to that haunted wind. Elena rested her shoulder against the wood pillar and gazed out over the greenish plane of snow, wondering if her Goddess had lied to her. If She wasn't everywhere, and could only be found in the desert sands of her valley. Elena still couldn't hear Her voice, and her head ached with listening.

She let herself back into the cabin, and made her way through the silent room to sit beside Grady again. She tipped her chin so she could examine the butterfly tape sealing the cut on her brow.

"*Bueno*. No more seeping, but you will have a nice bruise. How many fingers am I holding up?"

Grady glanced down at Elena's other hand, which was curled around her knee, and smiled. "I see no fingers, Curandera Montalvo."

"Then I have healed you, Professor Gringa." Elena patted Grady's face.

"I wonder what time it is. Coming up on midnight, you think?"

"Yes, about that." Elena rolled her head on her neck, trying to ease the grip hours of tension had on her muscles. "The night is passing very slowly."

"As long as it passes."

Theirs was one of three islands of murmured conversations, each at the edges of the wash of light from the fireplace. Pat and Maggie stood talking quietly near the kitchen. Becca sat on the deep couch next to Jo, whose hands were still bound behind her, a precaution Pat refused to lift.

"You were right, Elena," Grady said. "Jo didn't go after Becca with that poker, or after me. She didn't even look at either of us. She went straight for you."

"And it's lucky for me that you can move faster than a chubby Latina." Elena remembered poor Jo's white face flashing above her, the iron lifted over her shoulder. Then Grady's lean form streaking between them, grappling with Jo. "You may have saved my life, querida."

She felt Grady's hands slip beneath the fleece collar of her jacket to knead the tight muscles at the base of her neck, and she purred thanks. Her gaze was drawn again to one of the side windows of the living room. Elena had stood there only that afternoon, tracing a design onto the frosted glass while the others yammered nonsense about the storm. The image she had drawn on the pane was almost visible from this angle, but that had to be Elena's imagination; it would have faded hours ago.

"But why you, babe?" Grady's voice coaxed Elena's attention back to her. "We've all been worried about Jo taking a bite out of Becca, and she and I are still prickly, at best. I wouldn't think she'd have it in for you."

"Jo has nothing against me, Grady." Elena tried to quell a flare of impatience. "It was not Jo who attacked me, but the Cannibal Beast that has infested her body. Of course the Windigo would not go for you or Becca first. What does it care if you are fucking Jo's wife? But it sees a real threat in me. It knows I can truly harm it."

Grady's fingers had stilled on her shoulders and Elena saw stunned denial rising in her eyes. She replayed what she had just said in her mind and touched Grady's face in dismay.

"Querida, I'm sorry. I didn't mean to say such a thing. I don't know where—"

"Hey? Excuse me." Pat came up behind their sofa and rested both hands on it. "I'm sorry to break in, but I think it's time we came together again."

❖

Pat didn't like interrupting Grady and Elena when they were so intent on each other, but she couldn't shake a sense that their time was running short. She waited while Maggie settled on the floor in front of the warm hearth.

"Deputy Daka?" Becca used Pat's title without malice, but she sat protectively close to Jo in the deep sofa. "About these hand restraints. Really? It's been three hours."

"I'm afraid I can't remove them, Becca."

Jo grimaced and shifted in the plush cushions. "At least let me move to an armchair, Pat. I'm uncomfortable."

"You can get out of an armchair too quickly." Pat regarded her, not without sympathy. "We can do it, but I'd have to tie your ankles as well. Your call."

With her hands bound behind her, her broad shoulders covered by a blanket, Jo reminded Pat of a captive warrior, subdued but still dangerous. She glanced at Becca, and the resentment drained from her features. "You're right. I'll stay here."

Pat nodded. She waited for Grady to take the lead, but she looked distracted, unsettled as she watched the fire, and finally, Pat began.

"Since none of us seem real sleepy, at this point..." Pat paused, hoping for rueful smiles, but saw only grim agreement. "I thought we should talk about what to do if the cavalry doesn't show up in the morning. I ski pretty well, and Maggie says she does too. Anyone else?"

"I can't even inner tube," Elena sighed, and Becca shook her head.

"I skied when I lived up here." Grady took Elena's hand. "But I'm not leaving Elena." They exchanged a long look, and Grady kissed the back of her hand.

Pat hooked her thumbs in her pockets. "Well, if we have to, Maggie and I can try to reach a working radio to get help, once it gets light. Or we can try starting the snowmobiles in the back shed—"

"Oh, please, Pat, the snowmobiles won't start," Becca snorted. "You've really never read *The Shining*?" She rubbed her face and tittered weakly into her hands. "I'm sorry, guys. I think I'm getting a little slaphappy."

"You need rest, Becca." Jo scowled at her. "You hardly slept last night, and this afternoon..."

Jo trailed off, and Pat figured they were all remembering how Becca's nap had been interrupted.

"Anyway," Elena said, "Pat's truck won't start, the generator won't start, none of our toys work. We have no reason to hope these snowmobiles will be any different."

"Maybe we should try to heat some soup over this fire," Becca said. "I'll need calories if we're going to plot an escape."

She picked up the large bowl Jo had piled with chips, but it was almost empty. She held out a few fragments to Jo. "Here, poor thing. Trussed up like this, you can't even wrestle us for crumbs."

Jo turned her head. "Please. I couldn't possibly."

"You feeling sick, Jo?" Maggie was watching her.

"I'm just not hungry."

"That's funny. You were plenty hungry earlier today."

"What is it, hija?" Elena asked. "Tell us what you're thinking."

Maggie glanced at Pat, and her features took on the indifferent cast of someone who didn't expect to be believed. "It's just that it happened that way with Selly too. First, she acted like she was starving. She ate everything in sight, a lot more than her share. Then, nothing."

"When we met Selly yesterday, she looked like she was badly malnourished." Grady was finally engaged again, to Pat's relief. "I was afraid she had some wasting disease."

"Well, like Selly told you, doctors checked her out," Maggie said. "She was very old, but there was no disease."

"She just stopped eating?" Becca glanced at Jo uneasily, then at Maggie. "I remember Selly's room was stocked with food."

"Yeah, we tried to force meals on her for months." A flicker of regret crossed Maggie's face, and grudging affection. "She hardly touched any of it, not even after we brought her out here."

Elena shook her head. "Just because your abuela wouldn't eat, Maggie, doesn't mean she wasn't hungry."

"No, it doesn't." Maggie blinked at Elena. "You're right about that."

"Jo, I've noticed you keep swallowing." Elena's voice was kind. "Are you sure you don't feel ill?"

Pat looked at Jo, who was staring into the flames with her jaw clenched.

"Your mouth is watering, isn't it?" Maggie asked. "I'd say you're feeling damn ravenous, Jo. What are you hungry for?"

"I don't know. What difference does it make?" Jo snapped. "Forgive me, Maggie, but I can't believe I share much in common with Selly Abequa, or your entire family. From what you've told us, Selly's odd eating habits came on over a course of months. I only met the woman yesterday."

Maggie's face flushed. "Maybe whatever came after Selly is a lot closer now. Closer to *you*, now."

"Jo." Grady rested her elbows on her knees and addressed Jo respectfully. "Listen to what we've been telling you about rituals, and how powerfully they can sway us. Yes, it's only been one day since we inhaled that smoke, but one hell of a long, stressful day—"

"Grady?" Pat wasn't given to interruption, but it was necessary. "One thing we should learn from the Abequas. They relied on this young woman, and they trusted her." She nodded at Maggie. "In spite of her youth, Maggie was the main caretaker for her family. I think we should listen to what *she's* telling us."

A smile flickered across Maggie's lips as the shadowed room grew quiet.

"You're right, Pat." Becca gave Maggie a contrite look. "You probably know more about all this than any of us, honey, and I'm sorry if we haven't listened very well. Maybe it's time we stopped dumping your butt in the snow long enough to pay attention."

"I'm good with that." Maggie stared into the crackling flames. "I don't know where to start, though. I still hardly believe any of this shit myself."

"With your family stories, Maggie." Pat found she couldn't sit; she didn't want to relax her vigil over the others even as far as bending her knees. "Tell us what the Abequas, and the Chippewa, know about this Windigo."

Maggie nodded, but she didn't speak right away. Pat watched her face age in the reflected firelight. "Darkness is important to the Witiko. So is bitter cold. We call it the Spirit of the Lonely

Places, the Cannibal Beast, and it travels on the wind. It always attacks at night, and it always draws its victims outside to die."

Pat shivered, seeing it. A reeling chase through a wind-blown, freezing midnight, ending in bloody death. In murder. Her own face felt chapped from the searing cold.

"It draws them outside?" Jo shifted stiffly in the deep cushions. "What about that Cree family Grady mentioned? I'm not dismissing what you're telling us, Maggie, honestly. But on the drive to your compound, Grady told us about a man who killed and cannibalized his entire family. He blamed his crimes on the Windigo. And weren't their remains all found inside his cabin?"

"Not the first victim." Grady frowned. "The article said Swift Runner chased his son outside, into a blizzard. He killed him there, then returned to the family's cabin and murdered the others. And ate them," she added unnecessarily.

"The killings all happened in one night, I bet." Maggie sounded on surer ground. "Selly and the other elders were all real clear on that. The Windigo comes and goes before dawn. Which is only about six hours away, I hope."

"And that awful wind died away a long time ago." Becca adjusted the blanket around Jo's shoulders. "But it's still just as cold out there. Our moral so far is, no one goes outside." She looked at Pat pointedly. "Not to try to jump-start dead snowmobiles. Not for any reason."

"What about the moon, Maggie?" Elena gestured toward the faint moonlight leaking through a side window. "Pat says she's never seen one like this over her mountain."

"Sorry." Maggie shrugged. "Except for that weird green light, that's just Snow Moon to me, what most people called it, a big winter full moon. Well, my family called it Famine Moon. Obvious reasons."

Pat shook her head. "Snow Moon doesn't rise until February. I don't know any name for what's out there." She walked to a window and looked out at the strange orb that gleamed through the circular break in the cloud cover. It was foreign, alien, an insult to the mountain's night sky that had always brought Pat peace. If it had an odor, it would be a sour, rank smell. This moon was too *old,* and she didn't know how to explain that to the others, or to herself.

"It may not be February, but I'm not sure time is the same for us now, in this place." Elena drifted her fingers through her hair. "In this bad hour, this *mala hora*. This is the moon that rises the night of the Windigo, and that's what's important to know."

Pat realized they were all gazing at the painting over the fireplace; at the eerie green light the moon now spilled over the snowbound cabin.

"The Windigo has a heart of ice," Maggie said to the flames.

"Elena…heard this too," Grady said. "That its very center is ice."

"Well, maybe we can take some comfort in that." Jo smiled, and Pat could see her effort to ease their tension. "At least I'm not cold. The rest of you look a lot chillier than—"

"Selly was never cold, either." Maggie traced a line on the stone hearth. "Jo, when we were outside with you, a few hours ago, I thought Pat and I were going to freeze to death on the spot, it was so bitter out there. Steam gushed out of our mouths whenever we breathed, or talked. But not you, Jo. Your breath was invisible. Ice is your natural state now."

Jo stared at her, and silence fell over them again. "Becca?"

"Yes, honey." Becca smoothed her hand over Jo's chest, as if wondering at its warmth and hoping this belied Maggie's words.

"Do you remember the first time I kissed you?" Jo spoke to Becca quietly, as if they were the only ones in the room. "You had to teach me how to kiss you well. How to touch my lips lightly against yours, how to let my passion blend into that lightness. Do you remember?"

"I remember," Becca whispered.

"You taught me how to cherish your body, as well. Sometimes I want you so badly I ache with it."

Pat stood still, her eyes on the floor. She had never heard such intimacy in Jo's voice before, never knew such language existed in her.

"Becca, I'll die before I hurt you again."

"Mention dying one more time." Becca took Jo's chin in her hand, but gently. "And I'll have Pat stuff a sock in your mouth. I mean it. Hush, love."

Becca laid her head on Jo's chest and wrapped her arm around her waist, her eyes closing wearily. Jo rested her lips in Becca's hair. Elena and Grady curled themselves together on the other couch. The stillness lingered, and for now it felt good, just having them all here safe in one room.

Pat looked at Maggie and raised her eyebrows. Maggie shrugged, the slight lifting of one shoulder that was already dear. Pat had asked Maggie if she had anything more to tell them, Maggie had answered that she had no more to offer right now. The whole exchange was silent, their communication clear and easy.

Pat shifted in order to feel the weight of the pistol in her belt holster. She brushed her thumb over the prayer stick in her pocket and kept watch.

❖

Maggie lifted her head from her arms and looked around blearily. She must have fallen asleep, lulled by the warmth of the hearth, but probably not for long. The fire was still high and crackled brightly, shedding its gold light through their circle.

Pat had finally settled into an armchair, her head resting against its back, her eyes closed. Grady and Elena were still in each other's arms on one couch, motionless except for the slow lift of their breathing. Jo had managed to half-recline on the other sofa, and Becca was curled against her side.

Maggie's gaze was caught by a low, pulsing light from one of the side windows in a far corner of the large room. She tried to focus on it, but it faded, and Maggie let it fade. She had no urge to seek out any more mysteries tonight. She was too tired.

Pat Daka was another mystery. Maggie studied her handsome face, her first opportunity to do so openly, without Pat looking back. Her lips thrummed again with the memory of that sudden kiss, the moment when the cold, dark truck warmed around them into blissful comfort.

"Who is Sewa?" she whispered to Pat, who of course slept on.

Maggie rubbed her burning eyes and looked at the others. From babyhood on, she had always slept in rooms crowded with other people, except on those lucky nights she escaped to the bed of one lover or another. Sitting here on the floor, Maggie had the least comfortable spot of all of these strangers. She didn't understand why this felt like a good thing, waking up among these particular women.

And the next time, Maggie told herself as she rested her head back on her arms, *the next time I open my eyes, it'll be morning. I'll have a hellish crick in my neck, but the night will be over, and when I open my eyes…I'll see all of them again. I'll see her again.*

Maggie slept, and dreamed about the Chippewa woman and the brave who chased her through the night trees. She ran with them through the snow-choked forest of Minnesota, buffeted by the raging wind, cringing beneath Snow Moon.

CHAPTER THIRTEEN

Morning came. The sun didn't rise.

"No," Becca told the window quietly.

She was talking to the sky beyond the glass pane, the sky that stubbornly refused to lighten, despite her outrage and against all natural law. The sun rose late and set early this time of year, but Jesus, it never simply refused to appear at all. It was still jet-black out there, the air dead and still.

She heard the others behind her, moving restlessly through the large room. She remembered Maggie had a wristwatch, the only timepiece that seemed to be working.

Grady's voice. "Maggie, what time is—"

"It's fifteen minutes later than the last time someone asked me that," Maggie growled. "It's coming up on noon."

"No," Becca whispered to the darkness again. They had to get Jo out of here.

Pat was making her as comfortable as possible. Jo had been helped up, walked around. She was spared the indignity of personal assistance with urinating in the bathtub, but Pat had bound her wrists behind her again when she came out. Jo had been offered food, which she had refused. Now she sat in the deep sofa, her head resting against its back, staring at the high ceiling.

Becca closed her eyes, shutting out the freakish night and indulging in a childlike hope that when she opened her eyes again, the world would have come to its senses. A faint scent of fresh herbs reached her, and she knew it was Elena sliding her arm lightly across her shoulders.

"It's too cold here, away from the fire." Elena pressed her shoulders gently, staring with her into the blackness. "Too cold to be thinking frightening thoughts, by yourself."

"I'm thinking how badly I need to pee," Becca said, and then of course she did.

Elena chuckled. "I think we have taken to peeing in the bathtub. One problem solved."

Becca let herself lean against Elena, and felt again that pure wash of easy friendship that had flowered between them before all this weirdness began. She struggled with an almost irresistible urge to confess to Elena, to tell her she had kissed Grady, to receive her forgiveness. She had never wanted absolution, and a drink, so badly in her life.

"Do you think it's dark over Seattle?" Becca asked. "Is technology dead all over Puget Sound?"

"No. I think the six of us are in a different place, chica. We're caught in a point in time called *la mala hora,* the bad hour. I don't pretend to understand it very well. But I believe we're the only ones looking up at that strange moon." Elena was silent for a moment. "Becca. Are you ready to let me try to help Jo?"

Becca wanted specifics. She wanted to know exactly what Elena had in mind. Her methodology, and some documented proof that her peer-reviewed protocol had worked in the past. Becca wanted reassurance. And increasingly, she wanted a drink.

She glanced over her shoulder at Pat, who could imprison Jo but not free her. At Maggie, whose stories could trace a nightmare but not wake them from it. And at Grady, Jo, Becca herself, whose academic credentials were useless in fighting a demon. She looked into the strange, lingering night.

"Yes," Becca said. "Elena, please try."

Elena pressed her shoulders again, and Becca followed her back to the sofa. They sat on either side of Jo.

"Hey. How's my favorite space cadet?" Becca brushed a lock off Jo's forehead.

"Spacey." Jo's tongue sounded thick in her mouth. "I don't want to fall asleep again. Bad things seem to happen when I sleep."

"Well, you have to stay awake for the *Xena* marathon, once the power comes back." Becca didn't like Jo's pallor, the cool clamminess of her skin. "If we don't get power soon, we'll act out season two for you. In the meantime, though, I want Elena to try to help us, honey."

Jo turned her head on the back of the couch and regarded Elena. "Can you give me something to keep me awake?"

"I no longer think giving you any kind of stimulant, or sedative, is a good idea, Jo." Elena touched Jo's throat, taking her pulse. "But with your permission, I'd like to perform a simple ceremony. A very old one. It might bring you some relief."

The others were drifting closer now to listen, and Becca avoided Grady's gaze. She tried to inject some lightness into her tone. "Please tell us it's not an exorcism that might involve sacrificing a virgin, Elena. Pat would have to ski out to find one. Maybe out of state."

"It is a kind of exorcism." Elena spoke the word so calmly, she might have been referring to an inoculation under sterile conditions. "And it's not without risks. But I think this ceremony is our best chance to protect us all from whatever is coming."

"What kind of risks?" Becca asked.

"It doesn't matter." Jo's weary eyes were on Elena. "Let's try it."

"Excuse me, with the risks?" Becca frowned.

"Well, by calling on any kind of spiritual energy, we'll be challenging this demon on its own ground." Elena looked up as

Grady rested her hand on her shoulder. She covered it with her own. "I can reassure you, though, that my side has a sixteen and oh record."

Becca blinked. "A sixteen and oh record?"

"In my years working with my champion, fighting spiritual bullies with Her, She has won sixteen times." Elena waved one finger slightly at the ceiling. "She's very good."

A dimple appeared in Elena's cheek, and for some reason Becca found the teasing in her eyes as reassuring as her offer of hope.

"We should try this," Jo said, an old confidence in her again. "At least we'll be doing something. Get on with it, Elena."

"On Jo's planet, that means thank you, Elena," Becca translated automatically. "Tell us what to do."

"We'll need everyone's help." Elena's eyes searched Grady's face, then Pat's and Maggie's. "Whenever a healing takes place, we draw on the loving energy of friends of the afflicted."

"I'm a dead woman," Jo grumbled.

Pat snorted laughter, then stopped abruptly. Becca knew it was pure nervous energy, but poor Pat looked embarrassed anyway.

"No, you're not." Grady nudged Jo's shoulder. "Jo, we're all in this together. You're one of us. Of course we'll help."

Jo studied Grady's face and then nodded shortly, with quickly banked astonishment. Becca watched Jo because she didn't want to see Grady, but she was deeply grateful for Grady's words, her authority and sincerity.

"Sure, I'm in." Maggie smiled with a gamin charm, obviously relieved to have a plan, any plan. "Will this ceremony involve an orgy of any kind? Because I've heard about you Seattle lesbians."

"Regretfully, no," Elena chuckled. "Pat, please build up this fire for us. I need to get a few things from our room upstairs. The rest of you, just sit somewhere quietly and call on any deities that guide you." She leaned into Becca and whispered, "Don't forget to pee," and kissed her cheek.

Elena went to the mantel and took one of the tapered candles, then made her way up the dark stairs. The glowing circle of candlelight cast her straight, assured posture in shadow against the curving wall. Becca adjusted the blanket across Jo's shoulders until she feared she might spit into a Kleenex to scrub her cheek; her anxiety was driving her maternal urges to extremes.

"You don't have to go outside for more wood, right?" Maggie was talking to Pat, and she sounded a little maternal herself.

"No, I stocked the anteroom pretty well." Pat drew on her gloves. "Lend me a hand?"

"Sure." Maggie took another candle and followed her, color rising in her face.

Grady was half-lifting, half-sliding a heavy armchair out of the circle of firelight. Becca watched her muscle the other sofa back several feet as well, the lines of her body strong and supple.

"Can I ask what you're doing?" Jo asked politely.

"Just clearing a little space."

"Do you know anything about this ceremony, Grady?" Becca pulled her gaze from Grady and focused on Jo's features, on the most important woman in the room.

"Not really. I just know my wife." Such fondness in Grady's voice. "Elena grew up under desert skies. The woman likes space."

Out of the corner of her eye, Becca watched Grady kneel to roll up the small Pendleton rug, clearing a circular expanse of blond wood floor before the fire. She thought she saw a pulse of low amber light from one of the side windows, but it faded when she looked directly at it. Marvy. She was hallucinating too now. At least she and Jo had finally found something they could do together on this vacation.

"We can trust Elena." Jo had lowered her voice to speak to Becca alone, but that confidence was still in her. "I watched her face closely. There were no tells in her expressions, no indications of deceit or evasion. She was telling us the full truth. At least, the truth as Elena sees it."

"But what does that mean?" Becca shivered. "She was telling us the truth about fighting a demon?"

"Elena cares for me and she wants to help me. She meant that." There was muted wonder in Jo's voice. "This, in spite of my trying to kill her with an iron poker earlier, and braining her lover with it instead."

Becca smiled.

"Grady too," Jo murmured. "I still think she would happily flatten me, mind you, but she meant what she said about having my back. My being part of the clan."

"Well. That's the least Grady can say. You did give her a passing grade in your class, right?"

"Yes, I did. You're right, Becca. Grady owes me her life."

Becca giggled, half-giddy with sleeplessness and worry and fear, but enjoying the moment anyway. It was helping already, any kind of activity after the long, restless night. The other four women were moving with energy and purpose again, and Jo sounded much more herself. Better; this was the Jo she knew when they were alone together.

"I hope Pat doesn't feel she has to resort to heroic measures in all this." Jo sighed. "She's not much more than a kid. I forget that, at times, because she stalks around like some macho Stormtrooper bobblehead, but she speaks as if she's sixty years— Becca, I'm being entirely serious."

"I know. I hear you." Becca warmed her cold nose on Jo's sleeve. "You're right to be worried. Pat might pull something really heroic to impress Maggie."

"Maggie?"

"Come on. You haven't seen the way those two look at each other? They're working up to flammable."

"Pat? And *Maggie*?" Jo looked dismayed. "Maggie could inspire sexual addiction in a rock, for God's sake. Can Pat even handle Maggie?"

"I hope they get a chance to find out." Becca rested against Jo, relishing these last moments of peace before this strange party started. "Pat and Maggie will be fine, honey. We'll look out for them. They're clan too."

❖

Elena closed the bedroom door and sank back against it. She released a shaking sigh, and the candle flame she held jittered. She rested her head against the door and closed her eyes.

Okay. Last night I searched for You in my dreams, Mother. And I found only a terrible silence. So buenos días. It's time for You to wake up, please. I have a question. I didn't bring any asaga with me, so simple sage will have to do. If that's not all right... give me a sign. Hell, throw a tree through a window, anything, my Goddess.

Silence. For once, Elena cursed the opulence and space of this cabin, because she could hear nothing from the lower level. If her Goddess remained stubbornly silent, she wanted to hear the voices of her friends.

She fell back on the loved old words, the prayer she always offered before a healing. It had come to her for the first time when she was nine years old, and she had never seen reason to change it. The prayer fell from her lips mechanically, but still carried some measure of comfort.

Here we go. I'll trust You to guide me. Don't let me mess up. Don't let me hurt anybody, especially the gringa I'm supposed to help. Thank You. I love You. Go with me.

Elena waited for the tenuous breath of well-being that usually filled her after prayer. And waited some more.

❖

Grady knew Elena needed some time alone before she worked, but she didn't like her out of sight for long. She had mounted the stairs when a candle's glow appeared at the top, and Elena emerged from the hallway.

"Watch your step." Grady trotted up the stairs to take the bag Elena carried.

"You're the one with the possible concussion. Watch your own step." Elena tapped Grady's chin, then surveyed the large room. "Good. We have space to work in and a bright fire to keep us warm. Well, warmish. It looks like our friends are ready down there. Are you, querida?"

Grady nodded, grimly. "As ready as I can ever be for these things. Elena?"

Elena looked up at her.

This had been bothering Grady. "The darkness freaked everyone out. I think we're all a lot more receptive to trying your methods than we were yesterday. You didn't have to strong-arm anyone into this ceremony. But, sweetheart, I would have backed you up, if it had come to that. I trust you. I have faith in you. Just wanted to remind you of that."

There was a weariness in Elena's smile, in the distracted brush of her fingers down Grady's face, that did nothing to reassure her.

"Okay. Thank you. We need to focus on Jo now. Fold a blanket on the floor, please."

Grady followed her into the living room and lifted a blanket from an ottoman.

"It's time we start," Elena said to the others, and it was the curandera Grady loved who greeted them, calm and gracious. "Jo, we're going to want you here, close to the fire."

Pat and Becca helped Jo lever herself out of the deep sofa. Grady draped the folded blanket over the floor in front of the hearth, and Jo stepped onto it.

"Grady, would you and Maggie witness?"

Grady had been asked to serve as witness at a few rites, and remembered they stood to the afflicted's right. She took Maggie's arm and escorted her into place.

"Smokey Bear?" Elena used Maggie's name for Pat warmly, but then she grew serious. "I don't usually ask for physical protection during a healing, for someone to keep watch, but I'm asking it for this one. When we open these doors, we never know what will walk through. Will you look out for us?"

"Sure," Pat said softly. She moved to the edge of the circle where she could see everyone. She slipped her hand briefly into her pocket and then hooked her thumbs in her belt.

Elena looked into the fire for a moment. "All right. There are certain times a woman should not be alone. When she is born, when she gives birth, when she dies. When she needs healing."

Grady knew what was coming. She was going to enjoy this.

Elena settled cross-legged on the floor, her back against the hearth, and patted her lap. "Lie down please, Jo, and put your head here."

Jo frowned down at her. "You're serious?"

"Yes."

"I'm not overly comfortable with touch, Elena."

"All the same." Elena patted her thighs again.

Luckily, comfort wasn't their main objective, because Jo looked damned stiff stretching out on a blanket with her hands tied behind her. She rested her head in Elena's lap gingerly, as if she worried it might be too heavy.

"Relax, hija." Elena tussled Jo's hair as if she were a child, then reached into the bag on the floor beside her. She took out a small brass pot and lifted its lid, then dipped a lit candle into it. After a second, a thin white wisp of fragrant smoke rose, and she set the little pot on the stone hearth. Then Elena took a delicate chain from the bag, kissed its crucifix, and slid it around her neck.

"Excuse me," Maggie whispered beside Grady. "No disrespect. But I can't decide if Elena's turning into a midwife or a witch. Or a nun. What religion is this?"

"There's definitely a note of Catholicism," Grady whispered back. "Certain Mexican and Latin influences. But mostly, this is Elena. A curandera heals as her spirits instruct her to heal."

"But why is Jo lying in her lap?" Maggie looked fascinated.

"Elena believes no woman should have to go through something this hard alone." Grady touched the small shape in the breast pocket of her jacket. The image of that strange little mask kept coming to her.

"Becca, you kneel here." Elena gestured.

Becca looked uneasy, but she folded herself obediently onto the floor at Jo's left. She rested her hand on Jo's side without needing direction.

There was usually light music playing during a session, and Grady missed that comfort. The crackling fire held its own music, though, and Elena's low voice was soothing. The large room was taking on the hush of a cathedral. The air outside the cabin was dark and utterly still.

Elena looked up at them. "I don't think anything dramatic is going to happen, just yet. I just want to say a few prayers. Please remember that no one here is a passive observer. We're here because Jo is our sister, and she's decided to trust us."

She rested her hand on Jo's head. Jo shifted stiffly on the floor.

"The essence of healing is community," Elena said. "So we should ask Jo's community, her clan, for their wisdom. Do any of you have anything you want to say?"

Elena paused, and Grady remembered Elena was comfortable with silence. This one might go on for several minutes, if Elena read anything in their faces that said they needed time. She touched the shape in her breast pocket again, and unwound her arm from Maggie's.

"Elena, I'd like to remind you of this." Grady drew the mask from her jacket. "Pat, do you know this image?"

"Yeah." A wave of subtle emotions, pleasant ones, crossed Pat's face as she looked at the mask. "That's a Makah glyph, an image that appears on some of my tribe's canoes and shields. My grandmother used to tell me her story."

"Her?" Maggie peered at the mask with some trepidation; it wasn't a very cheering image; the woman was snaggle-toothed and glowering. "Who is she?"

"She doesn't have a name," Pat said. "She's just the Cannibal Woman."

"Oh." Maggie folded her arms. "Peachy."

"I dreamed about this mask earlier." Grady brought it to Elena. "No idea if it'll be useful, but for what it's worth..."

"Grady told me a little about this Makah legend, Pat." Elena touched the thin white pine delicately, drawing her finger along one of its feathers. "This Cannibal Woman threatened one of your clans a long time ago, but the children were able to stop her?"

"Right. They tricked her into a big pot of boiling water, and scalded her to death."

"Gee, the kids in your tribe sound as charming as the kids in mine," Maggie said, and Pat smiled at her. "Why would you guys put a cannibal on shields and canoes?"

Pat shrugged. "Because it's the image of a defeated enemy, a threat we conquered. But my grandmother seemed fond of the poor Cannibal Woman. When she told me those stories, she was always on her side."

"Well, if Delores Daka liked her." Jo looked glum. "Perhaps we should move directly to dousing me in kerosene."

"Let's keep that possibility in mind." Becca accepted the small mask from Elena and studied it. "You know, I think I like the Cannibal Woman too. She looks rather Xenic, Jo."

Grady was unfamiliar with *xenic* as an adjective, but Jo smiled reluctantly at the mask.

"I think she'll be good juju for us." Becca rested the mask on the center of Jo's chest. "She can be our shield in this Amazon battle."

Elena thanked Grady with her eyes, then waited another full patient minute for anyone else to speak. The quiet was calming them; even Jo was relaxing on the hard floor. A tendril of the white smoke from the pot reached Grady, a pleasant whiff of sage.

Elena nodded, then lifted the hood of her jacket over her hair, a pragmatic substitute for a *mantilla*, and rested her hands on Jo's shoulders. "Okay. I'm going to go check in again with my friend, upstairs. I would appreciate quiet while we begin, and each of you pray for protection, if you follow any god."

Elena closed her eyes, and her lips moved silently. Often her prayer was the entirety of the ceremony. Grady didn't count on that, in this case. She had never seen Elena take on an enemy this strong. The others closed their eyes too, either praying themselves or simply respecting those who were. Grady slipped her arm through Maggie's again, because she knew Maggie was scared.

You're still Someone I speak to through Elena. Grady stared at the flames and followed her own awkward process for prayer. *And right now, I know she's asking You to help Jo, and the rest of us, fight this Windigo. God, Gaia, Whoever You are. Protect Elena. This is the same prayer I always offer, the only one that matters to me. Protect Elena. I'm so afraid this girl You and I love is in more trouble than she knows.*

Grady let the words burble silently out of her. For a long time, the dark room held only the crackling fire and the softly scented smoke.

She felt the first faint vibrations through the pores of her cold face, and then the cabin seemed to tremble. Grady stepped closer to Elena, her Northwest roots warning her of an earthquake. But an earthquake would be normal on Mt. Rainier. What she was hearing was the abrupt onslaught of the wind rising again, howling against the walls.

CHAPTER FOURTEEN

Pat flexed her knees instinctively to duck a sudden threat that seemed directly overhead. It went from dead silence to deafening wind in a heartbeat, all but shaking the large house on its foundation. She saw the others blanch at the noise, and Jo half-lifted herself on her elbows. The Makah mask on her chest shifted, but stayed in place.

Elena may have cracked an eye open briefly as the howling filled their dark space, but otherwise her only reaction was to pray aloud, chanting in Spanish.

"I think our time-out is over." Maggie's voice shook.

"Fuck it," Becca said calmly, but her eyes were fierce. "Bring it on." She was still kneeling next to Jo, and Pat knew there was something right about that that was wrong with the rest of the room. She tried to grasp that thought, but it swam away.

"What the hell?" Pat touched the holster at her side, hearing a distant buzzing even over the wind, a faint but sinister high note threading through the dark air. She traced it to a side window, the one Maggie had pitched a rock through the night before. Even as Pat watched, a large, lumbering insect with scarlet wings buzzed through the jagged hole and into the cabin.

Grady noticed it too. "Jesus Christ. Elena, are you seeing this?"

Elena glanced up at the insect, which was hovering high in the eaves, then ignored it. She closed her eyes again and continued her prayer.

"What is that thing, Grady?" Pat turned to keep it in sight, yelling to be heard over the wind. The damn bug was the size of a small bird, and she'd never seen anything like it on the mountain.

"Yeah, it's deep winter," Maggie said. "What's a bee doing—"

"It's not a bee. It's a pepsis wasp." Grady's tone was sharp, and she pulled Maggie with her, closer to Elena, out from under the large wasp. "And no, it shouldn't be out in deep winter; it shouldn't be out of the damned *desert*. Elena?"

Pat figured her pistol was a little useless, and she looked around for a magazine to roll.

Three more huge wasps flew out of the night and into the room, long-legged, their red wings thrumming discordantly.

"Oh good, a party." Maggie emitted a laugh that sounded half-hysterical.

"Pat, be careful!" Grady snapped. "Pepsis wasps have the most painful sting known to humans. Do *not* fuck with these things."

Pat backed away cautiously, joining the others clustered around Jo.

"Go back to your places, please." Elena's voice, controlled but firm.

"Not likely," Pat murmured, having no wish to put any of them closer to the most agonizing sting on the planet. The wasps hovered in a formation of four at the top of the firelit circle.

"No. Do what Elena says." Grady took Maggie's arm again. "Pat, step back."

Pat cursed beneath her breath but complied, and Jo eased back down into Elena's lap. Elena's prayer continued, but the wind's roar smothered her words.

Pat felt naked and exposed here under the jittering wasps and was half-tempted to draw her piece again. Jesus, these were ugly things. Then she got a closeup view of the spider-like insect because one flew directly for her face.

Pat threw up an arm and heard Maggie cry out her name. The wasp's scarlet wings buzzed an inch from her eyes, an alien creature with prehensile legs. Then it snapped back abruptly, even angrily, and flew on.

"Elena!" Grady called, and Pat turned in time to see Elena make a quick, decisive gesture with one hand. The white smoke from the small copper pot swelled and flowed over the hearth, then began to fill the living room with its light scent.

"Maggie, watch it!" Becca hissed, and another wasp was bound right for her. Pat began to lunge toward Maggie to shield her, but the insect floated over her white face and then deserted her, darting off at an angle.

What happened next happened so quickly Pat could hardly track it. The four wasps seemed to find their targets just as the gushing white smoke from the pot filled their space, and Elena's voice rose above the wind on one commanding cry.

The wasps dived for Elena, for Becca and Jo and Grady.

They flew into the white smoke just as Elena's call cracked the air, and all four insects fell to the floor. Dead in less time than it took Pat to believe it.

And the wind faded. It didn't die entirely, Pat could still hear it out there, but she could think again. They could hear each other again.

"Blech." Becca stared at the dead wasp an inch from her knee. "I honestly can't think of anything else to say at this time."

Pat tried to draw an even breath. "No one was stung, right?"

"Oh, you'd know if one of us were stung." Grady used the side of her boot to nudge the wasp that had come for her, then kicked it beneath the sofa.

"Was it the smoke?" Maggie asked. They were drifting closer again, gathering around Jo. "Did you poison them or something, Elena? I can hardly even smell it."

Pat couldn't either. What had been a sudden, heavy fog of white smoke had never irritated her eyes or her sinuses, and its lingering remnants were fading. The air was clearing, leaving only a pleasing hint of sage behind.

"They're also called tarantula hawks, these wasps." Elena was a little breathless. She slid back the hood of her jacket and drew her hands through her hair. "Their larvae feed on tarantulas."

"I don't know *what* you could have said about these guys to make me like them any better." Becca was obviously still shaken, and she kept brushing Jo's shoulders off as if making sure she was waspless. "So how did bugs that eat desert tarantulas get all the way out here to attack us?"

They didn't attack all of us, Pat remembered, and she heard the words in her grandmother's voice.

"The pepsis wasp is the New Mexico state insect." Elena continued her bizarre nature tutorial. She looked at the floor, and then leaned over and picked up a dead wasp, tweezing its red-tissued wings in her fingers.

Grady hissed a warning. "Careful, babe."

"It's all right." Elena smiled at the dead insect, a disquieting sight. She leaned back and tossed its body over the rim of the fireguard. It bounced against a log and hissed into flame, curling blackly. "It makes sense to me that this demon would send a threat designed specifically for its enemy."

"Huh?" Maggie said.

"I find that 'makes sense' is kind of a relative term in these matters." Grady put her arm around Maggie's shoulders, where Pat's arm wanted very much to be. "But I think Elena is saying these wasps were used to target her personally."

"Well, does this mean we won, then?" Maggie raised her eyebrows hopefully. "Elena four, wasps zero? Can we get out of here now?" She looked at Pat as if she could lead them all out into a sunny and triumphant morning.

"Perhaps we could go as far as getting me off this floor, at least?" Jo said querulously. "I'm finally getting cold down here."

"I believe these wasps were intended to drive us outside," Elena said. "From what Maggie told us, this Windigo draws its victims out into the night to kill. At least we have shown it that it's not playing with fools."

Pat figured the satisfaction in Elena's voice was warranted, but the night was still black as pitch outside those windows. The gusting wind had slowed, but it hadn't stilled entirely. And she had not one clue in the universe what to do now.

"Jo, you're shaking like a damn leaf." Becca frowned. "Pat, come on. She's freezing down here. She needs to get up, and these wrist ties have to come off."

"And what in bloody hell *is* that, anyway?"

Pat tensed again, but Maggie sounded more irritated than frightened. She was pointing at one of the side windows, which pulsed with a mild orange glow.

"That light is back." Maggie stepped over Jo's long legs and went to it. "I saw it a while ago, and it's driving me nuts."

Pat experienced mild déjà vu, watching Maggie stand by that window. She remembered seeing Elena earlier in the same place, tracing a shape on the pane of glass with one finger.

"What is it, honey?" Becca sounded worried, and Maggie's hands slowly closed into fists.

Maggie's eyes were locked on the orange light glowing through the window. She took a step back.

❖

"Um, it's the face." Maggie swallowed past the cotton in her throat. "It's her."

Pat was walking closer, always a good thing. "You see a face?"

The light was growing brighter. Curving lines were marked clearly in the frost sheeting the pane, an oval shape. It was the image of the Makah mask, the Cannibal Woman. The same wild hair, angry, slanted eyes, the same snarl. She heard Pat's swift indrawn breath beside her.

"That's impossible," Pat whispered. "Any marks would have faded hours ago. Elena? Do you remember drawing this?"

"What are you talking about?" Elena sounded annoyed.

Grady's voice. "What is it, Pat?"

Maggie was thoroughly creeped out, and she reached for Pat's hand as naturally as a child seeking comfort from a mother. The moment their fingers touched, the light flashed brighter. The Cannibal Woman stood out in stark relief across the window, outlined by an orange glare that haloed Pat and Maggie.

"Son of a *bitch!*"

It was Jo and there was terror in her voice, and Maggie was jarred from the window. Pat was already running back toward the others by the hearth, and Maggie followed her quickly.

Jo was thrashing on the floor, and Becca was struggling to hold her still.

"Get it off me!" Jo bellowed, and she was staring pop-eyed at her chest.

The Makah mask was freezing into her jacket. Ice crystals were forming around it like snow around a lake, and the frost was spreading across Jo's breasts.

"Jo, lie still!" Grady threw herself across Jo's kicking legs, her glasses knocked askew across her face, and Elena joined her.

Pat knelt beside Jo, and Becca gripped the Makah mask. She cried out and released it, and Maggie could actually *hear* the mask freeze deeply into Jo's chest with a malign crackling sound.

"Easy, honey." Becca shook out her reddened fingers. "We're going to help you, just—"

"Get it *off!*" Jo screamed, bucking.

Pat whipped back her long coat and drew her knife from her belt. "Jo, don't move!" She barked. "Becca, I don't want to cut her."

Pat inserted the tip of the long knife beneath the edge of the mask, and Maggie drew in a hitching breath. Jo was obviously trying to lie still, but she was wracked with convulsive shudders.

Pat yanked—hard—and the mask ripped free of Jo's jacket with a tearing rasp.

It flipped into the air, and then it kept flipping. The frosted mask rose higher in a slow, lazy spin and hung in the space above them. A wave of dizziness swept Maggie and she locked her knees to keep from falling.

Orange light, the same disturbing shade of orange that had outlined the window, began to glow around the small mask. And it grew, right before Maggie's terrified eyes. Its sides spread to the size and shape of a human head, and the disembodied Cannibal Woman glared down at them.

"What the f-fu—" Jo's teeth were chattering so hard she couldn't speak.

"Jo, we've got this." Becca was behind Maggie so she couldn't see her face, but she took some courage from the strength in her voice. "Just lie still."

After a tense moment of silence, Maggie couldn't stand it anymore. "Is it going to do something?" she whispered.

The woman's primitive features regarded them impassively, and the large room was quiet.

"Jo?" Grady's voice. "You all right?"

"Yes. G-getting there."

Maggie pressed her hand to her hammering heart, willing it to slow the fuck down. To her great relief, Elena came up beside her, and addressed the cruel face with the ferocity of a street fighter.

"You're not welcome here, *abuela.*" Elena stood protectively close to Maggie. "You were not invited. Now get out of this house and leave these good women in peace."

The woman's gleaming visage was motionless. And then it wasn't. The slanting slits that served as her eyes shifted and turned toward the fireplace.

Maggie touched Pat's hand again.

The hearth exploded in flames.

"Becca!" Pat cried, and Becca was already pulling Jo back from the roaring column of fire.

It was fiercely bright but contained, a solid pole of twisting flame that shot up the chimney, flooding their circle in light. Not one spark made it through the cracked glass of the fireguard to the stone lip of the hearth, and Maggie clung to that comfort.

"Elena?" Grady was outlined in the gold light as she pointed to the painting mounted above the hearth. Maggie heard Elena gasp just as she saw it too. The trough.

The painting Delores Daka had painted twenty-five years ago had shifted again, drawn back. The mountain, their cabin, were small now in the distance, but still visible against the dark, cloud-choked sky. Half of the rusted trough now sat prominently in the snowy foreground. Instead of snow, the trough was filled with steaming water that appeared to be boiling.

Maggie was clenching Pat's hand bloodlessly. She glanced over her shoulder at the floating face, which still stared implacably at the painting.

"What's it trying to tell us?" Maggie whispered. "What's so damn important about a *trough*?"

"I don't think she's looking at the trough," Pat said. In the glare of unnatural firelight, her expression was filled with wonder. She patted Maggie's hand, then released it, and walked slowly over to the hearth.

"Pat, Grady, we need to get her up." Becca was struggling to help Jo rise, and Grady went to them quickly. Pat, however, rested her hands on the mantel and stared at the photographs sitting on it. Maggie hurried to snatch up the blanket that had snarled beneath Jo's legs, and Grady and Becca pulled her to her feet.

"What *is* this?" Becca hissed, scratching at the ice crystals that still formed a circle on Jo's jacket. The shape of the mask was a dark oval inside it. "Jo, you're shtill shaking like you're freezhing to death."

Maggie kept glancing at the high corner of the room to make sure that terrible face hadn't decided to open its maw to swallow them, and then the whiskey fumes hit her. She stared at Becca and realized how badly she was slurring her words. Her cheeks were flushed and she was blinking rapidly, bleary-eyed. Becca was, quite abruptly, drunk as a lord.

Maggie whipped around toward the hearth. "Uh, Pat? We need you over here."

❖

The Mexican girl is right, kid, Pat's grandmother said to her. *When you open doors, you never know who will come through.*

The small photograph of her grandmother, Jo, and Pat had changed. Her own laughing face, and Jo's, were the same. But her grandmother's toothless grin was gone. She no longer laughed into the camera. Her head had turned, and now her stern eyes were pinned on Pat's. Her lips didn't move with her speech, but it was unmistakably Delores's voice.

It's not okay with me that this monster fucks with my family. So listen, Patricia. All of these girls have part of your answer.

And then it was Elena's voice issuing out of the photograph, clear as a bell in Pat's ears. *We must meet this demon on its own ground.*

Becca Healy's voice, vibrant and ringing. *Fuck it. Bring it on.*

Then Grady's. *I have a feeling Jo's not alone in all this.*

❖

"Pat!" Maggie called again. Why the hell was she still ogling that damn picture?

"What were you thinking, Becca, putting that thing on my chest?" Jo's eyes were steely, and then they went blank in shock. "Becca. Are you *drunk?*"

"Of coursh not. Of *course* not, Jo." Becca released Jo's elbow and rubbed her face hard. "How could I be?"

"There's no liquor in the house," Grady protested, and Maggie shared her bewilderment. "We heard Pat tell us…uh, Pat, could you join us? Jo, Becca's telling the truth."

"This is a private conversation, Dr. Wrenn." Jo's voice went dangerously quiet. "Becca doesn't need you to come to her defense."

"Look," Maggie said testily. "Is anybody even a little bit concerned about the pillar of fucking *fire* that's shooting up the chim—"

"Maggie's right." Now Grady sounded pissed too. "Try to control yourself, Jo. This is not the time to give in to hallucinations, or what—"

"You enjoyed the hell out of mocking me after class, didn't you?" Jo's tone still held that frightening hush, and her eyes were still on Grady. "You and those cretinous jocks in the back row."

"*What?*" Grady sputtered. "Jo, you're certifiable. I never—"

"*And* that's scene." Becca stalked over to Grady, and Maggie could see it cost her great effort to speak clearly and walk without staggering. "Listen, people, we have a geysher—a *geyser* of fire to deal with, and that damn orange bitch is still floating on our ceiling, so could we…"

Becca had reached Grady and now she turned as if to protect her, to stand between her and Jo. But Becca stumbled and took a ragged step back, and Grady moved fast and took her shoulders to steady her.

Becca went still in Grady's grasp, and Maggie saw her eyes flutter shut. She let her head drop back on Grady's chest.

A low growl rose in Jo's throat, and Maggie was very glad Pat hadn't removed her wrist ties.

Then Grady closed her eyes too, and rested her chin in Becca's hair. Her hands moved toward her breasts.

Maggie yelled again for Pat and spun toward her. Pat was still standing at the mantel. Maggie had lost track of Elena, but she saw her now, moving silently up beside Pat.

Elena slipped the long knife out of Pat's loose-fingered hand.

❖

Jo has a lot of courage, more than you know. Trust her. She'll do right.

Pat's grandmother still looked at her with that grave sense of command. Then her eyes shifted over Pat's shoulder, toward the ceiling.

She's got part of the answer too, our old friend there, so you can trust her also. You can trust the fire she sends you. But mostly, Patricia, you trust your sewa.

Maggie's voice in Pat's mind. *The Windigo has a heart of ice.*

Her grandmother. *It's already done its worst to you two. It can't touch you again, so maybe you can beat it. I don't know. They don't tell me these things. But you'd be surprised how much this place here is like a good school, and I learned some stuff.*

The wise old eyes Pat remembered so well took her measure, and her own filled with tears at the love in the lisping voice. *You were plenty brave and strong enough, the first time. But you doubted yourself. Be that stupid again, and your friends are going to die tonight. It's your turn to look out for Jo, kid.*

CHAPTER FIFTEEN

M aggie smacked the back of Pat's shoulder powerfully with her fist, hard enough to rock her, but she couldn't linger to see if it was hard enough to wake the stupid woman up. She whirled before Pat's gasp faded.

Elena's back was to Maggie, but she had lifted the knife high enough to be seen in the roar of the column of firelight. Jo had planted herself solidly in front of Becca and Grady, blocking Elena's way to them, bound wrists or not.

"Elena, you *stop*!" Jo commanded, but Elena was shrieking curses at Becca, spittle flying through her clenched teeth. The cacophony of flame and their strident voices were all Maggie had time to register before she measured the angle of the blade and lunged for Elena's wrist.

Maggie had been in more than one street fight herself, and she hadn't grown up with two dozen cousins without learning about knives. She squeezed the bones of Elena's wrist as hard as she could and the knife clattered to the hearth, just as her weight on Elena's back toppled them both to the floor. They knocked into Jo's legs, who in turn fell back against Grady and Becca, and they all went down in a cascade of flailing limbs.

"Knock it off!" Pat bellowed, and it was over.

Elena moved beneath Maggie, but more with the sluggish confusion of a woman waking up than one bent on murder. Jo levered herself to a seated position and looked around immediately for Becca, who huddled against her side.

"J-Jesus," Grady stammered, straightening her glasses with oddly endearing propriety. "What was that?"

"Is anyone *not* injured?" Pat stood glaring down at their sprawled bodies, her fists on her hips. She looked taller.

Maggie realized she was seeing Pat through a reasonable wash of firelight. The column of flame had subsided, and the iron grate now held logs that crackled with a blessedly natural light. She clambered off Elena and scanned the high, dark ceiling. "I think our trespasser left." Her thumb brushed a shape on the floor and she lifted her hand. A chill went through her. "Yeek. I mean, our trespasser is right here."

She picked up the small mask with squeamish trepidation, but it was restored to a harmless oval of thin pine and feathers. She nodded toward the far corner of the room. "It looks like that weird light's gone too."

"Grady, I lost time. Are you all right?" Elena looked shaken. She sat up and leaned against the hearth, and Grady scrambled to her. She slid her arm around Elena's shoulders and held her.

"The last thing I remember is that spooky-as-hell face." Becca's diction was clear, and the flush had faded from her cheeks. Maggie stood two feet away from her, and she smelled nothing. The fumes of hard liquor that had surrounded Becca were gone. "Pat, what happened to us?"

"Yes, *Pat,* what happened to you all?" Maggie had been almost as rattled by Pat's zombie impersonation as she stared at that photograph as anything else in this freak show.

"I know what I saw when I turned around." Pat was absurdly calm. "Maggie, am I correct? Tell us what Jo was doing."

"What Jo was doing? You mean, after Elena took your knife and went for Becca's throat?" Maggie heard Elena gasp, but the tension was gushing out of her chest with her words and she couldn't stop. "Well, *Patsy*, Becca was drunk off her ass, and she was coming on hard to Grady. Who seemed just fine with that. And you went into some kind of freaking trance…" Then Maggie remembered Jo's face in that moment, her determination to place herself between Becca and the knife. "Wait. Jo was shielding Becca."

Pat looked around, then lifted her knife from the hearth. "Jo, I'm taking those ties off."

A squeak of protest escaped Maggie before she could stop it. Pat knelt behind Jo and freed her wrists.

"Pat." Jo grimaced. "Are you sure this is a good idea?"

"I'm not sure of anything, yet." Pat straightened and returned the knife to her belt. "But I think I have a plan."

"Elena." Grady sounded worried, and then Maggie was too. The color had fallen out of Elena's face in an alarming rush, and she sagged against Grady.

"It's not possible," Elena whispered, closing her eyes. "Becca, you must know I'd never hurt you."

"Hey." Becca's voice was clear and firm, and so was her hand on Elena's shoulder. "Of course you wouldn't hurt me, Elena. You'd never harm anyone. And I wouldn't drink, and I'd never betray Jo. It's time, Pat, isn't it?" She looked up at Pat with hollow fear in her eyes. "This isn't some mass psychosis. This is spirit shit. It's time we accepted that."

Pat nodded. "You guys just rest for a moment."

Moving with the same assured quiet, Pat tilted the fire screen and began to add fresh wood to the grate. Maggie shifted from foot to foot, tapping the mask nervously against her palm as she waited, but the others relaxed against each other. No one seemed in a hurry to get up. Outside, the wind remained banked but could still be heard, a sinister and distant whistle.

"Becca, you mentioned *The Shining* earlier," Pat observed, apropos of nothing, as she poked at the logs. "Are you a Stephen King fan?"

"Well, not tonight," Becca said pointedly.

Pat grinned. "Did you know King wrote a story about the Windigo? Scary as hell. But something bothered me about that story. Same thing that bothers me about most stories with demons in them."

"Um, Pat," Grady said politely. "This might be more words than I've ever heard you put together at one time, and I hate to interrupt. But will you be getting to that plan you mentioned soon?"

"Soon." Pat replaced the fire screen and brushed off her gloved hands, her face austere and lovely in the red firelight. "It's never seemed fair to me that demons get all this power in our stories, but normal human ghosts can never help us fight them." She looked up over her shoulder at the painting. "So tonight, we're listening to a new story. We're going to follow the advice of a ghost."

"Pat, I don't know what you heard." Jo's tone was entirely respectful. "But ghosts don't give advice. The voices of the dead are electrical impulses, data that can be measured. Please don't base our safety on some random message."

"Maybe Pat is listening to this message with wiser ears than ours." Elena lifted her head from Grady's shoulder. "Tell us what to do, amiga."

"We don't have much time." Pat swallowed visibly, and Maggie could see that in spite of this strange new confidence, she was as afraid as any of them. "And I don't know how to explain. I'm asking you guys for trust, and that's the hardest thing in the world to give."

She held out her hand to Maggie, and that disorienting déjà vu happened again. Maggie had seen this tall figure before, outlined by firelight, extending a hand toward her. She would have followed him anywhere. She would follow Pat now. When their hands touched, Maggie half-expected the pillar of fire to erupt again, but Pat just smiled at her.

"Becca, please take this." Pat took the little Makah mask from Maggie and handed it to Becca. "Keep it with you. It's all right. There's no harm in the Cannibal Woman. I think her story can help us."

Becca accepted the mask with a sickly smile and slid it into the pocket of her jacket.

"The four of you need to separate," Pat said, pointing. "Sit farther apart. Each of you, get out of arm's reach and stay there."

The others complied, shifting across the wood floor, probably with the same numbness Maggie felt.

"Watch each other," Pat ordered. "Jo, you're in charge."

"*Me?*" Jo squeaked.

"You. If anything happens in the next fifteen minutes—if anyone starts to look funny, feel funny, breathe funny, anything— yell out for us. Loud."

"Us?" Maggie repeated. "You and me? Where will we be?"

"Nearby. You and I have some history to address." Pat picked up a candle and turned, but Maggie tugged her back.

"We're leaving these guys?" Maggie had no desire to see either of them outside the safety of the clan, the company of the four women who were watching them with open concern. "Can't we address our history right here?"

"We couldn't *possibly.*" The high planes of Pat's face filled with color. She led Maggie out of the circle of firelight, toward the guest bedroom. "Remember," she called back. "Watch each other. We won't be far away."

❖

"Pat, it's a f-fucking freezer in here." Maggie had her arms clenched across her chest. "What do you want?"

"To be able to see you, for one thing," Pat made sure the door to the guest room was firmly shut, then rested the candle on a high shelf so its meager light fell on them both. "Would you take off your clothes, please?"

"Eat shit and fart fire," Maggie suggested.

"I'm serious." Pat bit the fingertip of her glove and pulled it off. She began to undress methodically, thinking harder and faster than she ever had in her life. Remembering her grandmother's words and trusting them, because there was no other choice.

Maggie was incredulous. "You want to do this here and now?"

"I know you." Pat could see the steam of Maggie's breath, and her lips were turning blue. She continued shedding her clothes, dropping her long coat to the floor, snaking out of her two flannel shirts. "I let you down once. I let it win, and it took me. My grandmother says it's already done its worst to me, and to you. It can't touch us again."

"Your grand…what the hell are you talking about?"

"I've been dreaming about us for weeks. The wasps flew for the others, Maggie, but they couldn't come near us."

"You're a crazy woman." Maggie was shivering spasmodically, staring at Pat's pale shoulders. "You're going to freeze to death in—"

"Maggie, I know you." Pat had to settle for removing her belt and unfastening her jeans. "You know me. We've been through this before. I'm telling you the truth."

She had to trust that Maggie would yell "no" or punch her or kick her in the crotch if she truly objected, because they couldn't waste more time on negotiation. Half-naked herself, Pat began undressing Maggie, swiftly and well.

Maggie didn't resist. She looked up into Pat's face, her eyes wide and searching, but she stood still beneath her hands. Pat reached the T-shirt Maggie wore and she simply ripped it open, baring her breasts. She slid her hands around beneath the soft fabric to press Maggie's naked back.

Maggie gasped and arched at the chill of her fingers. When their lips met, in the moment before Pat closed her eyes, she saw the frost coating the outside of the window begin to melt and recede. Maggie moaned into her open mouth.

The bed was right next to them but it was too far away, so they stayed on their feet. Pat opened her eyes because she wanted to see Maggie's body, her hands roaming feverishly over the cool swells of her breasts. They drew in air in harsh gasps, the steam of their blended breath gusting across their faces.

Maggie's features grew luminous in the candlelight. "Our baby saw the sun rise," she whispered.

"Yes, sewa." Pat was faintly aware that neither of them were speaking in English. She also realized she could no longer see Maggie's breath. The room was warming. She slipped her hands beneath Maggie's hair and kissed her again. Maggie's fingers skated up her bare back and she shivered, hard.

"We can't let it hurt them," Maggie murmured.

"We won't." Pat's fingers delved between Maggie's thighs and found her center, and her own sex tightened in welcome. Physical sensations more blissful than she had ever known, or at least hadn't known for over a century, surged through her sinew and filled her with liquid heat.

Steam swirled, rose, and enveloped them.

❖

"Are you guys hearing this?" Becca whispered.

Shivering on the floor, she gaped at the closed bedroom door. That dark corner of the large cabin was emitting an alarming series of wooden creaks and whistles, as if the walls holding it up were expanding suddenly with heat.

"Jesus. Is that *smoke*?" Grady pointed to the white vapor streaming beneath the door. Before anyone could respond, the door opened and Pat and Maggie emerged. Their figures were shrouded in a steamy mist, which dissipated swiftly in the cold air of the living room.

"Well, that answers that question." Pat held Maggie's hand and led her back to their circle, sounding almost cheerful. "Looks like we've got heat covered."

A high-pitched squeak of laughter escaped Becca, and she clapped her hand over her mouth. "S-sorry," she stammered. "I'm sorry. Do you two…need anything? Like clothing?"

Pat was still wearing her long coat, but in terms of attire, both she and Maggie looked recently and quickly reassembled. A sense of fragile relief coursed through Becca, her maternal worry easing as they returned unscathed.

"We need to bundle up, all of us." Pat stuffed her shirttail beneath her belt. The wind was kicking hard again, slapping against the cabin. "We're going out to the trough."

Becca turned automatically to the painting over the hearth, the metal trough now featured prominently in its foreground. It no longer appeared to hold steaming, boiling water, and its slanted sides glowed with a subdued gold-red light. No one commented on this, and Becca figured at this point they were so saturated in strangeness, a continually changing canvas was almost routine. She was not, however, getting a good vibe from any of this.

"Pat, honey, honestly." Becca folded her arms. "We'll take you tubing in the morning. What are you thinking we should do out there, with this trough?"

"It doesn't matter." Elena's distinctive brows were furrowed. "None of us should leave the cabin, Pat. We discussed this."

"We have to go outside," Pat said. "Hiding in here won't keep us safe. We've seen that. This Windigo is a bully. Like all bullies, it counts on fear to get its way. We're not going to let it trap us here. We're going out there to face it, head on."

"What are you thinking we should do *out there*, Pat?" Becca repeated herself, her pronunciation diamond clear.

"We're going to dunk Jo in boiling water."

Silence.

Jo nodded. "Okay."

Wind gasped and barked against the walls.

Pat went to the maple pegs that held their coats and began filling her arms. "The Windigo has a heart of ice, and now Jo does too. We have to melt that heart."

"By boiling her to death?" Maggie had one hand on her hip and she seemed to be shooting for sarcasm, but her voice was shaking. The flush that had filled her cheeks when she first emerged from the bedroom had faded to pale. "This is your big plan?"

"It worked for the Cannibal Woman." Pat tossed Maggie a heavy nylon jacket. "Put that on. But no, I don't think we're going to kill Jo."

"Mind you, I'm fine with the prospect of killing Jo," Grady said stiffly, "But, Pat, where are you getting all this? From your Makah legend? For one thing, how would we boil water out—"

"I'm not a physics major." Pat threw Grady a hooded coat, arcing it cleanly through the air into her hands. "The laws of nature are pretty fucked up around here right now. That painting's telling us the bad guys don't get to write all the rules."

Becca's mouth had gone paper-dry.

Instead of hurling a parka at Elena, Pat carried it to her and held it out politely. Elena still looked sorely troubled, but she turned and allowed Pat to slip it up over her arms.

"Elena, you were right. I'm listening to this message with wiser ears than yours." Pat lifted Elena's dark curls free of her collar and smoothed them across her shoulders. "You were right about a lot of things. You're amazing, my friend, but this isn't your story. It's Maggie's and mine, from Native people. It's our past. You brought us insights from a different culture, but now you have to trust ours."

Pat turned Elena gently to face her. She took Elena's hand and held it against her own heart, and in spite of her fear, Becca felt the thrum of Pat's pulse in her own palm. "Elena, I need you to watch my ass in all this. Because I have no real earthly fucking idea what's going to happen."

Elena blinked up at Pat. She glanced at Grady, then began buttoning the front of Pat's long coat. "You have the *cojones* of a grizzly bear, little sister." Elena patted her face. "Don't worry. We'll have your back."

"Oh yes? Will we?" Becca was ready to return directly to the mass psychosis theory. "Are we having Pat's back before or after Jo's bonfire?"

Blowing snow churned past the windows, and the night air filled with howling winds. They moved together, forming a tight circle in front of the fire, and Becca was comforted in spite of herself. They didn't hug or tousle each other's hair, and no one gazed adoringly at anyone else. She felt them drawing strength and courage from each other more simply than that; their presence was enough.

"It sounds like things are kicking up out there." Pat snuggled her gloves around her wrists. "We need to move now."

"Pat." Grady's gaze was on the floor. "How do we know this isn't exactly how the Windigo operates? That Canadian Cree, Swift Runner, who cannibalized his family...how do we know he didn't lure his son outside with some crazy diversion, just like this?"

Uncertainty flickered across Pat's face. It was an unsettling moment, and Becca was already unsettled to the point of nausea.

"Look, maybe I don't get this plan," Maggie said slowly. "This Cannibal Woman thing, how her story is supposed to help us. But, Grady, I don't think Pat and I can stop you guys, if you go for each other again. Sooner or later—"

"Maggie." Becca never interrupted anyone, ever. "Maggie, you told us yourself that this Windigo only attacks its victims outside. Now you're thinking it's a *good* idea to drag Jo out there in this blizzard and boil her like an egg?"

The wind had become a blizzard in full fury. Ice crystals of snow pattered against the glass windowpanes in angry bursts.

"Becca, don't you get it?" A pleading note entered Maggie's tone. "You need this almost as much as Jo does. So do they." She jerked her chin at Grady and Elena. "If we stay in here, how long will it be before you lose yourselves entirely? Selly said the Witiko changes the family in ways that drive the cursed one into a killing rage. Isn't that what we just saw?"

"Jealousy, pride." Elena closed her eyes. "You're right, little sister. This monster is corrupting our spirits in ways that can only end in bloodshed."

"We might be drifting from the point," Becca said loudly. "The point being—"

"Pardon me." Jo put her hand on Becca's shoulder. Becca had stepped forward when she barked at Maggie, but now she stepped back. Jo looked down at her narrowly, with a kind of courtly reproof. "I appreciate the sentiment, Becca, but this isn't your decision to make. I want this thing out of me, and I'm going with Pat. The rest of you can come or not."

"Nope," Pat said at once. "All of us or none of us, Jo."

"Joanne…" Becca said.

Jo winked at her. "Find some *cojones*, Rebecca."

No one spoke while the wind raged and battered the cabin.

"Oh, for heaven's sake." Jo rolled her eyes and stalked toward the front door.

Becca caught up with Jo, and the others followed.

CHAPTER SIXTEEN

Pat led them blindly. It was impossible to see through the churning vortex of wind and snow, but Pat knew the lay of the land well enough to have a fix on their direction. She imagined the sinister moon breathing overhead, looking down on six tiny, moving dots on a field of white, huddled together for warmth.

"Pat!" Maggie shouted to be heard over the wind. "Jesus, that sky…"

The heavy cloudbank above them couldn't possibly be more dense, save for the circle that emitted the green moonlight. But farther northeast, just over the horizon, a roiling blackness had appeared, darker even than the night. And it was coming closer, and moving fast.

Minnesota and the snow-choked, barren planes of Canada, the lonely places, lay northeast of Mt. Rainier. If this interesting geographical reality occurred to anyone other than Pat, they had no breath to discuss it. The snow was knee-deep, even thigh-deep in some places, and the ground was uneven. Pat had to kick powerfully to break a path, and the others had to focus on following her.

"Jo, how are you?" Elena shouted.

"Still fine, thank you," Jo called back. "Though I believe we called a moratorium on asking me that."

The metal trough swam into view ahead. Set on a small rise, it was only half-submerged in snow, a white drift cresting one of its slanting sides.

"Maggie!" Pat guided her to one end of the trough, and then kicked through the drift to its opposite end. They faced each other over its length, blinking furiously to clear their eyes of swirling sleet. The rest of them clustered along its sides.

"You want me on *that*?" Jo pointed at the mound of solid snow filling the steel rectangle. She looked ready to vault over the side and plant herself on it at Pat's word.

"Not yet." Pat looked up toward the rolling sea of black above the trees. "Maggie? Grab on."

Pat grasped the extended bar on one end of the trough in her gloved hands, and after a moment of hesitation, Maggie took hold of the bar at the other end.

"Sewa," Pat called to Maggie, "look at me."

They faced each other over the trough, and a quick vision came to Pat, the briefest glimpse into a realm Elena must inhabit daily. In the empty air above the trough, she saw a tall man with long, dark hair swirl into being. A young woman hovered with him, looking up into his eyes. He touched the woman's face, then handed her a small cloth pouch. She held it to her heart.

"Wh-wh-who are *they*?" Becca stammered, just as the ethereal figures melted into the freezing air.

"Who were *they*?" Grady echoed, through wildly chattering teeth. Pat saw they were all gaping at the now-empty space above the trough, but she returned her gaze to Maggie, and wondered if these visitors had chimed a deeply resonant note of recognition in her as well.

Without fanfare or flashing lights or special effects of any kind, the snow in the trough began to melt.

The entire white surface sank a visible inch immediately, and then steam started to boil up in the frigid air. Grady and Elena,

Becca and Jo stepped back in astonishment, but Pat and Maggie kept their hold on the swiftly warming steel bars.

"Pat!" Elena's call was urgent. "Are you being burned?"

"No. We're okay." Pat spoke for Maggie as well, who looked as bedazzled as the rest of them.

The sour green light of the moon began to fade, an ancient overhead eye closing in displeasure, and a bitter howling entered the wind.

The wind of the Spirit of the Lonely Places was composed of the death rattle of tribes lost to winter famine. Elena said she had first heard it in the trees as they drove toward Mt. Rainier. Pat had heard that wretched moaning in the recording of Selly Abequa. The mournful wail was rising again, and whatever rode on its back was coming fast now.

The sides of the trough began to pulse with a subtle light, a mild gold glow. The rest of the snow filling it melted in a wet swirl, still steaming mightily.

"Hey!" Becca grabbed the sleeve of Jo's parka. "No way are you diving into *that*!"

"Wait." Grady stepped to the trough and pulled off her glove. She held her hand just above the misting surface of the water, then patted it gingerly. Elena hissed, but Grady shook her head. "No, it's all right." She dipped her hand beneath the surface. "Hot, but bearable."

"Can I take it?" Jo asked Grady shortly.

"I think so."

Jo began unfastening her parka. She yelled at Pat, "You actually expect me to disrobe?"

Pat's shoulders hunched as an abrupt swell of the wind sent a harrowing and bereft quailing through her. "No time! Maggie, don't let go! Jo—move."

Jo stole an arm around Becca, pulled her close and kissed her, and the insane, entirely genuine passion of the moment hit Pat hard. Then Jo lifted one leg over the glowing edge of the trough.

Elena stopped her. "Jo. I'm coming with you."

"*What*?" Grady sputtered.

"No woman should endure such a healing alone." Elena turned to Pat, pleading. "And I need this healing as much as our sister, here. Pat, I feel this."

Pat raised her voice to be heard over the grieving wind. "My grandmother said each of us has part of the answer. Go on, Elena."

Elena shook off her jacket and dropped it, then yanked one glove free and pulled the silver ring from her third finger. She pressed into Grady's hand and touched her face. Then she turned and vaulted nimbly into the trough.

Hot water splashed Pat and Maggie to their waists, and Elena uttered a series of curses in Spanish as she settled into a seated position at one end of the trough. She waved reassurance, not to Grady but to Becca, as Jo climbed in and joined her in the steaming water.

The trough was deep, submerging Jo and Elena to their chests. Jo sat back against Elena, who wrapped both arms around her, bracing her. Jo clung to either side of the steel rim with both hands.

"Hot," Jo said clearly, her eyes clenched shut. "But do it, go on."

"Maybe we should take up the places Elena had us take in the living room," Pat called above the shrieking gale. "Becca, you're over here next to—"

"Right, like you could stop me!" Becca was already kicking her way to Jo's side.

"Grady, you stand there. You're our witness." Pat kept both hands around the steel bar, and Grady backed reluctantly away from them to stand to one side. The wind grew ferocious, and the sky darkened entirely. They were plunged into blackness broken only by the mild glow of the trough.

"What now?" Maggie's eyes were enormous. "Pat, it's starting to hurt them!"

Elena arched her back and hissed in pain, and it wasn't hard to imagine how it felt to submerge very cold hands and feet in very hot water. The stinging of blood racing to the surface of the skin had to be excruciating.

"This ain't doing it." Grady threw Pat a look of pure defiance and moved. She threw herself on her knees beside the trough and grabbed Elena's hand.

And apparently *that* did it, the joining of all six women around the steaming water again, because it abruptly began to boil. The surface roiled around Elena and Jo in great bursting bubbles.

"Jo?" Becca gasped.

"It's all right." Jo was breathing in deep pants. "It's no h-hotter."

Pat waited in unbearable limbo for anything to happen— for Jo's ice heart to melt in the churning water, for a gruesome demon to descend out of the gale, for the mountain to open and swallow them whole. The piercing wind slapped them, and they leaned in helplessly toward one another.

"Pat?" Maggie cried.

"Hold on, babe." Grady gripped Elena's hand hard, and Elena closed her eyes and rested her head against it, her lips moving in prayer.

"Pat!" Maggie screamed again. She was staring over Pat's shoulder, and as one, they turned to follow her horrified gaze.

It skittered like a spider over the top of the distant hill, an immense creature, towering above the tallest trees. The Windigo ran upright, all long, emaciated limbs and withered ribcage.

"J-Jesus." Becca's stunned whisper was lost in the chaos. "I thought it was a f-fucking *metaphor…*"

There was nothing ephemeral in the Cannibal Beast that scuttled swiftly down toward them with desperate speed. The monster had the head of a deer, and its broad antlers rocked as it sniffed the air hungrily. The Windigo was starvation made animate, with the crazed, greedy red eyes of utter famine, and those eyes were pinned on Jo.

"The mask!" Maggie's voice rang clarion-strong. For that moment, she was the mother of this clan, and she must be obeyed. "Becca, use the mask!"

Becca groped in the pocket of her jacket.

The towering near-skeleton was close enough now that its stench reached them even through the wind, a rank, foul musk, the scent of the cursed smoke from Selly Abequa's pipe.

Becca drew out the small Makah mask and slammed it down on Jo's chest with a fierce cry.

The pine oval ignited at once into sparking flame and sank deeply into Jo's breast. She thrashed convulsively in the water, and they screamed like terrified children.

The Windigo swept down on them, blanketing them in impossible cold. Ravenous need sparked briefly through Pat's blood, a killing need, a horrible craving that obliterated friendship and love and all her humanity.

Jo's body, and Elena's, glowed a deep gold-red in the boiling water. On either side of the trough, the same light flared briefly in the center of Grady's chest, then Becca's.

The Windigo's prolonged, cheated howl cracked the air, and then it melted into thin air and was gone.

CHAPTER SEVENTEEN

T hen the sun came up.

The sun didn't exactly come up, it was just there, serene and shining in the crystalline teal sky overhead.

This immediate transition to daylight and balmy weather wasn't as reassuring as one might imagine. The sudden silencing of that relentless wind made Maggie fear she'd gone deaf, and the sunlight was painfully dazzling after too many wretched hours of darkness.

They straightened out of their hunch and shared a moment of pop-eyed silence. Pat let go of the trough and turned in a quick circle, scanning the trees and the sky for any sign of their monster. They were alone. Mt. Rainier ruled over the valley again, stately and silent in the afternoon sun.

"Hoochie-mama!" Jo clambered awkwardly to her feet in the steel trough, sloshing the several inches of water that remained in it. "Now it's *so* frigging cold!"

"Hoochie-mama?" Grinning wildly, Maggie took Jo's arm and helped her over the rim. "Seriously?"

"It just came out," Jo mumbled.

"Hey." Grady was still kneeling beside the trough, clenching Elena's hand. "Let's get you out of there too."

Elena let Grady help her stand, but protested when she began to lift her bodily out of the trough. "Oh yes, Grady, by all means, throw out your back, I am perfectly capable of—" She broke off as Grady set her on her feet and pulled her close. "Ah. Never mind," she mumbled into Grady's shoulder. "This is a very good idea."

"Are you safe? Are you sane?" Becca demanded, kicking through the snow to Jo. "Are you whole? Are you well? Jesus, I'm Horton talking to a Who!"

Jo steadied Becca's flailing arms. "I believe I'm fine again, thank you."

They couldn't stop blinking at each other.

"This looks like a burn." Grady touched a red patch on Elena's throat gently. "From the water?"

Elena nodded, feeling her throat. "I think we're cooked, Jo and me, but we're not too badly boiled. Nothing a little aloe won't cure. I want my ring back now please, Grady."

"Here you go, love." Grady slipped the silver ring from her pocket and slid it on Elena's finger.

Their gasping breath steamed freely in the crisp air. Maggie didn't consider it Windigo-freezing anymore, but it was still a brisk January day at the foot of Mt. Rainier. The trough was simply a trough again, sans glowing light. The only surreal note came from the sudden chiming of music through the air, the faint melody of "Season of the Witch."

Grady looked around. "Is that…?"

"Sí, sí," Elena sighed. "It is my hoochie-mama."

Grady crunched through the snow to Elena's jacket and brought it to her. Elena took her cell out of its pocket and opened it.

"Hello, Mamá, we are fine, call you soon, good-bye." Elena pressed a key firmly to switch her phone off, and Becca rested her head on Maggie's arm and tittered in frazzled amusement.

Grady slipped Elena's jacket over her shoulders. "Wow. It's two o'clock, Monday afternoon. Just as it should be."

"Now that's a lovely sight." Becca nodded toward the cabin in the distance. Power restored, it was lit from within with humming light, and Maggie could almost hear its large rooms warming with welcome heat. Becca slid her arm through Jo's. "You guys are soaking wet. We need to get you in out of this cold."

Pat hadn't spoken, and it had taken her this long to make her way around the trough to Maggie. She put her hands on Maggie's shoulders and turned her. Then she tipped her chin and kissed her, in front of Rainier and Elena's Goddess and everyone. Maggie smiled at her, and they kissed again, long and slow and sweet.

"Please, Patricia." Jo was already on her way back to the cabin. "Get a room."

They followed.

CHAPTER EIGHTEEN

Two hours later, Jo was on the cabin's front veranda, blissfully ensconced in the hot tub with Becca and Grady. The clear water bubbled merrily and predictably, behaving itself, providing nigh onto perfect ecstasy for those immersed in it.

"You need to join us, Maggie," Grady drawled.

"No, thanks." Maggie patted Grady's head, which rested on the cushioned lip of the tub. "This thing is too full of Seattle lesbians. I'll get a private soak in later."

"You and Smokey Bear?" Becca simpered coyly, chin-deep in the water. "Woo-hoo."

"Please," Jo sighed, her long length languid beside Becca. "Don't start with the lascivious woo-hooing. You should hear Becca with her girlfriends, Maggie. The air turns purple when they get going."

"Well, the tips of Jo's ears turn red when we woo-hoo," Becca purred. "It's almost irresis—awp!"

The sliding glass door slapped open and Elena streaked out of the cabin, naked as the day she was born. Jo nearly covered Becca's eyes automatically. Elena vaulted nimbly over the rim of the tub and splashed hugely as she landed, soaking Maggie.

"*Seriously*!" Maggie shrieked, shaking out her hands. "Again? What *is* it with you people!"

"Sweet Diosa, your Elena is in heaven!" Elena sighed and stretched out between Grady and Jo, letting her legs float. In the name of modesty or practicality, Jo and the others had opted for T-shirts and shorts, but Elena closed her eyes as the warm water kissed her bare skin.

"Did you jog down the stairs like that?" Grady tapped her sternly. "Is poor Pat in there passed out on the floor, after that wanton display?"

"Poor Pat is in there building up our fire again." Elena struggled erect in the deep tub and held up several small mesh bags of tea leaves. "She'll be here soon. And I had to go upstairs because I had to get these."

"What are these, witchy one?" Becca asked. "Are you going to brew us?"

"I am." Elena scattered the sealed teabags liberally around the surface of the hot tub. "This is a mild mix of curative herbs. They'll help Jo's legs and my back."

"Excellent," Jo said. Her legs were patched with red splotches, remnants of the heat-bewitched water in the trough; Elena's back was similarly marked. They were no worse than a respectable sunburn. "What about Becca's hand?"

"Yes, it will ease Becca's hand too," Elena said.

"Yeah?" Becca brightened. She slipped the plastic bag off her left hand and dipped it cautiously into the water. Her palm bore the only discernible injury that qualified as a war wound in their battle—a rough oval burn, not deep enough to blister, but painful.

Aside from these discomforts, they had emerged from the endless night exhausted but unhurt. Once it was determined that everyone's limbs were intact, Jo had assumed their first need would be for sleep, as it had been nearly three days since anyone slept. They stood in the living room discussing everyone's need for sleep, and then adjourned promptly to the hot tub. Without getting all fraught about it, Jo realized, they weren't ready to separate yet, even as far as private bedrooms.

"So how will we know if all of this took?" Grady asked, eyes closed. "Yeah, everything seems normal again now. But how do we know Jo won't turn back into a cannibal or a werewolf at midnight, or some such?"

Jo eyed Grady narrowly.

"I wouldn't worry too much, Professor Gringa." Elena nestled against Grady's side. "I think it's over. She's talking up a storm now."

"She is?" Grady asked. "Your mother? Or your Goddess?"

"Both of them," Elena said. "But we'll be happy to listen to any rational argument you have in favor of boiling Jo like an egg again, Grady."

Grady opened one eye and squinted at Elena's breasts. "Don't ask me to be rational with those floating right next to me."

"I know what Grady's talking about, though." Becca moved her arms through the swirling water. "I'm kind of afraid to feel safe too. Just look at us. We're lesbians relaxing in a hot tub, for heaven's sake. Any decent porn would have us attacked by a serial killer next, at the very least."

Elena giggled.

"But yes, I'm now reasonably sure Jo's not going to eat me," Becca added.

Jo scowled at the top of Becca's head. "Rebecca, while you're entirely safe, I can assure you that you are going to be eaten quite thoroughly, and soon."

Becca looked up at Jo, and flushed pink to the tips of her ears. She smiled wickedly.

"Woo-hoo," Maggie crooned.

"Hoochie-mama." Grady splashed Jo lightly. "Get a room."

The glass door slid open again and Pat stepped out, studying the small framed photograph in her hands.

"Pat." Jo snapped her fingers peremptorily. "Assuming your truck works now, please drive down to Longmire. Take Grady with you, and leave her tied up at the side of the road somewhere, but bring steaks for the rest of us. In fact, get enough food for three days."

"Three…are we staying?" Becca asked.

"Why not?" Jo shrugged. "We have minor wounds to heal, sleep to catch up on, women to ravish, and soon, steaks to consume. What's our hurry?"

Sloshing, Becca raised up and kissed Jo on the cheek, then smiled at the rest of them. "Yeah? Can you guys hang out for a few days? We promise Jo won't eat any of *you*."

Grady looked at Elena, who smiled back at her. "Yeah, we'll stay." Grady grinned. "Thanks."

"We'll have a *Xena* marathon," Becca promised.

"Thanks?" Grady said. "Pat, okay with you if we stick around for a while?"

"Uh." Pat hadn't looked up from the photo she carried. "Have you guys seen *It's a Wonderful Life*?"

"Only ten thousand times," Becca snickered. "Why?"

"Is that the picture of your grandmother?" Maggie asked.

"Uh huh." Pat stared at the photo.

"Don't tell us she's been rewarded for saving us from the Windigo, and she now has a new pair of wings," Jo said.

Pat shrugged. "Kind of." She handed the frame to Jo.

Jo squeaked in surprise, and the others crowded in around her to look. Delores Daka now beamed out of the photograph with a full set of shining, perfect white teeth.

"But I would have bought the woman excellent dentures," Jo protested, "any time she—"

"My grandmother speaks from the spirit world, 'No need now, white girl.'" Pat grinned and knuckled Jo's hair, a dimple appearing in her cheek.

An irresistible smile tugged at the corner of Jo's mouth as she studied the happy old woman. Then she turned the photograph carefully facedown on the dry table next to the tub. "I'm sorry, Pat, but I can't possibly relax in a bath with a naked witch lesbian if your grandmother is watching us. Not with her leering like that."

"We do owe Pat's grandmother some thanks." Elena seemed half-asleep on Grady's shoulder. "And also her tribe's Cannibal Woman. I find our mothers come through for us, when they can." She opened her eyes and sat up. "Hey."

"Hey?" Grady said.

"Does anyone else remember that vision we had, just as Pat and Maggie put their hands on the trough out there?"

"Whoa. I did see something." Becca sat up straighter too. "A man and a woman, right? Looking at each other?"

"And both had long dark hair," Jo murmured. Even given the chaos that followed, she remembered the love in the couple's eyes clearly.

"And the guy gave the woman something," Grady said. "I saw it too."

"This is *so* cool." Becca flicked water at Elena playfully. "Finally, a sweet vision in my head, instead of that nightmare deer-spider-thing crawling down the hill…" She shivered, and Jo slipped an arm around her shoulders.

"Did you see it?" Maggie asked Pat.

Pat shrugged casually. "I was there, right?" She walked over to Maggie and extended her arm, an oddly gallant gesture. "It's a beautiful day for a walk."

Maggie squinted up at her, then at the women lounging in the hot tub. Becca flicked her fingers at her subtly, urging her on.

"Oookay." Maggie accepted Pat's arm, scowling. "But if I get dumped on my butt in the snow again, I'm giving up on you Seattle lesbians for good."

"Have her back by dark," Grady called to them as they stepped off the porch. "Pat, you be a lady, now. Maggie's real shy and modest and inno—" Grady spluttered satisfyingly as Elena dunked her head beneath the water.

They heard Maggie titter as she and Pat walked together into the sunlit field of snow. Becca and Elena sighed sentimentally.

"What's going to happen to that young woman?" Jo nibbled her lip. "I can buy her a ticket on a flight back to her family in Minnesota, if she wishes."

"Or *we* can help Maggie find a home here." Becca patted Jo's arm. "I think she's halfway home here already."

Grady stretched, yawning. "Well, we've got a few days to figure things out. Jo, after we've had some sleep, you and I should try to hit that paper for Chambliss."

"Stating what, exactly?" Jo frowned.

"Um, the truth?" Grady said.

"The truth about *this* weekend?" Jo scoffed. "Only if we can omit any embarrassing parts about me and say that you did them."

"I'm just talking about the data," Grady protested. "We don't have to use any names or clinical descriptions of—"

"Dr. Wrenn? Dr. Call?" Becca never interrupted anyone, ever. "Elena and I are entirely too comfortable in this lovely hot tub to move, so we can't escape you. But I promise, if you persist in arguing about this, or anything at all in the next three days, Elena and I will cheerfully drown you both."

Elena opened her eyes and winked at Becca, then they settled back into the healing water.

❖

The silence between them was easy, and always had been.

Sanity seemed fully restored to the land. The snow beneath their boots was deep and crisp, but not the heat-sucking maw of the long night before. There was no wind, not even a breeze. The air was sharp, crystal clear, and blessedly still.

"What is it with you and this trough?" Maggie griped cheerfully as they reached their destination. "I know I'm a cheap date, but come on. Not even a Burger King?"

"I figure this place has good juju for us, now." Pat folded her arms and sat back against the trough's edge. "Jo and I fed deer out of this trough when I was a kid. We had fun here. We beat the bad guy here. And you've never been here at sunset, so I wanted you to see this."

She nodded toward the mountain and Maggie turned, and the breath was sucked out of her chest in the most pleasant way possible. Rainier gleamed in all its craggy glory in the gold light of the setting sun, and Maggie couldn't speak for a moment.

"Hoo," she whispered finally, and Pat nodded, but she kept her arms crossed over her chest.

"You'd be giving up a lot," Pat said.

"Huh?"

"You might have a lot of dreams, Maggie. Places you've always wanted to live, lovers you've wanted to meet. I'd be asking you to choose this mountain, and one woman."

"You mean choose her again."

Pat nodded, then gave her time to think.

Something colorful flicked at the edge of Maggie's vision, and she grasped the moment of distraction. "Wow. I don't believe this." She walked around the trough and crouched next to the spray of wildflowers peeking out of the snow.

"Glacier lillies." Maggie recognized Indian paintbrush and alpine asters too, a small cluster of blossoms that had no business blooming in the dead of winter. Maggie drifted her fingers through their richness, reluctant to disturb them—and then she imagined Pat's lonely little camper behind the cabin, and how beautiful these flowers would be there. She plucked a handful carefully and brought them back to Pat.

"Here." She handed the flowers to Pat gruffly. "Enjoy the moment. This is about as mushy as I get."

Pat smiled down at their vibrant colors, and then reached into her pocket. "Here." She handed Maggie her prayer stick. "Enjoy the moment."

"Are you serious?" Maggie stared at the small stick in her palm. "Pat, you're giving this to me?"

"Yep."

"But you said no one could touch this except you." She swallowed and tried to think of something to say that might unlock her throat. "You're giving me this because I brought you some stupid *flowers*?"

"Yeah, actually. It's a story the Makah tell. A very special man once fell out of the stars to visit our tribe. He brought a lot of wisdom with him, a lot of healing. He was with us for years, and he was very much loved. When he was finished teaching us, he went back to the stars. And the moment he rose into the sky, the field he left us from exploded in wildflowers. Beautiful blossoms everywhere."

"Okay. Cool story." A smile played around Maggie's lips. "So wildflowers are special to you guys."

"Yes, and so is the woman who carries them." Pat folded Maggie's fingers around the prayer stick, and then held her closed hand to her heart. "She's the best woman we'll ever meet, if we're lucky enough to find her. She's the love of our lives."

Maggie waited.

"We have a name for this woman. We call her 'she who carries flowers,' or *sewa*."

"Ah," Maggie whispered.

Pat kissed the back of her hand. "Will you stay?"

Maggie thought about it, but she didn't have to think hard.

They sat together and watched the mountain.

End

About the Author

Cate Culpepper has resided in Seattle for the past twenty-five years. She's the author of the *Tristaine* series, *Fireside, River Walker,* and *A Question of Ghosts*. Her books have won three Golden Crown Literary Society Awards, a Lambda Literary Award, a Lesbian Fiction Readers' Choice Award, and an Alice B. Medal for her body of work.

Books Available from Bold Strokes Books

The Quickening: A Sisters of Spirits Novel byYvonne Heidt. Ghosts, visions, and demons are all in a day's work for Tiffany. But when Kat asks for help on a serial killer case, life takes on another dimension altogether. (978-1-60282-975-6)

Windigo Thrall by Cate Culpepper. Six women trapped in a mountain cabin by a blizzard, stalked by an ancient cannibal demon bent on stealing their sanity—and their lives. (978-1-60282-950-3)

Smoke and Fire by Julie Cannon. Oil and water, passion and desire, a combustible combination. Can two women fight the fire that draws them together and threatens to keep them apart? (978-1-60282-977-0)

Asher's Fault by Elizabeth Wheeler. Fourteen-year-old Asher Price sees the world in black and white, much like the photos he takes, but when his little brother drowns at the same moment Asher experiences his first same-sex kiss, he can no longer hide behind the lens of his camera and eventually discovers he isn't the only one with a secret. (978-1-60282-982-4)

Love and Devotion by Jove Belle. KC Hall trips her way through life, stumbling into an affair with a married bombshell twice her age. Thankfully, her best friend, Emma Reynolds, is there to show her the true meaning of Love and Devotion. (978-1-60282-965-7)

Rush by Carsen Taite. Murder, secrets, and romance combine to create the ultimate rush. (978-1-60282-966-4)

The Shoal of Time by J.M. Redmann. It sounded too easy. Micky Knight is reluctant to take the case because the easy ones often turn into the hard ones, and the hard ones turn into the dangerous ones. In this one, easy turns hard without warning. (978-1-60282-967-1)

In Between by Jane Hoppen. At the age of 14, Sophie Schmidt discovers that she was born an intersexual baby and sets off on a journey to find her place in a world that denies her true existence. (978-1-60282-968-8)

Secret Lies by Amy Dunne. While fleeing from her abuser, Nicola Jackson bumps into Jenny O'Connor, and their unlikely friendship quickly develops into a blossoming romance—but when it comes down to a matter of life or death, are they both willing to face their fears? (978-1-60282-970-1)

Under Her Spell by Maggie Morton. The magic of love brought Terra and Athene together, but now a magical quest stands between them—a quest for Athene's hand in marriage. Will their passion keep them together, or will stronger magic tear them apart? (978-1-60282-973-2)

Homestead by Radclyffe. R. Clayton Sutter figures getting NorthAm Fuel's newest refinery operational on a rolling tract of land in Upstate New York should take a month or two, but then, she hadn't counted on local resistance in the form of vandalism, petitions, and one furious farmer named Tess Rogers. (978-1-60282-956-5)

Battle of Forces: Sera Toujours by Ali Vali. Kendal and Piper return to New Orleans to start the rest of eternity together, but the return of an old enemy makes their peaceful reunion short-lived, especially when they join forces with the new queen of the vampires. (978-1-60282-957-2)

How Sweet It Is by Melissa Brayden. Some things are better than chocolate. Molly O'Brien enjoys her quiet life running the bakeshop in a small town. When the beautiful Jordan Tuscana returns home, Molly can't deny the attraction—or the stirrings of something more. (978-1-60282-958-9)

The Missing Juliet: A Fisher Key Adventure by Sam Cameron. A teenage detective and her friends search for a kidnapped Hollywood star in the Florida Keys. (978-1-60282-959-6)

Amor and More: Love Everafter edited by Radclyffe and Stacia Seaman. Rediscover favorite couples as Bold Strokes Books authors reveal glimpses of life and love beyond the honeymoon in short stories featuring main characters from favorite BSB novels. (978-1-60282-963-3)

First Love by CJ Harte. Finding true love is hard enough, but for Jordan Thompson, daughter of a conservative president, it's challenging, especially when that love is a female rodeo cowgirl. (978-1-60282-949-7)

Pale Wings Protecting by Lesley Davis. Posing as a couple to investigate the abduction of infants, Special Agent Blythe Kent and Detective Daryl Chandler find themselves drawn into a battle over the innocents, with demons on one side and the unlikeliest of protectors on the other. (978-1-60282-964-0)

Mounting Danger by Karis Walsh. Sergeant Rachel Bryce, an outcast on the police force, is put in charge of the department's newly formed mounted division. Can she and polo champion Callan Lanford resist their growing attraction as they struggle to safeguard the disaster-prone unit? (978-1-60282-951-0)

Meeting Chance by Jennifer Lavoie. When man's best friend turns on Aaron Cassidy, the teen keeps his distance until fate puts Chance in his hands. (978-1-60282-952-7)

At Her Feet by Rebekah Weatherspoon. Digital marketing producer Suzanne Kim knows she has found the perfect love in her new mistress Pilar, but before they can make the ultimate commitment, Suzanne's professional life threatens to disrupt their perfectly balanced bliss. (978-1-60282-948-0)

Show of Force by AJ Quinn. A chance meeting between navy pilot Evan Kane and correspondent Tate McKenna takes them on a roller-coaster ride where the stakes are high, but the reward is higher: a chance at love. (978-1-60282-942-8)

Clean Slate by Andrea Bramhall. Can Erin and Morgan work through their individual demons to rediscover their love for each other, or are the unexplainable wounds too deep to heal? (978-1-60282-943-5)

Hold Me Forever by D. Jackson Leigh. An investigation into illegal cloning in the quarter horse racing industry threatens to destroy the growing attraction between Georgia debutante Mae St. John and Louisiana horse trainer Whit Casey. (978-1-60282-944-2)

Trusting Tomorrow by PJ Trebelhorn. Funeral director Logan Swift thinks she's perfectly happy with her solitary life devoted to helping others cope with loss until Brooke Collier moves in next door to care for her elderly grandparents. (978-1-60282-891-9)

Forsaking All Others by Kathleen Knowles. What if what you think you want is the opposite of what makes you happy? (978-1-60282-892-6)

Exit Wounds by VK Powell. When Officer Loane Landry falls in love with ATF informant Abigail Mancuso, she realizes that nothing is as it seems—not the case, not her lover, not even the dead. (978-1-60282-893-3)

Dirty Power by Ashley Bartlett. Cooper's been through hell and back, and she's still broke and on the run. But at least she found the twins. They'll keep her alive. Right? (978-1-60282-896-4)

The Rarest Rose by I. Beacham. After a decade of living in her beloved house, Ele disturbs its past and finds her life being haunted by the presence of a ghost who will show her that true love never dies. (978-1-60282-884-1)

Code of Honor by Radclyffe. The face of terror is hard to recognize—especially when it's homegrown. The next book in the Honor series. (978-1-60282-885-8)

Does She Love You? by Rachel Spangler. When Annabelle and Davis find out they are both in a relationship with the same woman, it leaves them facing life-altering questions about trust, redemption, and the possibility of finding love in the wake of betrayal. (978-1-60282-886-5)

The Road to Her by KE Payne. Sparks fly when actress Holly Croft, star of UK soap Portobello Road, meets her new on-screen love interest, the enigmatic and sexy Elise Manford. (978-1-60282-887-2)

Shadows of Something Real by Sophia Kell Hagin. Trying to escape flashbacks and nightmares, ex-POW Jamie Gwynmorgan stumbles into the heart of former Red Cross worker Adele Sabellius and uncovers a deadly conspiracy against everything and everyone she loves. (978-1-60282-889-6)

Date with Destiny by Mason Dixon. When sophisticated bank executive Rashida Ivey meets unemployed blue collar worker Destiny Jackson, will her life ever be the same? (978-1-60282-878-0)

The Devil's Orchard by Ali Vali. Cain and Emma plan a wedding before the birth of their third child while Juan Luis is still lurking, and as Cain plans for his death, an unexpected visitor arrives and challenges her belief in her father, Dalton Casey. (978-1-60282-879-7)

Secrets and Shadows by L.T. Marie. A bodyguard and the woman she protects run from a madman and into each other's arms. (978-1-60282-880-3)

Change Horizons: Three Novellas by Gun Brooke. Three stories of courageous women who dare to love as they fight to claim a future in a hostile universe. (978-1-60282-881-0)

Scarlet Thirst by Crin Claxton. When hot, feisty Rani meets cool, vampire Rob, one lifetime isn't enough, and the road from human to vampire is shorter than you think... (978-1-60282-856-8)

Battle Axe by Carsen Taite. How close is too close? Bounty hunter Luca Bennett will soon find out. (978-1-60282-871-1)